When the doorbell rings, thinking it's Eve, I grab my robe and rush downstairs. I should have known better. That would have been too easy. The handsome man standing on the threshold takes my breath away. His masculine scent surrounds me. The dark blue single-breasted suit appears to be tailored to fit and is set off by a tasteful two-tone tie. His hair seems a bit shorter. It has a healthy-looking shine to it and is neatly combed, as usual. I see I'm not the only one who paid a visit to the hairdresser. I'm pleased.

"You're early," I say.

"I apologize for that. I had business in the area that finished up earlier than I anticipated. I didn't want to risk driving all the way back to Canton, so here I am. I could wait in the car if. . . ."

"No, no. Don't be silly. It's just that, as you can see, I'm not altogether ready." I say, self-consciously pulling my robe closer to my body.

"You look all together to me," he claims. His eyes sweep up an down my body before returning to collide boldly with mine. I clear my throat and look away.

"Won't you come in? Make yourself comfortable in the living room. I'll be down shortly."

I don't give the Answer-To-All-My-Male-Fantasies a chance to say anything else; I dash off, practically running up the stairs. I will never be entirely certain, but I could have sworn I heard him chuckle.

⁓⁓⁓

THIS LIFE ISN'T PERFECT HOLLA

SANDRA FOY

Genesis Press, Inc.

INDIGO

An imprint of Genesis Press, Inc.
Publishing Company

Genesis Press, Inc.
P.O. Box 101
Columbus, MS 39703

All rights reserved. Except for use in any review, the reproduction or utilization of this work in whole or in part in any form by any electronic, mechanical, or other means, not known or hereafter invented, including xerography, photocopying, and recording, or in any information storage or retrieval system, is forbidden without written permission of the publisher, Genesis Press, Inc. For information write Genesis Press, Inc., P.O. Box 101 Columbus, MS. 39703

All characters in this book have no existence outside the imagination of the author and have no relation whatsoever to anyone bearing the same name or names. They are not even distantly inspired by any individual known or unknown to the author and all incidents are pure invention.

Copyright © 2008 by Sandra Foy

ISBN: 13 DIGIT : 978-1-58571-331-8
ISBN: 10 DIGIT : 1-58571-331-7
Manufactured in the United States of America

First Edition

Visit us at www.genesis-press.com
or call at 1-888-Indigo-1-4-0

DEDICATION

"He raises the poor from the dust
and lifts the needy from the ash heap;
he seats them with princes,
with the princes of their people."
Psalm 113: 7-9.

CHAPTER 1

I suck in the gut, hold it, and manage to zip my jeans. I'm flat on my back 'cause gravity aids in the process. Don't know how I let myself get to this shameful state. My big ass is now an unmentionable two hundred eight pounds of shameful blubber struggling to fit into a pair of jeans I slid into a month ago, for goodness sake. If I hadn't inherited my height from my dad, I would be a hot mess. I swear, for every pound I have ever lost, I have gained back double for my effort. Even at five foot nine, I cannot hide the fact that I'm in serious need of some self-control. I struggle to my feet, adjust the straps on my 18-hour Playtex double-D bra, and slip on a loose sweater.

Standing in front of the mirror, I carefully and strategically stretch the center of the sweater. This way I only look overweight all over without drawing attention to my pouch. No trace remains of my pear-shaped-body-with-attitude. My husband was fond of calling it that because I had tight abs, definition in my wide hips, a toned behind, and was a perky B cup to top it all off. Those were the days of healthy eating, daily exercising, and eternal optimism.

After fourteen years of stubbornly blaming my weight on motherhood, I fess up to what I've inwardly known all along. "My children are not to blame for my swollen midsection, jiggling thighs, and sagging bottom. The sixty or so extra pounds I'm hauling around are not surplus from my two pregnancies; but they are instead the result of years of gluttony."

Taking off my headscarf, I run a brush lightly over my microbraids. I'm thinking it's about time for them to come out. I've had them in for more than two months, and they're starting to loosen up. That's all I need—to walk into the office Monday morning, go about my business, and then have a braid fall out. Katherine would really get a kick out of that. I can just hear her now. "Kimberly, you dropped a piece of your weave!" That is one spiteful heifer. She's always smirking while offering me celery sticks. I don't ever see her skinny ass eating any. I'm positive she brings that nasty shit every day just to harass me—her way of reminding me, and everybody else in the office, that I'm overweight. As if the state of my body isn't obvious at a glance.

I give my appearance a long, hard, critical look—something I would not dare do in the nude these days. My skin is pretty good. Not a blemish in sight. I scrutinize my upper lip, looking for any sign of hair. Satisfied I'm still hair-free two weeks after last using Nair, I focus in on my big, black expressive eyes. They reflect the misery that is at my core. I spare a few moments to fuss with my long lashes and add a dab of lip-gloss to my full lips. I step back and take in my whole frame. "Sista child, you better start working out soon. You're only thirty-four, for goodness sake." Saying it aloud underscores the seriousness of my sorry state. I'm not an obsessive woman; I don't need to be a size two. I just want to look good in my clothes and feel good about the reflection staring back at me when I step out of the shower.

I walk over to my wall calendar and circle Monday, March 11, and underneath in big letters I write, "Start diet and work out today." Then in small letters, I ever so lightly write down my weight. I heard somewhere that when you decide to lose weight, you should set a day and prepare yourself mentally for the changes to come. I'm not sure I buy that, but I do it because it gives me two days to drink as much Pepsi and eat as much Ben & Jerry's Chunky Monkey ice cream as I want without feeling guilty. That is one of the benefits of starting a diet—you get to drink and eat all the no-good stuff and promise yourself it is the last time you will. My longest diet lasted three weeks. I lost nine pounds and felt great, and then my husband lost yet another job, and off the wagon I fell with a loud thud. I've been off the wagon ever since.

The door to my bedroom opens without a warning knock, so I know without looking it's my husband. Daniel Riley the second, in my opinion, is the handsomest man on the planet. At six and a half feet he has an air of authority that still, to this day, makes my heart skip a beat and swell with pride because he's mine—on paper, anyway. His daily visits to the Y on Huntington Avenue account for his well-toned, muscular body. A nightly ritual of doing about a bazillion stomach crunches is the secret behind his enviable abs. His smooth, even-toned cocoa complexion comes from his late father, as does his sandy-colored wavy hair.

Daniel has had it going on since the first day my terrified black eyes met his shocked hazel ones in the parking lot of Frank's Burger Pit, when I had mistaken the gas pedal for the brake pedal and ended up running him down during my second driving lesson. Luckily for his future kids, I had a light foot; otherwise, I would have mowed him down instead of merely tapping him with my father's new station wagon. After my panic-stricken mother had made sure he was all right, we exchanged phone numbers. Daniel and I have been a couple ever since.

I mutter a curse. I was secretly hoping to get the kids together and be gone before he got back from visiting his mama. Every Saturday morning, without fail, he makes the twenty-minute drive from our house in Boston's historic neighborhood of Jamaica Plain, commonly known as JP, to his mother's house across town in the more urban district of Ashmont. I wish he could be half as dedicated to me.

"You guys going out?" he asks, tossing his jacket on the bed.

"For a bit, yep," I say, being evasive, not because I mind telling him where I'm off to but because I know this man. I've been exclusive to him for eighteen years. There is no way Daniel hasn't already asked his children where we were going. And I know they told him. He is asking me because I haven't invited him along, and it is his way of giving me a chance to make amends. I don't.

"Mama invited us all over for dinner tonight, Kimi."

"Including me?"

"Yes, of course."

"Why, what does she want with me?"

"What's that supposed to mean?"

"It ain't Thanksgiving or Christmas, so why does she want me at her house, Daniel?"

"She's just trying to be a good mother-in-law, Kimi."

"She's about two decades too late for that, don't you think?"

"You're always accusing her of not liking you, but as soon as she reaches out, you talk trash. She's damned if she doesn't approach you and she's damned if she does."

"That's cause she always finds a way to make me feel like shit, whether in person or by messenger."

"She doesn't make you feel like shit."

"Daniel, don't stand there and try to tell me how that woman makes me feel!"

"I know she doesn't make you feel like shit on purpose."

"Let's not talk about your mother and me."

"Fine by me. Anyway, she's having the new reverend from her church over and thought we'd like to come by and meet him and his wife."

"And you wanted me to believe she was reaching out for no good reason. Please. I knew better. And I'm not going over there to play the happy in-laws—no way."

"Fine, don't come, but I'm taking my kids."

"They have homework to do later on."

"It's Saturday. They'll do it tomorrow."

"They always do their weekend homework on Saturday night so that they can have Sunday to do whatever they want."

"It's just dinner, Kimi. They have to eat."

"Fine, but have them home by 8:30."

"I'll bring my kids home when I'm ready to bring them home."

"You'll bring them home at 8:30 or I'll come and collect them—embarrassin' your ass in the process!"

"I'll give Mama your love."

"She'll know better," I say, sucking my teeth. "Where are my kids, Daniel?"

"Went out to fool around in what's left of the snow. Said to tell you they're ready when you are."

"Good, 'cause you and I need to chat seriously about a few things."

"What things?"

"Your mama called about ten minutes before you walked in. Said to remind you to pick up a new paint roller. She didn't mention dinner, by the way."

"She didn't mention it because she knew I would."

"I suppose. So is she redecorating?"

"A little paint here and there."

"Who's paintin' here and there, you?"

"Kimi."

"I don't believe you! I asked you to trim the hedges leading up the walkway over a week ago. It's starting to look like a forest out there, and you still haven't done a thing about it. The neighbors are gonna start complainin' soon."

"I'll get to it tomorrow."

"So you'll get around to takin' care of *our* household tomorrow? But you have time for 'paintin' here and there' for your mama today?"

"It's only one more day, Kimi, damn!"

"What about *our* gutters?"

"I'll do those, too."

"And the quotes for repaving the driveway, Daniel?"

"I thought you were gonna call around?"

"Nope, not after the way you bitched and moaned over the price I got on the fence last year. You do it."

"You're supposed to haggle; you took the first thing offered, Kimi."

"It's not the first time I made *that* mistake."

"Care to elaborate?"

"Do you care to elaborate why you were out 'til after two in the morning—again. That's three times in two weeks," I say, crossing my arms over my ample bosom.

"Bobby and I had a few Buds. I wasn't aware my grown ass needed your permission to hang with my friend."

"My husband and father of my two impressionable young children quit another damn job for no good reason and goes off to get drunk without so much as a phone call. You could have been dead for all we knew! Do you really think that shit is all right, Daniel?"

"Not the way you tell it. I go for months at a time without an ounce of liquor . . ."

"Exactly! So why would a man who can care less about drinkin' spend three nights away from his family, supposedly to drink? Anywhere is better than here, is that it?

"The fellas and I . . ."

"The fellas? What fellas? You said it was you and Bobby."

"A couple of his cousins stopped by."

"Maria allowed a bunch of guys to get drunk around her kids? Is that what you're telling me?" I ask, really suspicious now.

"Not everyone's an uptight ass."

"Daniel, you're full of lies, and that leaves no room for the truth. You had your ass at a bar! Didn't you?"

"Not the whole time."

"We're done here. Get out my face!" I say, pinning him with the evil eye I inherited from my mama.

"It was just guy time, Kimi. No need to make something tiny into something big."

"You're right. Your lying *is* no big deal; it's now the norm."

"Anyway, I called the temp agency Cleve gave me. They said I should just come in Monday." *Smooth, Daniel, real smooth!*

"That's what I told you to do in the first place, Daniel; just go your ass in."

"Things change all the time, Kimi. When was the last time you temped?"

I stare him down. I'm on the verge of telling his ass to pack a bag. But *excuse me* is all that comes out.

"Nothing, Kimi."

"No, it is somethin'. It's always somethin' with you, Daniel Riley." My husband is now gawking at me. He has known me for eighteen years now, and in all that time I've never called him Daniel Riley except when pissed off to the point of showing my ass. As any black person brought up in the South will tell you, if you hear your mama calling you by the full name on your birth certificate, seek police protection. It means you are in big trouble. Daniel was born in Steele, Mississippi, and lived there until age fifteen. He knows he is in a whole heap of trouble.

Like any man, he knows there are three levels of trouble he can get into with his wife. Daniel is at trouble level one. When he is late bringing his black behind home after work because he "stopped by Bobby's place for a quick sec." I retaliate by forgetting to tell him I'm meeting Yvonne after work. When he calls looking for me, he gets my voice mail because I've "accidentally" turned off my cellphone. Such childish behavior doesn't solve anything, but it's my small way of making a point.

Level two trouble is reserved for when my loving husband tells me, straight-faced, he got the custom-made rims for his '97 'Beamer' from a mechanic friend of Bobby's and it cost a hundred bucks. I can think of a hundred other useful ways to spend a hundred dollars, but my husband's pleading, slanted hazel eyes sway me. Then I discover a faded receipt from Goodyear in the washer. It's made out to Daniel Riley for two sets of brand-spanking-new rims. My husband's life flashes before my eyes when I notice he paid with MasterCard— not just any MasterCard, but a MasterCard I didn't even know he had. The betrayal I feel over Daniel's deception cannot be expressed in words. I don't speak. I slam the crinkled-up slip on the coffee table so hard my hand aches. And before his innocent "What?" has left his lips, I've left the room.

Daniel quit his job last Monday after a row with a coworker over the thermostat. He has now succeeded in reaching trouble level three.

"This has been coming for a long time, Kimi. You know that fucker was making my life a living hell."

"All I know is you can't keep a damn job, Daniel Riley. You and work are like fire and ice. Every time you take your hotheaded ass to work, the job dissolves."

"That's bullshit! I've been wasting away at that place for over a year—"

"Yeah, you were overdue to quit."

"I don't have to stay where I'm not appreciated, Kimi."

"What the hell you talkin' about? Somebody at work doesn't want to turn up the thermostat and that means you're undervalued?"

"It wasn't about the damn thermostat! You're twisting my words. And don't act so surprised that I quit. You know I wasn't happy at that damn parts factory. I want to paint! I want to draw!"

"And I want to make more than ends meet, Daniel. I understand you got dreams, but you need to live in the here and now. We got bills, this mortgage, Angela's braces, their school—"

"Alex's football gear, Angela's dance lessons, your sister— Whose fault is all this shit, Kimi?"

Hold up. This man is not blaming me for our financial obligations. "With righteous indignation comes the burden of valid principle!" I shout.

"Where the hell you pull that shit from?" he asks, eyeballing me up and down. "You must be writin' again."

"F you, Daniel."

"Speak English, then," he says, and sort of smirks, but not quite.

"I'm sayin' I've got a job. I'm makin' my share," I say, placing my hands on my thick waist.

"Yeah, you got a job, busting your ass in that fancy accounting office year in, year out. You front, but you ain't happy and it's showing all over you."

"You've figured me out, *Sir Isaac Newton*. I ain't happy—with your lyin' ass." I'm steaming now because Daniel has touched some real sore spots. He knows I hate the weight I've gained and that I want to write full time.

"What you saying? You want me out, Kimi?"

"I'm sayin' I can do bad all by my damn self."

"You want me to get my shit?"

"I'm not stoppin' you. You want to get it, get it." He doesn't. He just stands there with a look that says *I'd rather be anywhere but here—with you.* I wish he would leave the room first. That way, I won't have to walk out knowing he has more to say. It's a sick idiosyncrasy I wrestle with at times and one that can be traced back to my well-meaning mother, who would force my sister and I to sit together and hash out our disagreements—no matter how long it took.

I do not look at Daniel anymore. After about a minute with not so much as a sigh from him, I walk out of our bedroom, down the stairs, and slam out the front door.

———∿∿∿———

"Mom, are you and Daddy fighting?"

"We were discussing *loudly*, Alex," I tell my wise fourteen-year-old. He doesn't say another word on the subject; he just sits in the passenger seat, looking expectant. I rub the top of his head and look away. I glance in my rearview mirror. My thirteen-year-old is looking long-faced—in my direction. My kids are no different from kids everywhere. The thought of their father and me splitting upsets them. They do not understand or care who did what. All they ask is that we not break up their family.

"Mom?" Alex lets me know he's still waiting.

"Nobody is fighting, Spudmuffin," I lie, turning onto the expressway. Alex looks unconvinced but accepts my playfulness and smiles. I do not want to hurt my kids, but I need to change the course of my life. I feel as if I'm drowning in misery.

When we arrive at the mall, the kids briefly argue about where to go first. Alex wants to visit the video store for the latest game for his PlayStation 2, but Angela is adamant about going to the Gap and the music shop. Seems there is a pair of Converse All Star lo-top sneakers—in red—her girlfriend was sporting yesterday and now Angela has to have, along with a Beyonce CD.

"Look, you two, we have all the time in the world today, so it does not matter which store we go to first."

"But, Mama, Alex takes forever, drooling over games you're not even gonna buy him. All the red Converse All Stars lo-tops may be gone by the time we get to the Gap, and the music shop will only take me a sec."

"It's Saturday, Angela. The music shop never takes a sec on Saturday and you know that. And I don't feel like long lines and hassling today. So that's out. We'll go to the Gap and then the video store," I say, thinking that settles it.

"That's not fair," Alex complains. "Angela whines like a brat, so she gets her way."

"Fine, Alex, we'll go to the video store first, where they have tons of games, one of which I've already reserved for you. But be warned, if we get to the Gap and they are sold out of the sneakers Angela wants, your game goes back. Let's go." I do not know for sure if I'm being fair, but it is the best I can do today. My mind is back in my bedroom on my last words to Daniel.

"Okay, okay," Alex says now, not willing to chance it. Two hours later, my jeans are cutting into my middle and my underwire bra is torturing me. The kids are pleased with their purchases and discussing lunch plans. I want so badly to get home and pop the button on my jeans. I'm tempted to tell them we are leaving, but do not. I know the highlight of mall shopping is the food court. I'm thirty-four but I still remember when my mom would take me to the mall; my best friend, Yvonne, and I would tolerate being shuffled from one clothing store to the next, taking comfort in the knowledge that we would get fast food as a reward for behaving while Mom tried on outfits and shopped for household items.

We're finally on our way home when a thought occurs to me, and I turn off before getting to our street.

"Where are we going?" Alex asks.

"Never mind where, Alex Riley. You best be worrying about your game."

"Oh, shoot, Alex, Mama told you," my thirteen-year-old beauty queen goads him.

"Bring what you got—both of you," Alex says, joining in the fun. "But be warned, I'm gonna treat you to my usual total annihilation. Blood don't mean nada when it comes to the hoop."

"We've been practicing, Alex, so get prepared for a *real* challenge this time," I warn playfully.

"Please," he scoffs. "I saw that tired, totally whacked game you two got. I'm not worried."

I smile to myself. Alex is a mirror image of his father, with long limbs and big feet offering a glimpse of the tall and strapping man he will likely be one day.

"You haven't seen us recently. We've improved a lot," I respond.

"What up now, huh, Alex?" Angela resumes baiting her brother. Alex falls silent, obviously digesting the bombshell I just dropped on him.

"Ain't nobody worried, uh, uh, uh. Won't be no smiling faces, uh, uh, uh," he soulfully sings in a near-perfect rendition of a Staple Singers song.

"First one to twenty wins," I say confidently, parking next to what I've come to think of as our court.

For the next twenty minutes Angela and I employ every underhanded trick we can come up with, but it was all for naught. It ends in another futile attempt to defeat Alex.

In the end he beats us twenty to six—an all-time best for us. Alex pounds his chest in victory. Angela whines, but there is sparkle in her eyes despite our loss. I chuckle despite the pain of having my heart slamming into my chest and the extreme discomfort of being sweat-drenched from hair root to toe and clammy in every private spot in between. I am happy; we have successfully escaped our present uncertain existence for twenty sanity-sustaining minutes. It doesn't matter what life throws at us once we drive away from the safe haven of this basketball court. Our time at the count will carry us—for a while.

When we arrive home Daniel is leaning his handsome ass up against his car, clearly waiting for the kids. As soon as I hit the brakes, they jump out of my car and make a bee-line to their father. I don't fault them for being excited about going to see Ma Riley; she's nice to them. All the hugs and kisses they can stand, along with her undivided attention and all the unconditional praise they can stomach.

I make eye contact with my pathetic husband and stare his ass down until he gets into his Beamer and drives off. I do not return his insincere air kiss.

As soon as I'm inside I undo the button on my pants and head down to the basement to throw in a load of laundry. My basement is what you would call finished. The house is a typical middle class, contemporary and economically furnished home. It consists of a small entranceway crowded by a flight of stairs that lead up to three rooms and two bathrooms. Turn right and you are immediately greeted by a cozy living room. The rooms' only effects worth mentioning are a floor model forty-six-inch television, an antique cherry wood coffee table with brass claw feet inherited from my grandmother, a stereo system, and a three-tier corner shelf that houses my large collection of dog figurines. A doorway to the right of the living room leads into a medium size eat-in kitchen with appliances that have seen better days. There's a half bath off the kitchen and a door across from it that leads down to the basement. The basement houses a laundry room, a storage room, and Daniel's work area, which is always locked up—tight. I've tried forcing the door several times. It's where he goes to paint. In all the years I've been with him I've only seen one of his paintings. It was a picture of his mother, and I had foolishly criticized it. He hasn't shared his work with me since, preferring instead to disappear for hours on end behind the door in the rear of the basement. Once I'd charged in behind him, determined to see what his big secret was. I caught a glimpse of what looked to be the beginning of a portrait of a young female. Daniel managed to slam the door in my face before I could even get a look around the room. He started working under lock and key after that. I don't know why I didn't think to sneak a peek inside before he'd taken such drastic measures. I actually wasn't interested until it became apparent he was keeping it from me.

I notice light spilling from under the door and try the knob. It's locked, as usual.

It's 11:30 and I've just come downstairs and heading out to collect my kids when the front door opens. Daniel, looking weary, is the first through the door. I glimpse Alex and Angela behind him playing peek-a-boo.

"I've called your ass at least ten times, Daniel Riley!"

"Yeah, you've been calling nonstop since 8:45."

"Why didn't you answer?"

"I decided to let you get it out all in one shot."

"You're not making any sense," I say, but an uneasy feeling is starting to settle over me. Why are my kids so quiet, and why are they still cowering behind their father?

"I told you to bring my kids home at a decent hour. You just couldn't do it, could you?"

"Look, Kimi—"

I show him the palm of my hand, not interested in what he has to say—at the moment. I'm slowly, apprehensively, moving around his tall, stock-still frame.

"What the hell happened?" I wail, finally getting a look at the kids.

"It looks bad, but . . ."

"What did you do to my babies?" I scream at him, grabbing Alex and Angela by the arm and pulling them forward. Alex's left eye is swollen shut and Angela's top lip has grown two sizes.

"It's not as bad as it looks, I promise you. I took them to the emergency room . . ."

"Emergency room?"

"The doctor said they're fine."

"Fine? Look at them!"

"Mama had a bee's nest."

"And?"

"They got stung and had a bad reaction. The doctor said the swelling should be gone, or almost gone, by morning. He said we should keep ice on it and just watch them overnight."

"They went for dinner, damnit! Your mama got a bee's nest at her dinner table?" I ask sarcastically, eyeing my kids' soiled clothes.

"We were outside for around five minutes. I knocked down the nest and they got stung. End of story."

"*End of story*? My kids are swollen! What kind of fool are you? Why would you have my kids anywhere near a bee's nest? That is idiotic, Daniel Riley!"

"It was an accident. Accidents happen, Kimi. They were helping me in the yard."

"You were working in your mama's yard when our yard is a freakin' mess? I'm sick of placing a distant second to that woman, Daniel."

"Mom, don't be mad at Daddy, please," Angela pleads, wiping at the drool she can't control.

"Please, Mom." Alex seconds his sister, tilting his head to the side so that he can look at me with his one good eye.

"Oh, my God, look at my babies!"

"Kimi."

"Don't talk to me, Daniel Riley. I can't stand the sound of your voice! There is no excuse for this shit!"

"I'm not excusing anything, I'm only trying to explain what happened. You going all crazy."

"We are outta here!" I say, surprising us all. I rush out the front door, pulling both kids with me.

CHAPTER 2

"Mom?"

"Yes, Alex?"

"How long are we going to be staying here?"

"This is one of those extended-stay hotels. We could stay for quite a while if we wanted to."

"I don't want to."

"How's the icepack?"

"Getting warm."

"What about yours, Ang?"

"It's already warm."

"Well, hopefully you've had them on long enough. You two try and get some sleep now. I need to think," I say lightly, adjusting the pillow on the strange bed for the millionth time. It's a wasted effort; I can't sleep in a strange bed. But I can't face Daniel right now. I've had it with his ass.

"Mom?"

"Yes, Ang?"

"I don't want to stay either. I miss Daddy."

"We've only been gone for three hours, Ang. And if you don't stay on your side of the bed, you are going to go sleep with Alex."

"No way!" Alex pipes up. "She's drooling every-where."

"She can't help it, so be nice, Alex, before I send her over there."

"That's not fair, I only have a small bed. You guys have a large one."

"Sometimes life is not fair, Alex," I say, and we all fall silent.

The next morning both are looking almost as good as new and complaining nonstop about being homesick. I manage to distract them with a visit to I-Hop, where I linger and overeat in the process. Afterwards, I foolishly suggest a walk around Jamaica pond. Slow as a turtle, I drag my big butt halfway around the mile and a half trail and then insist on turning back the way we've come. After which the kids double-team me all over again with pleas to go home. By now I'm longing for a hot shower and my own bed, but I want to avoid Daniel more than I want either. Alex's sudden and dubious assertion that he's now worried about not having enough time to complete his weekend homework tips the scales, and I decide to take them home.

The first thing I notice when we enter the house is that the television, DVD player, and stereo system are missing. I know we haven't been robbed, because I turned off the burglar alarm when we came in. Besides, everything else is still in place. I know damn well the culprit has to be Daniel's black ass.

"Mama, what happened to our stuff?" Alex asks.

"Your father happened. Get upstairs, both of you. I need to call Daddy."

"Mama, why—?"

"Just go, Alex." As soon as my children disappear I head down to the basement and straight for the rear room. The door is wide open and the room is completely empty. Heart racing, I rush back upstairs, and then up to my bedroom and throw open the closet door. Most of Daniel's clothes are gone. I grab the phone, pause to unbutton my jeans, and then dial Daniel's mom's house. His mom answers on the first ring. She doesn't even try to hide the fact that she was sitting by, waiting for my call.

"Hello?" she ventures pleasantly in her manly way. When I began dating Daniel, I was sure his mama was a man in drag. She is a big-boned woman, and tall to boot. She has to be close to six feet—seriously. God definitely withheld the beauty when he made this woman. She reminds me a lot of Dennis Rodman. I honestly think she is his sister and just doesn't want to admit it.

"Hello, Ma Riley. May I speak to Daniel, please?"

There is a long pause before she answers. This woman has never forgiven me for getting pregnant at nineteen and trapping and coercing, as she saw it, her twenty-year-old *baby* into dropping out of art school in order to do the right thing by me and his unborn child.

"I don't know what's going on with you two, but Junior showed up here with some of his things."

"Well, *Junior* had better bring those things back home. May I speak to him, please?"

"Hold on," she says.

She might as well have said "whatever." I can hear it in her voice, anyway. I do not know what it is about my

21

mother-in-law; she acts as though I'm her enemy—always. She never misses an opportunity to make me feel like crap. She should be thanking me for taking her sorry ass of a son off her hands. By the time Daniel gets his sorry behind to the phone, I've stripped down to my underthings. I'm definitely more comfortable.

"Yeah?" I hear him ask as if he hasn't the faintest idea what I want.

"Why did you take that stuff, Daniel? You know damn well some of my money went into it, too."

"Mostly my money, Kimi. That makes it more mine."

"I want it back."

"I'm not bringing it back, Kimi. Tell the kids I will talk to them later on in the week."

"I'm not your messenger pigeon!"

"Fuck it!" he shouts and hangs up.

I strip down to the nude and then rummage around in the dresser drawer until I find my favorite lounge dress. I slide it on and plop down on my bed. I do not know if I'm upset or relieved that Daniel left. Part of me is pissed that I did not technically put him out, and part of me is breathing a lot easier because I will not have to deal with deciphering the truth from Daniel's lies of omission.

Having many hours before I have to start dinner, and needing a distraction before I attempt to talk with the kids, I take a hot shower and then call Yvonne.

"Hello?"

"What's up, girly girl?" I ask, straining to sound normal.

"Nothing much. Just getting settled. I just got in from church. You should have come, girl. It was great. Pastor Roland talked about people abandoning God and how we don't put God first in our lives. It was good."

"Ahh, sounds like it. If we lived closer I would come," I say. That's my usual lame excuse. Yvonne knows I'm full of it, but seldom calls me on it. The church is in Holbrook, which is only half an hour away from me. I travel farther to get my favorite pizza in Watertown.

"Where are Alex and Angela? I don't hear them."

"We went to the mall yesterday. Most likely they're admiring their purchases."

"And Daniel?"

"What about him?"

"Any word on what he plans to do for work?"

"Nope," I say in a "that's the end of that topic" sort of way. But I know Yvonne is not going to be satisfied with my answer, and I don't want her to be. I want to tell her what happened; I just don't know how to start.

"Where is he, Kimberly?"

"Not here."

"Well, that's obvious. You sound upset. Where is he? His mom's?"

"You guessed it."

"Did you tell him to go, or did he leave?"

I wonder why that is the first thing people think to ask. Why is it so important to know who left whom? I think it is so that people know, or think they know, whom to pity.

"Does it matter?" I snap.

23

"What did he say before he left?" Yvonne asks.

I hate her. She is such a smart-ass. "We had it out about his quitting his job and his unmanly habit of putting this family second. The kids and I stayed at a motel last night. When we came home today he was gone."

"It must have gotten pretty bad for you to walk out."

"That fool let my babies get stung by bees!"

"What? How?"

"By doing what he does best, putting his mama first."

"Explain that."

"He had them helping him knock down a bee nest at his mama's house."

"He had them helping?"

"They were in the yard with him."

"Are they okay?"

"A little swollen still, but they're fine now."

"So you left your husband because your kids were accidentally stung by a bee?"

"It's not just that. This was a long time coming, Eve. You know, he attacked me, claiming the mortgage, the kid's school tuition, etc., are my entire fault. He even hinted that I'm somehow to blame for Angela needing braces. Can he get any more foolish?"

"Some black men are like that."

"Black men? Eve, any man can be an a-hole." I say a-hole out of respect for Yvonne's aversion to swear words. She is the most religious person I know. She would go to church eight days a week if she could. I've lost count of all the different committees she is involved with. I did not know there were so many different committees in church, and Yvonne is on at least half a billion of them.

I've given up trying to keep up with which one she does from day to day. I always get it wrong when I try and guess. Now I just say, "You had church tonight, right?" Yvonne will usually just fill me in on the particulars.

When I do go to church, I pray and leave, never to be heard from again until my life seems so screwed up I need to get as close to God as possible. I envy Yvonne's unwavering belief that God has everything under control and He will answer any prayer—always. I've seen plenty of spiritual movies where people put all their faith in God no matter the adversity they face. I even know a few older folks who will not start the day without praying to God for guidance. Nor will they close their eyes at night without thanking him for bringing them through another day in one piece. Yvonne is working on carrying on that tradition.

I believe there is a higher power at work, and that all mankind will eventually answer to Him. I just don't live every day as though it were my last to make amends for my sins the way Yvonne does. She is the daughter my mother tried to raise. Yvonne is the type of person who could get hit by a speeding car, lose both her legs and still be grateful she still had her hands to raise high in praise of all God has given her. If that isn't devotion, I don't know what is.

"White men are just more responsible," she says now.

"You've obviously been married to that fair-haired, blue-eyed paragon too long, my friend. You've been brainwashed, Eve," I charge. "Irresponsibility isn't inherent in a particular race—or gender, for that matter. No matter what Mike says."

"Hmmm."

"What's that supposed to mean?" I ask, pushing the issue.

"Let's drop it, Kimberly. You're in a mood, and I don't want you taking it out on me."

"Standing up for my people means I'm in a mood?"

"No, your snapping at everything I say means you're in a mood."

"I'm sick of hearing Mike's bigoted views coming out of your mouth."

"I speak my own mind." Yvonne defends herself with trademark calm.

"Black men are bums and white men are saints. That's speaking your mind?"

"Yes, most black men leave much to be desired these days, and you can't accept that Mike has nothing to do with my feeling that way."

"I don't accept it because it's stereotypical bullshit! America was built on the backs of hardworking, responsible black men, the likes of Benjamin Banneker, who in 1753 built a wooden pocket watch. Phil Brooks, who in 1974 invented a disposable syringe. Dr. Charles Richard Drew, who managed in his short 46 years of life to develop the blood bank, establish the American Red Cross, and organize the world's first, the very, very first, blood bank drive, for goodness sakes."

"Only because they couldn't send their black women to do it for them," Yvonne retorts.

"Black women such as Marie Brown who invented a video home surveillance system, or Dr. Patricia Bath who invented a method for removing cataracts."

"Girl, you need to check your history, your black history, and stop taking Mike's word for it."

"No, Kimi, I just check your history and that of your sister at the hands of black men to prove my point," she tells me smugly.

I'm not a violent person. I can only recall getting into one fight my entire life. I was around eleven at the time and my two-year-old sister Nicole had a bad habit of pulling the heads off my Barbie dolls. One day she had the misfortune of doing the same to my friend Brenda's favorite doll—Baby-alive. Brenda up and pushed Nicole down for the offense. I retaliated by smacking Brenda and pushing her down.

These days I would rather curse and walk away or curse and hang up, which is what I do.

I haven't the slightest idea what attracted me to the pintsize roadrunner in college. I'm kidding myself. We have so much in common, its still gives me goose bumps; we are both from Georgia and were both raised Baptist, and both our families moved to Boston when we were twelve years old. We are both thirty-four. I'm older by exactly two weeks. Our professions, however, are totally different; she could have played professional tennis—she's that good—but after falling in love she quit. She opted for a more conventional path; she went to college and became an emergency-room nurse.

I faint just having my blood drawn during a routine physical. I've wanted to write novels since I was fifteen years old. Not short stories or articles, but full-blown novels. Yvonne will not even read a grocery list. She says it's because she is required to read so much at work. She refuses to read anything outside of work unless it's church-related. I spend hours surfing the net, reading a little bit of everything. It helps me broaden my scope. Whenever I'm suffering from writer's block, I surf. It clears away the backup and my creative juices flow.

Before I get halfway downstairs the phone rings. I'm thinking it's Yvonne again, but a quick check of the caller ID box and I see it is Nicole calling.

"Hey, Nicky, what's up?"

"Hey, I'm surprised somebody answered. Didn't you say you guys were going to the mall today?"

"Yesterday. And yes, we did go. But even if we had gone today, we'd have made it home by now. Unlike some people, going to the mall is not an all-day affair."

"I know you aren't hinting in my direction. I don't have enough money to linger in the mall."

"That doesn't stop you from lingering with other people's money."

"Kimi, if I wanted a lecture, I would've called Mom."

"Yeah, right. You only call Georgia when you need more money."

"Wrong, I only call Georgia when you don't give me enough money. Speaking of which—"

"Don't ask, unless you want to get your feelings hurt. I gave you an extra forty bucks two weeks ago, Nicky. I'm not the bank."

"I didn't say you were. One day I'll pay you back the hundred and forty bucks."

"Hundred and forty?"

"Yep, the forty, plus the hundred I need today."

"Nope."

"Come on, Kimi. I would give it to you if you asked me."

"I would be borrowing my own money. Don't you get a check from Mom and Dad on Thursday, Nicky?"

"Every week."

"And you're broke? You sure you don't have an addiction of some sort—drinking, drugs, gambling?"

"I got addictions, all right. They're called Natasha and Nicholas."

Natasha and Nicholas are her kids. They are five and four, and quite a handful. Nicole's doing her best to be a good mom, but it is hard. Being a twenty-five-year-old mother of two is hard even with a partner—I know. Alone, it's nearly impossible. That is why I make a point of taking the kids every other weekend. I don't want Nicole to become burnt out, not when she is trying so hard to do the right thing.

Our parents' decision to move back to Georgia three years ago was a tough break for Nicole. She had a one- and two-year-old at the time, was a student at Northeastern University, and working six to eleven at Super Stop & Shop in Dedham. She had been dependent on them to help out with Natasha and Nicholas. But after almost twenty-five years my dad retired from his job at Hatchett Waterproofing and my parents had decided to move back to their small farm in Georgia. I sometimes think Nicole would have been better off following them as they asked her to, but she was head over heels in love at the time.

Robby Whales had captured her eighteen-year-old heart and taken it on a reckless journey of lies and betrayal that lasted for seven demoralizing years before derailing, leaving Nicole a single mother of two struggling to make ends meet while at the same time pursuing a college education.

I regret many of Nicole's decisions, some of which have led to her struggle. But I mostly admire her unshakable belief in herself. She has this air about her. I can't say exactly what it is, but when I'm around her I feel as though her life story has already been written, and God has slipped her the ending and she knows she is going to be a success. Even when she finally ended her failing relationship with Robby, I couldn't help but marvel at her show of strength. There she was, barely able to take care of her kids, with minimal help from Robby's trifling ass, and without a tear she unblinkingly tells him to hit the road. It was as if she woke up one day fed up with his whoring, his lying, just him period, and refused to hear any more excuses. Her abrupt about-face left me speechless.

I had spent the two years prior to Natasha's conception trying to get her to end it with Robby; telling her over and over again how attractive she was despite her beanpole shape. Assuring her that what she saw as bug-eyes and big lips were in actuality magnet pools and luscious lips that made up for any perceived flaws with her body. I all but got down on hands and knees begging her not to settle on Robby. But she wouldn't listen, not even when he had slapped her at a family cookout for chatting what he considered too long to my mother's handsome next-door neighbor. Daniel had beaten him down that day, and Nicole had never treated my husband the same again—always quiet and withdrawn whenever Daniel was around. It was as if she was mad at him for coming to her defense.

"I thought you said Robby was going to bring some money by."

"He was supposed to. I'm still waiting for it."

"He said Friday, right?"

"Yeah, Kimi, he said today. Look, when you and Mom and Dad came to me with the idea that I go to school full time, I said I didn't think it would work. But you guys wouldn't take no for an answer. You promised to support me financially," she says with attitude.

"True that, and we are. All I'm asking is, have you heard from Robby?"

"No, you're complaining. Robby was never a guarantee. You guys knew that."

"Why are you getting so defensive, Nicky?"

"Because I don't need you emphasizing what I already know, Kimi. Robby didn't bring the money as he said he would. Are you happy to hear me say that?"

"Hold up! What's that supposed to mean?"

"You are such a Gemini. My chart said I should avoid conflict today—Gemini conflict, to be exact."

"What kind of nonsense is that? Nicky, don't call my house being disrespectful. I'm hanging up now. You bring your skinny, broke ass by and Alex will meet you out front with the money. Don't even think of bringing your ungrateful ass in my house. Bye!"

I slam down the receiver. I'm pissed. If that skinny chick was not my flesh and blood, I would go out front and wait for her to show up and then knock her on her ass. While she was down I would dust my driveway with her unconscious body.

At about eight o'clock the doorbell rings. I'm pretty sure it's Nicole, but poke my head out to yell for Alex, anyway.

"Alex! Make sure that's your auntie before you open the door. There is an envelope on the coffee table for her."

"Okay, Mama," he calls over his shoulder as he rushes down the stairs. I think a part of him is hoping his father is on the other side of the door. I know better. I position myself at the top of the stairs so I can hear what's being said. It is Nicole, and she is alone. I'm guessing she got Mrs. Leigh, who lives across from her, to babysit. I can hear her asking about Angela, then about me. Alex tells her what she wants to know. That boy got a big mouth.

"Tell your mama I said thank you, and I'm sorry for earlier, okay?"

"What happened earlier?"

"None of your business, nosy." I yell down, saving Nicole from having to answer one way or another.

"Thanks, big sis," my sister calls out.

I don't answer back. I slam my bedroom door instead. Let her sleep on that for the night. If I wanted to be treated like crap I would call up my no-good husband.

CHAPTER 3

"Kimberly, the Bronzen account should've been ready Friday." Those are the first words that greet me when I walk into Thature Mathematics at seven forty-five Monday morning.

"Good morning, Mr. Stevens. My input on the Bronzen account was submitted Friday afternoon at two," I tell him nervously, as I make my way past curious eyes to get to my small office near the end of the hall.

"Submitted to whom?" he asks, on my heels.

"I finished double-checking Christine's numbers and passed the file on to Katherine. Why?"

Mr. Stevens doesn't answer my question; instead, he closes the door to my office. I'm beginning to sweat. I start to get an uneasy feeling that there is big trouble with the account and I've been pegged as the scapegoat.

"I have a copy of the work I did on my computer. If you want to see it, I'd be happy to print it out for you."

"I'll need that. I'm meeting with Jeremy at ten. I need to get all the facts together before then."

"The facts?" I asked, seeking clarification.

"The Bronzen account never made it over to Cauplum Enterprises."

"What? How could that have happened?"

"I'm still trying to figure that out, but what I do know is the auditors are there, demanding Cauplum's books on Bronzen, which they don't have because we never sent them over."

"Can't they reschedule? This can't be the first time something like this has happened," I say, sure my suggestion is reasonable.

"Any other time, Kimberly, I would suggest the same thing, but with Python going belly-up and hundreds of its employees losing millions in now-useless retirement investments, people are nervous, and rightly so. I saw a lady on the news the other night. She had saved for over twenty-seven years for her retirement. Python comes tumbling down, seemingly overnight. She wakes up to find her savings have been decimated, and she has less then ten thousand dollars to show for all her years of sacrificing."

"What does that have to do with Cauplum's Bronzen account? The retail end of their company has always flourished. They're not in danger of folding. Their stock is the strongest it has been in five years, and their health centers are no longer under state receivership. The auditing firm of Bernard and Myers gave them a clean bill of health last year. Their last quarterly exam showed membership up at all ten of their healthcare sites."

I doubt I'm telling Mr. Stevens anything he hasn't already thought through. With this in mind, I cover my face with both hands and take a deep breath. I heard somewhere that deep breaths send extra oxygen to the brain, enhancing its function. I need all my wits about me now. If Ted Stevens, CEO, Harvard graduate, class of seventy-two, and twenty-year veteran of Thature Mathematics Inc. is scared, so am I.

"If the media gets wind of this, they will blow this way out of proportion," I say aloud, finally seeing what the potential problem is.

"I have word that is just what the auditors are slyly threatening. If word starts to spread Cauplum is stalling the state auditors, Kimberly—"

"Cauplum Healthcare Division runs the risk of finding themselves right back in the hole they spent a great deal of time and money digging out of for the past five years," I finish for him.

"What do we do to fix this?" I ask, looking to Mr. Stevens with total confidence. He is the one man here who has treated me like I have a brain from day one. Him being white sort of makes his fair treatment even more special—not because he is better than the blacks or any other ethic group working here, but because he is a corporate male, conditioned to believe he is better than any other being in existence. But in the seven years I've been with Thature Mathematics, Mr. Stevens is the only person who ever offers to get me a cup of coffee when he steps out for a break.

"Katie says you never gave her the Bronzen files on Friday."

"That's a flat-out lie. I sent them to her at around two. I know that because my daughter called me not two minutes later to confirm after-school arrangements."

"Are you sure you pressed send on your computer, Kimberly?"

"What? Yes! I'm sure. If Katherine didn't receive the files, why didn't she say something to me on Friday?"

"She says she did."

"Not true, Mr. Stevens. I'm not, I repeat, not taking the blame for what sounds like a major screwup. I did my job."

"Well, I haven't the time to figure this out right now, Kimberly. I need that checked copy. I'll go over the numbers myself and pray there aren't any missed discrepancies. Their man Klein has a lot of questionable charges for work supposedly done for Bronzen."

I'm a little taken aback to hear him say this. I was not aware he was following the developments so closely.

"I didn't get where I am by totally detaching myself from the goings-on, Kimberly. Brad was instructed to e-mail me with any pertinent developments regarding Cauplum," Mr. Stevens explains, seeing my surprise. "Check your e-mail; there's a brief outline about the meeting at ten. I've called my own for nine in conference room seven. Have Mildred reschedule everything you have for today."

"Everything?" I ask, suspicious now. "Why not just my morning agenda? Making plans to throw me under the bus, Mr. Stevens?" My voice is joking, but I'm dead serious.

He looks me straight in the eyes and doesn't flinch. "Jeremy may very well fire whoever is found responsible, Kimberly, not because this is such a big deal, but because it is such a big deal right now."

My printer starts to print at that exact moment. Like the telephone ringing or an unexpected knock at the door, it brings a welcome end to an awkward moment.

Well, that is how it feels in my small ten-by-ten office as I look up at my boss of seven years. He has just informed me my job is on the line and I feel *relevant* and, in a strange way, excited. *I'm important here.* My actions can make or break a multimillion-dollar deal. It was my word against that of my nemesis Katherine. Suddenly, I'm not worried anymore. I'm looking forward to what is to come. I gather the pile of papers from my laser jet printer and hand them to my boss, and then I pop in a blank disk to copy the data.

"I will see you at ten," I say calmly.

"If you should get any calls between now and then pertaining to Cauplum, please refer them to my office," he orders, real businesslike, glances at his watch, and then leaves, closing my door softly. I immediately dial Yvonne and tell her the whole story in three minutes flat.

"You did everything you were supposed to do. You follow their repetitive protocol. You've got nothing to worry about."

I don't answer right away. I can hear Yvonne speaking with someone. She is at work and I can tell by the background noise she is busy.

"Listen, Eve, you sound busy, so I'll let you go, but I'll call back and let you know what happens."

"Okay, but call me, no matter what," she says. I can tell she is concerned.

"Promise promise." I say, Two minutes later, I'm calling my mother-in-law's house.

"Yeah?"

"Hello, is Daniel there?"

"Who wants to know?"

"His wife," I say indignantly.

"Hold, please," a male voice says, now trying to sound businesslike. I hear music playing in the background. Curious, I listen intently. I make out that it's Usher singing "You Don't Have to Call." I hang up. A minute later my phone rings, and it is Daniel.

"You called?"

"Yeah, but I hung up. I didn't want to interrupt what sounded like a get-together. You celebrating something I should know about, Daniel?"

"Nobody's celebrating, Kimi."

"Whatever, Daniel. Know what? I shouldn't have called. I don't have time to deal with this shit."

"Well, I was going to call you, anyway, to let you know I took three hundred out of savings this morning."

I'm about to curse this fool out when I hear laughter in the background—female laughter along with male laughter; I know his mama has gone to work by now.

"Who the hell is that, number one? And two, I know you didn't take your lying, can't-keep-a-job ass self to my bank and withdraw money!"

"Kimi, I'm not trying to get into an argument with you this morning," Daniel says, sounding bored with the whole matter. "I just didn't want you to be surprised when you checked the account."

"Daniel, I'm so through with you. You have no idea how through."

"Bye, Kimi."

The phone goes dead, and I literally have to count to twenty to regain my composure. My marriage of fifteen years is coming to an end, and for all I know, so is my job. If I were a weaker person, with just an ounce less dignity, I would get my coat and run for the nearest exit. I reach for my lunch bag and devour one of two tuna salad sandwiches meant for lunch and then chug down half the bottle of Pepsi.

When I arrive at Mr. Stevens's office at eight fifty-five, everyone else is already there, including Katherine Rings, who is usually shamelessly half an hour late for everything. I give her a hard stare before heading to the opposite side of the long conference table. I have not confronted the liar yet. I was afraid if I did and she insisted on lying to my face, I would strangle her by reflex. I stayed in my office with the door locked the entire time while waiting to present myself in conference room seven as ordered.

"I've reviewed Cauplum's books on the Bronzen as best I could, focusing my attention mainly on any seemingly questionable expenditures," Mr. Stevens says. His eyes seem to linger on me. I look away. "The six of you were given the task of handling the Cauplum account, handpicked by me out of a staff of one hundred and fifteen. Brad, Charley, Katie, you three alone bring over thirty years of experience to this project. Three master's degrees. Harvard University, Howard University, Suffolk University. You can't get much better than that," he says, waving a hand at each one as he called out his or her respective alma mater. "Christine, Jennifer, Kimberly, all of you are CPAs. It's not as if I placed a multimillion-dollar account in the hands of a bunch of incompetents," he says, sounding defensive.

And so it went. He spent the next forty or so minutes justifying his decision to give us the account and explaining why he hadn't personally made sure the final papers were received at Cauplum by the close of business last Friday.

"I think the way to address this problem construc-tively is to pick up where the chain broke down," I say, waging a war within for the courage not to be intimi-dated. I receive a variety of looks. The other two flawed minions in the room, Christine and Jennifer, have the deer-in-the headlights stare going on. The three men shift their bodies, looking extremely uncomfortable, and Katherine flips her hair and smacks her thin, overly glossed lips. I'd love to snatch a knot in this bony blonde chick. "I sent the file to Katherine after checking and rechecking Christine's work, just as I was instructed to do. I echo her concerns regarding one Thomas Klein. There are several causes for concern regarding the man's expense account."

"Katie says she never received the file, and when she asked you about it, you said everything was all set. She assumed you had taken care of getting it over to Cauplum," my boss explains.

"So what—Katherine can't speak for herself? You're her advocate, Mr. Stevens? I thought we were here to ascertain what happened, not record Katherine's version for the record. I do have a side." I say this all in one breath. I'm sitting on my hands; otherwise they would be flying this way and that way.

"I'm not going to get into that just yet, Kimberly. However, I agree completely with your findings. Cauplum should have been made aware of Mr. Klein's dealings. It would be incompetent of us to drop this in their laps at this late date. They won't have time to react before the auditors are all over it."

"What then?" I ask, not caring if I appear dense. I want to hear him say plainly what I suspect.

"Klein's questionable expenses will be deleted—for the time being."

"How can we do that?" I ask, practically rubbing the skin off my forehead. "That's got to be against the law, Mr. Stevens."

"Not if we're careful about it," Mr. Harvard University assures us. Bradley Worther is a walking ency-clopedia. If he says there is a way out of this mess, I believe him. He studied law before switching to business. There is not a law passed that Bradley doesn't know inside and out, along with knowing a way around it.

"We submit a report, minus Mr. Klein's accounts, with a vague footnote stating, 'Processing, final draft to follow'. In the interim Cauplum avoids looking shady, we escape with minimal damage, and the auditors get most of what they want." Bradley smiles broadly and I shake my head, relieved.

"Cauplum isn't going to be happy with our pussy-footing, but this just might work," Mr. Stevens agrees.

"If we get them out of this mess, they'll be more grateful than annoyed," Charles predicts. I silently concur.

"This decision doesn't leave this room, understood?" Mr. Stevens says suddenly. I feel as if I'm a part of a conspiracy. Now I know how those people feel on television when they wind up in court being charged with conspiracy or obstruction of justice. No one believes them when they say they were hoodwinked into breaking the law. I know I never believe them.

"I don't care what you do. I'm not signing anything or altering anything," I announce to the room. Several of my coworkers simultaneously echo my declaration. I am reminded of a scene from school: the teacher asks, "Does anyone have any questions?" Not a single hand goes up until some sorry soul, whose fear of facing his mama with a F is greater than his fear of looking stupid in front of his peers, speaks up—followed by a chorus of 'I dos.'

"That isn't going to be necessary," Bradley assures us. "I'll get something typed up and personally have the courier service take it over." His mention of the service takes us back to the undelivered Cauplum books.

"Okay, that's settled. That leaves us with the matter of last Friday," Mr. Stevens says, voicing what we all were thinking, I imagine. "There appear to be two vastly different accounts of what happened after the draft left Christine's possession. Kimberly, you say you sent the file via office computer to Katie. According to Katie, she never received it. She says she was under the impression that you had sent the complete report over to Cauplum by courier. You say you thought Katie was taking care of getting the files over to Cauplum. Does that sum it up, ladies?"

I'm about to call Katherine a liar to her artificially tanned face, but she gets her words out first. "I would just like to reiterate what I told you this morning, Ted. I'm so sorry. I take the blame for Kimberly's confusion. I should have made myself clearer. I should have seen to the package getting to Cauplum. I should not have assumed she would follow through. No offense, Kimberly, but my father always said, 'If you want something done right, you do it yourself.' "

This could get ugly. I take a deep breath because my mother always said, "Think before you speak." I would like nothing more than to walk over and yank out every one of Katherine's bleached blonde strands, but that would only get me fired. What the hell.

"You should have seen to it, Katherine. It was your job to see that Cauplum got the damn report—right after I sent it over to you. We all agreed it would be done that way. You dropped the ball, not me. Offer up as many fake apologies as you want; it won't change a thing. But I'll tell you this only once: the next time you call me incompetent, you'll need another nose job."

"Kimberly, enough!" my boss commands, a clear warning in his voice.

"What?" I shout back, banging my fist on the table. I know my behavior is pushing the limits of what he is expected to accept, but I can't help it. I'm steaming. The expressions of shock my coworkers are sending my way tell me my ass is in hot water.

"I want to speak with you, Kimberly, before I meet with Jeremy. Everybody else, out!" Mr. Stevens orders, his face beet red.

Everyone scrambles to exit, the scraping of chairs against the floor further jarring my already jumbled thoughts. My fear of being jobless is second only to my embarrassment. I've become what Katherine has spent the last seven years trying to reduce me to. I just went "ghetto" in a multimillion-dollar corporate boardroom.

"Threatening an employee at Thature Mathematics is strictly forbidden and will never, never be tolerated. Am I clear?"

"What about favoritism? Is that tolerated here, Ted?"

"Pardon?"

"Favoritism, *Ted*. An example would be how you call your boys by little pet names, as you do the little bimbo. I'm Kimberly, but Katherine no-brains is adoringly called Katie. Christine versus Brad, Jennifer is Jennifer but Charles is Charley."

"If you're looking to make a case for discrimination, young lady, you're welcome to try. You just head on down to human resources and file whatever kind of complaint you want. Now if you will excuse me, *Mrs. Riley*, I have a meeting." His language is deliberate and crisp as he storms from the room.

I rush back to my office and gather my belongings. I don't call Yvonne. I do tell Mildred I'm leaving sick. I don't know why I bother; it's not as if I have anything awaiting my attention, anyway.

CHAPTER 4

I turn off the car engine outside my mother-in-law's house. I don't know why I'm here, really. I suppose I want to confront Daniel, but not as much as I want a confrontation, period. He answers the door after about the fifth knock.

"Kimi, what are you doing here?"

"What the hell is going on, Daniel?"

"Go home, Kimi," he tells me and then moves to close the door.

I'm not having that. I shove my way in, managing because he's not expecting me to be so forceful and because I put all my two hundred pounds into it.

"What the fuck you trying to hide, Daniel?" I don't wait for an answer; I charge past him. I know my way around the place; I'd been here countless times when Daniel and I were dating. I head straight for what was once Daniel's bedroom. He grabs me before I can turn the doorknob.

" You can't barge into my mama's house and act like you own the place, Kimi!"

"Get the fuck off me! You got a skank up in here, don't you?" Not giving him time to answer, I turn on him, swinging. I hit him everywhere I can reach—his chest, his face, the side of his head. I even manage to punch him hard in the stomach. He doesn't fight back. He knows his ass is guilty and deserves my rage.

"I'm calling the cops, Kimi, if you don't get your ass out!"

His threat is wasted on me. I make a run for the bedroom while he's still recovering from my attack. I have to see for myself who is in there. Otherwise I will wonder if every woman I pass on the street is the one. As I grab the doorknob, I feel Daniel's arm come around my waist, pulling me back. I cannot describe my frustration at being restrained.

"I'm not leaving until I see who it is, Daniel!" I scream at the top of my lungs.

My husband keeps the hold he has on me and lifts me off the floor. He is moving back toward the front door when the door I was trying to open suddenly opens and out walks Daniel's friend Bobby. I freeze. Daniel releases me. I don't move. I'm totally confused and sort of relieved. I had expected a female to appear.

"What's all the commotion about?" Bobby asks, rubbing his eyes as if he had been sleeping—only he doesn't look as if he has just awakened. His black eyes are wide and alert. He covers his mouth as if to hide a yawn, but it looks forced. I know these two fucks are hiding something or someone.

"Bobby, how's Maria these days?" I ask. Lord knows I don't care how his gossiping-ass wife is doing. Maria Locus is worse than Daniel's mama when it comes to dishing dirt on people. She's always nice enough to me whenever Daniel has brought her and Bobby around, but the woman always has something bad to say about some-body—Bobby, her sister, her own mama, even her dead father. I don't trust people like that. My philosophy is, if you can bad-mouth your own family then that doesn't say much for what kind of relationship we could have. She should be putting her energy into losing some of her excess weight.

"She's good. You know Maria, always trying a new diet," Bobby says, snickering.

"Good for her," I say, slowly walking forward.

"I'm sorry I woke you, Bobby, but I got a little crazy. I was sure Daniel had a woman up in here."

"Nope, just us guys here," Bobby claims.

I don't believe him, especially when it seems he's pur-posely blocking the bedroom.

"Kimi, about the money. I'm going to put it back next week. Bobby got a lead on a job. I'm going to check it out tomorrow."

Now, is it just me, or is Daniel rambling on, trying to pacify me all of a sudden? "That's good, Daniel," I lie. Right about now I couldn't care less about the freakin' money or some dead-end job Bobby the mechanic hooked him up with.

"Something is not right here, Daniel, but I don't have time to figure this out. I've got to get going. I only left work for an early lunch. I better get back. Bye." I brush past Daniel without another word, and he knows better than to try to stop me. By the time I get to my car, I'm almost running. The sooner I drive off, the sooner I can circle back and see what's really going on.

I leave my car down a side street two blocks away and half walk, half run back to Daniel's mother's house. My feet are killing me by the time I inconspicuously take cover at a convenience store. I pretend to be using the filthy pay phone out front as an excuse for being there. About ten minutes after I start my amateur surveillance, out walk Daniel and Bobby—alone. It's possible they could have left a girl behind. But why? And why doesn't Daniel turn to lock the door? I know he has a key. It always irked me that he kept his keys to his mama's house handy on his key chain.

"What the hell are those two up to?"

"Looks like they're about to go for a ride."

I jump about a hundred feet in the air. I was not expecting an answer. I look behind me and see a middle-aged black man with a shiny bald dome smiling at me.

"You scared me." I say it as if I think he did it on purpose. And I kinda do.

"I didn't mean to," he claims, a bit too late.

"I'm just trying to use the phone."

"Are you done?" he asks, gesturing toward the phone with large yellowish eyes. My Uncle Edward had eyes like that from drinking every day, my father says.

"Here you go." I gladly hand him the cootie phone. I'm about to duck inside the convenience store when he calls out to me.

"You should hire a professional. Looks like you could afford it."

Before I can pretend I don't know what he's talking about, Mr. Bald Dome turns his back and starts dialing.

I steal a quick glance up the street and see my husband's Beamer backing out of his mama's driveway, so I make haste to get inside the store. But what the bald dome said sticks with me as I watch Daniel's Beamer cruise by.

When I get home, I immediately make two phone calls. I call my answering service at work to see if I have any messages. Mildred transfers all my calls there when I'm out of the office. I have no unheard messages, so I call Mildred's desk line. She answers the phone in her usual overly bright soprano voice. I remember being twenty; I was never that bubbly.

"Mildred, it's Kimberly. I'm just checking to see if perhaps you forgot to forward my phone to voice mail." I squeeze my eyes shut, wishing I could just hang up and put myself out of my misery. I sound desperate, and pitiful.

"Afraid not, Kimberly. I transferred your phone as soon as you stormed out."

I hate this child-woman.

"I did not storm out, Mildred. I left early because I'm not feeling well today."

"I don't blame you. I would have left early, too, if I were you. So much drama around here today. I wish I could just pick up and go, but somebody has got to man the phone. Speaking of phones, these are ringing off the hook. Hold, please."

Mildred puts me on hold and I hang up, relieved and pissed. I don't deserve this shit; first my marriage collapses, then my job. Now some inexperienced secretary thinks it is okay to disrespect my ass.

After wandering aimlessly through my house for a time and mentally replaying the disaster at my office, I find my thoughts repeatedly returning to what Bald Dome had suggested, and before I think to question why, I'm surfing the net for private detectives. After surfing three sites, not sure what I'm really looking for, an ad jumps out at me.

The name, Discreet Detective Agency, was in comic-book-style typeface in the center of the page. "We find them and tell you what they've been up to" was in smaller typeface beneath the name, along with a local number. I'm seriously thinking about calling. I print the page, but I don't make the call after all. I would love to say I came to my senses and blame the whole crazy idea on my having been severely rattled by what happened to me at work and then at my mother-in-law's, but the truth of the matter is that I realize I am in danger of running late picking Angela up from cheerleading tryouts. I promised her we would head over to Three Scoops Homemade Ice Cream Café for cappuccino crunch with extra sprinkles to celebrate her efforts whether she made the team or not.

I'm about a block away from my daughter's school when my cellphone starts ringing. A quick glance and I see it is Yvonne. I'm so tempted to let my voice mail pick up, but I don't.

"I told you to call me, no matter what."

These are the first words out of Yvonne's mouth. I expected no less from her. According to my sister, the wannabe astrologer, Yvonne is a born worrier.

"I got tied up, girly girl."

"Too tied up to call me, even though you know I'm sitting here worrying about you?"

I smile to myself. "I'm sorry, Eve, but things went from bad to worse and I jetted. I don't even know if I have a job."

"What happened?"

"Katherine happened. That lying backstabber always happens."

"You need to be more specific, Kimi."

"Can't, don't have time, but I promise to fill you in on everything later on tonight."

"But—"

"This time I truly promise, Eve. I see Angela in front of her school, girl. I'd better let you go. I don't want her hearing what I have to tell you."

"Great. Now I die of curiosity for the next zillion hours."

"Sorry, Eve."

"No, you're not."

"Whatever. I told you Angela went out for junior cheerleader, right?" I ask, coming to a stop in front of my daughter's prep school.

Angela doesn't see me right away. She is in a circle of about six girls, all of whom are at least a head shorter than my statuesque beauty. She inherited height from me and Daniel. But her smooth, even caramel complexion and symmetrical facial features, the narrow slightly upturned nose, the faintly pink bow lips, and big black eyes enhanced by long lashes, are all inheritance from me. The kid is going places. God truly saw to that with her looks. I'm making sure she has the brains to know what to do when she gets there.

"Did she make the squad?" Yvonne asks, not bothering to answer my question. I can tell by her slightly strained tone that she is hot and bothered.

"By the look of her sixty-watt smile, I'd say it's a pretty safe bet Ms. Angela Riley made the squad," I say, smiling.

"Tell Angela I said congrats, and I want to hear all about who she dusted."

"Sillyhead. I'll tell her you said congrats. She sees me. I'll talk to you tonight—promise, promise."

"We'll see. Bye, Kimi."

My daughter races to the car and, before I can ask if she made the squad, she pokes her head inside the passenger side window and screams, "Mom, I made it!" at the top of her lungs.

"I knew it. Baby, I'm proud of you. Get in. We have a date with the ice cream man. What is it, Angela? Is everything okay?" I ask, scanning the area for something amiss, because she makes no move to get in the car.

"Mom, you think my friend Ashley can come along?"

"Ashley? I've never heard you mention an Ashley before now. Who are her parents? Where are her parents?"

"Mom," my daughter whines.

"I'm not joking, Angela."

"She lives with her dad. He's some type of advisor," she says. "We got introduced today at tryouts. You haven't heard her name before because she isn't in any of my classes. Mom, please can she come? She called her dad, and he's running late at work. But he says it's okay if she comes with us, and he will pick her up when he gets off."

"He knows where we live, how?"

"I told him?"

"Ang, we don't even know the man and he doesn't know us. Where is the child's mother?"

"In Texas."

"Angela—"

"I'm for real, Mom. Ashley and her mother moved back to Texas after her parents divorced two years ago. But she was having trouble adjusting, so she came back. She started Gorman Leaver last September. She doesn't have any brothers or sisters. Her dad's really busy with work. If we don't bring her along, she'll have to take two street buses home and that'll take forever."

"I didn't know you were so skilled at the violin, my dear."

"Mom."

"You got all that info, and still managed to make the squad—now I'm really impressed."

"Come on, Mom, say yes, please."

"Okay, she can come, but I better not find out later her dad's some deranged madman."

"Thanks, Mom. I'll be right back."

I watch as half my reason for existing rushes off. I don't know who among the excited group is supposed to be Ashley because Angela doesn't appear to speak to anyone in particular. After about a minute of watching the group, I honk. Angela latches on to a petite redhead and hurries back to the car.

"Sorry, Mom," she says, sitting directly behind me. "Mom, this is Ashley. Ashley, this is my mom, Mrs. Kimberly Riley."

"Hello, Ashley. It's nice to meet you, and congratulations on making the squad." I meet the child's eye in the rearview mirror.

"Thank you, Mrs. Riley. And thanks for taking me along."

"You're welcome, dear." I catch my daughter's eye and send her a warning look that says clearly, *There better not be any problems later because of this.* She is wide-eyed and looking innocent.

Three Scoops is abuzz with a hodgepodge of clientele: hyper adolescents, young couples, old couples, and everyone in between. We order and the girls choose a booth near the front of the café, guaranteeing we will suffer every draft as customers come and go. I withhold my objections and indulge my daughter and company. I nod, smile, and occasionally offer up my two cents worth during discussions such as: Summerset and Carver having their tryouts at the same time, whether or not Linda somebody who left Gorman Leaver and now attended Carver had made cheerleader there and, if so, was it be because she was good enough or because her boyfriend's mother is a judge, and the monumental difference between just turning thirteen and having turned thirteen seven months ago—to name a few vital topics.

As soon as we get inside the house, I abandon the girls for the privacy of my bedroom and call Discreet Detective Agency. I make an appointment with a pleasant-sounding woman and call Yvonne.

"Unless you're ready to tell me what's going on with you, this is going to be a real short call." These are the first words out of Yvonne's mouth.

"Some people should be barred from caller ID, Eve," I tell her with a forced chuckle. Yvonne doesn't join in; she is oddly silent. "Eve?"

"I'm still here—for now."

"You want the long drawn-out version, or will a summary of my world caving in suffice?"

"Whichever tells me what is going on."

"I ran out like a coward, Eve."

"Kimi."

"Yes?"

" I want the long drawn-out version."

"Shut up, Eve," I say, feeling a tad better, thanks to her dry humor. I go on for about half an hour telling Eve everything, including my appointment with the private detective. "Eve?" I prompt after there's nothing more to tell.

"You hired a private detective to spy on your husband? Kimi—"

"I haven't hired a private detective—yet. I only have an appointment to speak with one."

"Split hairs all you want, but when it's all said and done, I think you've lost it."

"I've lost a lot—my marriage, my belief in happily ever after, possibly my job, but not my damned mind."

"I don't mean to make you feel worse or put you on the defensive, Kimi, but you need to take a deep breath and try to see reason. You've been through a great deal today—"

"This day has been a long time coming, Eve. We talk daily, and if you've listened to half of what I've said for the past year and a half, you'd know that for yourself," I say, my voice rising.

"Mom?"

I turn quickly—startled to see Angela at the door of my bedroom. "Eve, I'll call you back later, okay, bye."

I end the call without Eve's concurrence. I'm afraid of how much of our conversation Angela has overheard. Damn. I should have waited until much later to call Yvonne back. But I had needed to vent—I still do. Everything seems to be closing in on me, leaving me feeling as if some invisible force is restricting my very will.

"You should have knocked, Angela. Haven't I always said if my door is closed you should knock before you barge headlong into my room?"

"Yes," she says in a small, pitiful voice. I've stolen my daughter's joy. It was unintentional, but I've done so nonetheless.

"You didn't answer when I knocked, Mom."

"I didn't hear you, Angela. What do you want?" My words remain sharp, but now it's only a smokescreen. I don't want my self-reproach showing. Why? I don't know. Perhaps I fear appearing vulnerable or, worse, weak in front of my child. "Ashley's dad is out front. He's waiting to meet you."

"What! How long has he been waiting out there?" I ask, alarmed I might make a bad first impression. I shouldn't care, but I do. For as far back as I can remember, I've always cared what others thought and said about me. Nicole says it's the Gemini's fate to worry endlessly about how the world views us, even to the point of obsessing about our posture. I would normally blow off Nicole's zodiac readings as nothing but "hogwash" as my big mama Rosa used to say, but I've caught myself adjusting my hand until it rests just so, or crossing and uncrossing my legs in hopes of capturing some elusive pose I wasn't even sure existed. Too bad my obsessing hasn't stopped me from spooning and drinking myself to death with all things fattening.

Ashley's ivory hand is frantically waving at me from the passenger side of a 2008 black Bentley convertible.

"So Daddy is a player or wannabe player."

"Mom," my fearful thirteen-year-old pleads.

Her fear of being embarrassed by me is comical and somewhat fitting. We've come full circle and it's only taken a decade or so. I vividly remember my own pleas to a three-year-old Angela that she lower her voice in church, or that she not slurp her pasta when we have guests over for dinner. And if it pleased her, could she not ask her Uncle Leroy, when he invites himself over for Christmas dinner, if the silky, chestnut-colored wavy *thing* sitting in the center of his kinky jet-black locks is indeed his real hair.

"No need to fear, Angela, Mama Cool is here," I whisper superhero-like, pulling her close for a playful squeeze as I go to the Bentley. I'm envious—shame on me, but it's true. My life, as it is, never allowed for such selfish purchases. By the looks of this blinding babe magnet, it had to set him back at least two hundred grand.

A lean, fit male emerges from the showpiece. My envy meter rises. He has Hollywood casting-call good looks: beautiful come-hither blue eyes, a finely chiseled face with a square chin, and not-too-thin lips. Short and glossy dirty blond hair completed the look.

I've never been envious—okay, jealous—of a man until now.

"Hi, I'm Thomas."

"I'm Kimberly." I manage to introduce myself, despite the sudden wave of shyness washing over me. Out of the blue, I'm wishing I had started dieting six mouths ago, not that I have ever entertained the notion of an interracial relationship. I just feel uncomfortable going one-on-one with a man I find so attractive knowing I'm so far from looking my best. Vain, but true.

"I'm really grateful to you, Kimberly. I don't know how I would have managed if you hadn't taken Ashley along."

"Don't mention it. She was no trouble at all. As a matter of fact, she kept Angela company and out of my hair."

I don't know why I said that. I should have simply let him thank me and allowed that to be that. If he is anything like the man I'm married to, he needs to be reminded that childcare isn't just a one-way street. The man had probably taken on his kid after much arm twisting. Of course he could have volunteered to get out of paying child support. Why am I being so cynical? I'm unfairly judging him based on my own life experiences.

"I'm grateful nonetheless, Kimberly. Perhaps I could treat you—and your husband—to dinner some evening soon?"

Did this handsome devil just try picking me up? I know I didn't imagine that calculated pause in his invite. Sounded like an inquiry about my marital status to me. I'm still wearing the microscopic diamond Daniel gave me sixteen years ago and has never considered replacing, as I've hinted he should.

"Maybe," I say, my smile strained. I'm uncomfortable in my own skin, and I want this man gone—now. Abruptly I move away, interrupting the girls' conversation to say good-bye to Ashley. Without another glance, I usher Angela inside. From the safety of my living-room window, I watch until the black Bentley is out of sight.

CHAPTER 5

It is past midnight, long after my kids have finished their homework, filled their bellies, given me the third degree regarding their father, and finally settled in for the night. I'm still sitting in front of my computer, unable to type so much as a word and unable to fall asleep, either. There has been no word from my office. Should I go to work tomorrow?

Twelve-eighteen. Dreading the sleepless night ahead, I abandon my room.

Insomnia. I've suffered from bouts of it in the wake of every crisis in my life: like when my Grandma Rosa died; when Alex was three months old and came down with whooping cough; and again when Angela got lost in Wal-Mart. That was the longest ten minutes of my life; I didn't sleep for two weeks afterwards. "Here I go again," I lament to the empty kitchen, just before opening the refrigerator to scan its contents. I'm not hungry, the nagging voice of salvation tries to remind me, but I ignore it, as usual, and go to town on two cold drumsticks, chasing them down with a tall glass of Pepsi.

At two thirty-seven I call my sister Nicole. She can stand to lose a little sleep. She doesn't have class tomorrow, I reason. She answers around the seventh ring.

"Somebody better be dead or dying, Kimi. Because if this is one your insomnia calls, I'm hanging up. Kimi? I can hear your big ass breathing. I know you're still there."

"Why I call you of all people, I'll never know. I'm hanging up now, Nicky."

"You do and I'll crank-call your ass until six in the morning."

"Go ahead, it'll give me something to do," I challenge her. My voice must have conveyed my dejected state because Nicole's next words, while still gruff, were also laced with concern.

"I told you to buy some NyQuil and take a good swig whenever you can't sleep. I don't know why you won't do it."

"I don't need drugs, Nicky. We have this discussion every time I can't sleep."

"Cause you're a hard head. You won't get addicted to NyQuil, Kimi. We'll both get some sleep, that's all."

"Whatever, Nicky; you're not a doctor. I might end up a NyQuil addict."

"Now you're being silly. Typical Gemini behavior."

"Don't start that zodiac shit."

"You called me at three in the morning. I'll talk about shit-stained drawers if I want to."

"Now I know I'm hanging up; you done gone and lost your mind, Nicky," I declare. Then I can't help but laugh my head off. I don't know why this girl didn't try to be a professional comic; she could get a laugh out of a dead man.

"Do you feel better?" she asks when my laughter dies down.

I'm convinced God made sisters so that we would have a permanent paradox in our lives. Why? I've no idea.

"I feel as good as I can considering my marriage is over, I may be jobless, and another diet appears doomed before it ever gets started."

Nicole is silent for a good ten seconds. As a matter of fact, I have to call her name to get her to acknowledge I've said something. Even then, her "I'm here" is hardly sufficient.

"That is all you going to say?" I prompt, getting pissed. "A few sisterly words of encouragement would go a long way right about now."

"What's that old saying? If you can't say anything good, etc. . . . Besides, I have studying to do in the morning."

"Can't say anything good about what? My marriage? My job? My weight? What?"

"All of the above," she says straightaway.

"What are you itching to say, Nicky?" I ask, not because I really value or care to hear the opinion of a twenty-three-year-old, but because I can't stand not knowing what my sister thinks of me and my life.

"Nat and Nick are invited over this weekend no matter what—right?"

"What kind of nonsense is that?"

"And you're gonna cornrow Nat's hair?" Nicole asks without bothering to answer me.

"I already promised Nat I would do her hair. Besides, I would never punish my niece and nephew for shit you do and say. You should know that without checking."

"You've never asked my uncensored opinion of *you* before. I feel it's wise to set a few ground rules," she says, attempting to sound carefree, but I catch the hint of seriousness that slips in.

"You've given me your point of view numerous times over the years, Nicky, whether I've asked for it or not. I don't see what's so different tonight."

"That's because you're confusing regulated, for-what-it's-worth advice with uncontestable, you're-fuckin'-up-your-life facts."

"My life's not fucked up, number one. And you would do well to sort your own dirty laundry before you try to sort mine, Miss I got two kids, no father for them, no child support, no prospect for a father figure for them, and not enough hours in the day to get half the crap done that must be done, let alone time to get your black ass back in the dating game. Mr. Wales has done quite a number on your life."

"Are you done, Kimi? Because now I'm looking forward to this intervention."

"Intervention? Girl, you crazy. You actually believe I need my kid sister to rescue me?"

"Who better than me? I know everything that's going on. You need to divorce Daniel, not because he's a no-good, untrustworthy nigga, but because he's a no-good, untrustworthy nigga who's taken eighteen years of your life and unconscionably filled them with mostly grief.

Look at you—you're a fatty. I'm sorry if my saying it so bluntly hurts, but the truth is the truth. You act as though it doesn't bother you that you've given up your dream of becoming a published author to be the sole stable support system for your kids. You pretend the stress of being a one-woman show doesn't bother you, but I see it does. It manifests itself no matter how hard you try to hide it from everybody, and probably deny it to yourself. Once upon a time I envied your bangin' body. Not anymore."

"Funny, I thought it would take you about six or eight years of college to become a full-fledged advice-giving psychologist with the credentials to dispense therapeutic advice."

"Doesn't take a therapist to figure out what's going on with you, Kimi. I've firsthand knowledge—"

"Firsthand knowledge, my ass. You just can't resist the opportunity to pick my marriage apart. You're still bullshit with Daniel for giving Robby the beat-down he deserved. Only God knows why. Guess you were so used to receiving it that you resent Daniel putting a stop to the ass whoopin' you had come to expect from good old Rob."

"I don't resent being saved per se, Kimi, though I'm an independent spirit. I resented being saved from the big bad wolf by a wolf in sheep's clothing," Nicole says evenly.

Her words are surprisingly calm, lacking all trace of defensiveness. That's not good, especially when I'm trying my damnedest to draw blood.

"At least Daniel tried to be a good husband and father. Robby never once asked you to marry him, and poor Nat and Nick are about as important to him as mud on a new pair of Jordan's. I'm sure they monopolized his mind for about a good minute. But by and large, he chalked the whole parenting experience up to an unfortunate misstep."

"Why you bring my kids into this, Kimi? I'm trying to help your fat-ass self."

"Do you really think I need a poverty-stricken, know-it-all chick to help me? You obviously let your psychology thing, which I largely am paying for, go to your big-ass head. The day I need your help, Nicky, is the day I slit my wrists. And you best get to making other arrangements for your Bébé-Bébé kids. I'm busy this coming weekend and all the weekends after that," I inform her, my voice as high as it can go.

I slam down the receiver before Nicole can tell me what she thinks of my backpedaling disregard for her kids. I've never been this angry with my sister. I can't even think a complete thought for close to an hour, during which time I manage to chow down on two ham sandwiches and down two glasses of Pepsi.

I shouldn't have asked Nicole to tell me what was on her mind. Her hesitation spoke volumes. I knew I wasn't going to like what she had to say, and I hadn't.

Trying to get some sleep proved just as futile as I expected. At six I give up and roll my fat butt out of bed. I can't decide whether to put on my Buns of Steel tapes that have been gathering dust for six months—the last time Daniel quit a job—or hop into the shower.

Ten minutes later I'm still prowling about my bedroom, undecided, when my son yells my name. Now I'm no track star. I don't even know the world's record for the fifty-meter dash, but I'd bet my life's savings I broke it getting to Alex's room.

There is a moment of raw anguish when I throw open the door and can't locate Alex right away. A second later he yells "Mom" again. Relief flows through me, giving me the energy to move. I locate Alex on the opposite side of the room wedged between his bed and the wall. He is all tangled up in the bed sheet.

"Alex, wake up!" I command, bending down and gently shaking his shoulder. At first he just thrashes about, as if he is fighting with someone or something in a dream. All of a sudden, he bolts up to a sitting position. His slanted hazel eyes are huge and roving to and fro.

"Alex! Wake up, baby. Wake up. You're dreaming, Alex," I say, shaking his shoulders. The force causes his head to jerk back and forth like a rag doll's. I'm afraid I may have hurt him.

"How'd I get on the floor?" he asks suddenly and calmly. He's serious, and I'm relieved.

"Apparently, you were dreaming. You don't remember any part of what happened?" I ask, helping him to stand. As if this future skyscraper needs my assistance.

"Well, sort of. Somebody knocked me down. You were there, Mom, but you're not the one who did it," he quickly adds.

"Well, that's good to hear," I say, reaching up to grasp his chin for a brief reassuring squeeze. "What else happened, Alex?"

"Well, let me see. I was dancing—"

"Dancing?"

"Yeah, dancing, Mom," he says. He's frowning now. Alex hates to be reminded that he has two left feet. Like mother, like son, in this case.

"I was dancing. I think I was at a party for you. Your birthday, I think."

"God, no. I've had all the birthdays I wish to have, Alex."

"You're only thirty-four. That's not so old," he says, trying to reassure me and failing.

"Yeah, well, thirty-five is my limit, and I have no intention of celebrating it. I'd like to grow old quietly, thank you very much."

Alex chuckles for about five seconds, and then clears his throat. "Anyway, I'm not totally sure it was a birthday party, but you were laughing and dancing—"

"I'm dancing, too? Was I any good? Please tell me I didn't make a fool of myself."

"Mom."

"Don't 'Mom' me. If I'm dancing with other people around I need to know."

"You looked good to me, but you fell, and Dad and this other guy were fighting over who would help you up."

"Hmmm."

"But no one laughed at you."

"Okay, what else?"

"That's it, really."

"You said somebody pushed you down. Who?"

"I don't know. I didn't see his face."

I smile briefly at my son's male chauvinism, assuming only a "he" could have pushed him down.

"That's a pretty confusing dream, Alex, at least to me. I can't make heads or tails of it. My mom used to say that what we dream really isn't what it seems. Whatever that means. Are you okay now?"

"Yeah, but I think I hurt my booty bone when I fell."

"In your dream or falling off the bed?"

He's about to answer but glimpses the laughter in my eyes and sucks his teeth instead.

"I got to get ready for school."

"I thought you said you hurt your behind? Sounds like you hit your head as well."

"Mom."

"You worried about being late for school? Something is wrong up in here, Alex." I pretend to examine his head, receiving a louder teeth sucking and exasperated sigh for my efforts. I take that as my cue and leave.

I arrive at my office at seven forty-five sharp, as usual, but I don't get up the nerve to step onto the elevator until eight. The ride from the lobby to my ninth floor office seems to take only a few seconds instead of the usual forever; today the elevator doesn't stop on every floor along the way to load and unload. Fate seems to be in a hurry to play itself out. I'm the only one to get off on the ninth floor. It adds to my feeling of me against the powers that be. In my case it's Ted. It's clear he's waiting for me. It's also clear that the two security guards with him are also waiting for me. I stop dead in my tracks.

Unfortunately for me, my office is bustling with activity already. Mildred is staring openly, while everyone else milling about appears oblivious to my being there. For once I prefer Mildred's naively honest response to a situation that has to be the talk of the office. I'm mentally aware of my every facial twitch, every bead of perspiration, especially the telling bead on my nose.

"Kimberly, I would like a word with you—in my office—now."

I suppose Ted added the last because my misgivings about accompanying him are showing.

"Sure thing. Just give me a minute to put my things in my office."

"Why don't you hold on to them for now, Kimberly," Ted suggests gently, and then holds out an arm, gesturing for me to precede him. My stomach drops to my shoes. I attempt to walk in the direction he has indicated, but my legs seem suddenly to be made of lead. If not for the certainty that if I didn't move on my own the security guards would move me by force, I don't think I could have willed my betraying limbs to obey my commands to get a move on. Halfway to Ted's office, I glimpse Katherine exiting the ladies' room. Ordinarily, I probably wouldn't have given her presence a second thought except that she is on time. She is empty-handed except for the Kleenex she uses to dab at both eyes. This means she has already had time to hang her coat and what have you in her office.

The guards don't accompany Ted and me into his office, but when I emerge twenty minutes later, they are right on my heels. As a matter of fact, the taller of the two beats me pressing the elevator button. I'm not sure if it's because he was faster or because the tears I can't contain despite my struggle to do so are beginning to blur my vision. I spot Katherine exiting the ladies' room—again. A smirk appears and disappears from her face so fast I can't swear I didn't imagine it there. I stop, and so does she. She places her hands on her narrow hips and I make a move in her direction. The security guard on my left takes hold of my elbow. I get a grip on my temper and head for the elevator instead.

Security doesn't just follow me to the main lobby—that was humiliating enough—they escort me to the parking lot and wait nearby until I exit the premises.

I drive for about two blocks before I'm forced to pull over. I can barely see two feet in front of me now. Tears are blinding me. That skank. She finally succeeded in partly doing what she has spent every working day trying to do. Katherine Rings got me suspended indefinitely—without pay.

I have a self-pitying cry for a good fifteen minutes, and then I drive to the drive-through of the nearest McDonald's and order a breakfast consisting of four pancakes with syrup, four sausages, three eggs with cheese, two hash browns and a large orange juice. I pull into the parking lot and I devour the sumptuous, yet fattening, meal. Gluttony sooths the ache of despair I feel about my part in what happened back at work.

According to Mr. Stevens, Katherine had taken my threat to heart and had gone to human resources, saying she feared for her safety—and I was the reason. When human resources investigated by asking Ted, he claims he had no choice but to corroborate Katherine's story that I had threatened her with bodily harm. Damn—how could I've been so stupid? I should have gone to human resources myself—before Katherine had the chance. To do so now wouldn't accomplish a thing. They would assume my claims of discrimination to be made up after the fact to counter Katherine's charges against me.

"There has to be something you can do. What about filing an appeal?" Yvonne wants to know.

We're sitting at my kitchen table. A true friend, Yvonne had rushed right over when I called her from my driveway. That's where she found me when she arrived. I don't remember coming into the house or entering the kitchen. In fact, my last conscious act since leaving McDonald's was placing the call to her, after which I totally zoned out. Yvonne's hopeful words draw me back to the present.

"Kimi? You haven't said two words since I got here."

"Then how do you know what happened at my job today?" I ask, confused.

"I can see you're dressed for work. I'm assuming you went. Now you're back. Your only words to me when you called were 'I need you now.' I put the pieces together. I can't believe they would fire you. What's going to happen to Ms. White Contrary? She was just as involved as you."

"I wasn't fired, Eve."

"What?"

"I wasn't fired."

"Now I'm confused. You went to work, yes?"

"Yes."

"You left of your own free will?"

"No."

"Kimi, what do you call it?"

"Suspended indefinitely—without pay, Eve."

"Oh, my, I never dreamt that could happen."

"That makes two of us. I was prepared for the possibility I'd get fired over the Cauplum incident. I'd even started plotting my course of action. But I never imagined I'd get suspended over a few harmless words. I tell you, even if it turns out they want me back, I can't face my coworkers knowing they know I've been suspended for threatening Katherine Rings."

"You threatened her with bodily harm?"

"Is there any other type of harm to threaten with?"

"God, yes, but you don't look like you're in the mood to hear it, so I'll refrain from elaborating."

"That's mighty big of you, Eve. I'm floundering here, at the end of my rope. I'll take whatever grace comes my way. You shutting up is definitely God's grace shining on me."

"Whatever. What's new with Daniel? Have you two talked?"

"Nothing to talk about."

"If you're not talking to him, how do you know there's nothing new up with him? Marriage is forever, Kimi. The sooner you get cracking on patching yours up, the better. What God has joined together let no man—"

"Eve—"

"Don't even think of saying some smart comeback, Kimi. I'm being serious here."

"What year were you born, Eve?"

"Here we go. I was born 1973, same as you, darlin'."

"You could've fooled me. I would have guessed you came along at about the Stone Age myself."

"Make fun all you want, but the Bible is clear on the subject of marriage. One man, one woman, joined in matrimony forever before God. Your body is Daniel's temple, and vice versa."

"Eve, I'm not in the mood to debate today. But I will say this: Daniel hasn't come to worship at this temple in a month. And before that his visits had become sporadic. He claims it's because we are using the rhythm method to make love, but I know better. We can't even get through sex anymore without a fight breaking out."

"You use the rhythm method?"

"I wish Daniel could see your face right now."

"Why?"

"He swears I tell you everything, but that's one that slipped by you. Anyway, we've been using it since my physical, not this year, but last. My blood pressure was a little elevated so I'm off the pill. Now Daniel claims he feels restricted because we can't do it any old time. And having to take it out if we do it around my ovulation doesn't seem natural. What a bunch of bull."

"All I know is, God's way is best—natural. Mike and I practice the rhythm method. Have for years. I'm not totally comfortable doing it because it feels a bit like cheating fate. You know, like we're interfering with God's will."

"It's not God's will for you or me, or any female, for that matter, to end up with a houseful of kids we can't afford to care for properly."

"You're right, but not for the reason you're thinking. God doesn't want us to be unable to take care of our kids, but he said be fruitful and multiply. So I know the God I serve would make a way for me to provide for however many kids he blessed me with. I know he would because he's an awesome God."

"So awesome, this God of yours—"

"He's yours, too. Don't be afraid to claim Him."

"Oh, excuse me. So awesome, this God of *ours*. I wonder why he chooses to allow all those children of third-world countries to starve to death. I'm sure their parents are praying to Him, begging Him to intervene. They're no doubt just as trusting as you are—until they bury their blind, malnourished child, that is."

"That's not God's doing; it's man's. Man is greedy and corrupt," Yvonne is quick to point out.

And I silently applaud her observation. But I still go down fighting.

"But man is no match for God. He still has the final say in what happens. You're not implying that man is in control, are you, Eve?"

"Go ahead and make sport of me. Just be warned, God sees all and hears all."

"Now you're attempting to scare me. When all else fails, use that old Christian scare tactic."

"What Christian scare tactic?"

"The one where you and other well-meaning Christians condemn anyone who challenges your interpretation—cause that is what it is—your interpretation of the Bible. I can line up a Jew, a Muslim, and a Seventh-Day evangelist who will disagree with some, if not all, of what Pastor Roland teaches in his Bible class."

"And they're welcome to their opinion, but—"

"Here you go with your but."

"Can I finish? I didn't interrupt you. Lord knows I wanted to."

"Go on," I say on a sigh, getting up to pour myself another cup of Pepsi. When I return to my seat, Yvonne is frowning at me. It doesn't take her long to start in on my choice of morning drink. "Pepsi, Kimi?"

"Always, Eve."

"How's your diet going overall?"

"Same as all my diets go, to pot."

"You just started it Monday."

"Revenge is such an ugly thing, Eve, especially coming from a Christian."

"What are you talking about?" Yvonne asks, pretending to be baffled.

I know better, and tell her so. "You're attacking me by hitting my vulnerable spot—my weight. What next, you going to ask after Daniel again?"

"How is he?"

"I don't concern myself with the well-being of my estranged husband."

"I mentioned your family at a prayer service last night. Pastor Roland was terrific, as usual. He'll have you all in his prayers."

"Good of Pastor Roland, I guess. Close the door on your way out, Eve."

I don't stay around for more of Yvonne's goodwill babble. I do what I've been itching to do for the last twenty minutes or so—leave her sitting there. I don't know why I called her righteous ass in the first place.

CHAPTER 6

For four days I lie around feeling sorry for myself and imagining ways to do away with Katherine without having to go to jail for my crime. After sleeping most of Friday away, I take a shower, not because I have snapped out of my melancholic state, but because I can no longer stand the odor emanating from different areas of my body. I haven't returned any phone calls. My children have received the barest minimum of my attention, and mail has gone unopened. I'm in the process of drying off when I hear the doorbell. By the time I get to the top of the stairs I hear Angela saying, "Hi, Auntie Nicky." I slip on my bathrobe and join them downstairs. I can hear my niece and nephew before I locate them kneeling by the antique coffee table. They don't see me at first. They're busy racing two miniature Corvettes across its surface.

"Nick and Nat, if you two don't get off my antique table—" I don't finish my threat. I don't have to. They get my meaning and move their car race to the floor. "What are you doing here, Nicky?"

"Same thing I do every other Friday night—dropping off Bébé-Bébé kids," she says smart-ass-like, but she's whispering so her kids don't hear.

"Hmm," is all I say in return. Then I silently move to relieve Natalie, then Nicolas, of their jackets and hats. They manage to keep playing without missing a beat.

"Don't you have somewhere to go, Nicky?" I grouch.

"Yes, I do," she cheerfully confirms.

"Don't let me stop you. Please get out—I mean, get going. Just make sure you're back here on time on Sunday. I've a life, too, believe it or not."

"Look, Kimi—"

"I don't wanna hear it, Nicky. Believe that." After roughly ordering Angela to keep an eye on the kids, I head back upstairs without a backward glance. That's the last I see or hear from my sister until 10 P.M. Sunday.

I answer the door, a curse on my lips, but my words are cut short when I see Nicky is not alone; Yvonne is in tow. They look nervous but determined. I'm suddenly feeling uneasy and apprehensive.

"What's this?" I venture slowly, eyeing them suspiciously.

"Can we come in?" my sister asks, leaving me in suspense.

I'm seriously contemplating slamming the door in their faces when Nicolas's mommy radar goes off and he comes charging, seemingly out of nowhere, to tackle his mother.

While Nicole is distracted, I give Yvonne a long hard *I don't like this* stare. She raises her chin a notch and looks away, clearly ill at ease, but still resigned to do whatever they've cooked up. I leave them at the door without an invite to enter and head for the living room.

"You think Angela and Alex can mind Nat and Nick for a bit, Kimi?" Nicole asks, trailing closely behind me. "It won't take us long to say what we've come here to say," she assures me.

"I don't know, Nicky. They've been helping mind your kids since Friday. They may be fed up with it. You think?"

"It won't take us long to say what we came to say, Kimi."

"But it may take you both some time to deal with what I have to say in turn."

Again we're interrupted, this time by Angela and Natasha. Angela's frustrated expression leaves no doubt she hadn't wanted to come downstairs. Hands on her narrow hips, she lets out a long sigh. Nicole hugs Natasha and settles her on one hip; Nicolas is wiggling on the other.

"Auntie Nicky, I'm trying to finish Nat's hair," Angela says, explaining the obvious. One side of Natasha's head is in thin, neat cornrows, and the other is still a wild bush.

"Girl, you braid nice," Nicky says admiringly. "I didn't know you had skills like this. When you gonna hook up your auntie?" she asks playfully.

Angela beams, something she hasn't done since her father left home. I don't doubt Nicole was aiming for just that sort of response.

"I can't do anything fancy yet, Auntie Nicky, but I'm practicing on Mom's old mannequin."

"Oh, yeah, I forgot all about that mannequin," Nicole declares, and then giggles for a good twenty seconds.

"What's funny?" I ask, obviously a glutton for punishment.

"I'm just remembering when you fancied yourself a professional hair stylist. Remember that, Yvonne? Kimi was gonna be a stylist to the stars."

"You know what you can do with your sick humor, Nicky," I tell her, at the same time giving Yvonne a murderous look that succeeds in killing any response she was on the verge of giving. But her telling smirk does not fade.

"You have until Angela finishes Nat's hair, then out—both of yah," I happily inform my sister and my best friend.

On that note, Nicole makes short work of getting the kids squared away upstairs, despite Nicolas's protests. When she rejoins us, she starts right in on me. "You have to make some major changes, Kimi, major. Call it an intervention, or whatever else you want, but we're concerned, and we're here to help you help yourself."

"I hit a bump in the rocky road of life, and you two think I need rescuing? I applaud your willingness to jump headlong into my business, and I don't doubt you're both eternally sincere in your efforts, but I do not need, nor will I accept and/or tolerate, either of you interfering in my life without an invite."

"We're not here to interfere in your life, Kimi. Yvonne and I are here because someone we both love dearly is in trouble—emotionally and physically."

"My sister, the wannabe psychologist."

"Kimi, there's no reason to attack Nicole. God put the love in our hearts and the determination in our souls, and here we are."

"And best friend—Mrs. Holy as She Wannabe."

"I noticed the stack of unopened mail on the table in the entranceway, Kimi."

"Daniel usually sorts the bills, Miss Know-It-All."

"Still not taking care of business isn't like the Kimi I know and love. My big sister wouldn't fall flat on her face just because she hit a 'bump on the road of life.' No, my sister would catch her balance before her knees touch the ground."

"Go and pedal that yes-you-can bullshit somewhere else, Nicky love. Because not only has your big sister hit the ground, I've hit it so hard I've cracked the pavement. Shit, I feel sort of like Humpty Dumpty, and all the words of flattery and praise you two heap on me can't put me back together again."

"You're not like Humpty Dumpty, Kimi. You're God's child, and He loves you. Turn to Him now. Ask for strength and guidance."

"I'm not going to hear all the Lordy, Lord stuff right about now, Eve." I'm suddenly pissed all over again, and I'm not entirely sure why.

"Why are you so set against turning to God, Kimi? He's all you need. He's the power and the glory."

"Oh? In that case, you two can get the hell out. And next time, call first." I'm up and out of there before either one of them can respond. My bedroom door is locked, and I'm buried under the covers before the first knock sounds.

"Open up, Kimi!" my sister orders. She sounds mad; I couldn't care less.

"Go away, Nicky." My voice is overly pleasant.

"Come on out, Kimi. You can hide from us, but God sees you. He knows you're hurting. He knows how much

81

you can take. He will never burden you with more than you can handle. He's waiting for you to call on Him, Kimi. He already knows what you want. He's already prepared your blessing. He's just waiting for you to call on Him."

I know I'm not supposed to swear, but I swear to God, Yvonne was born the wrong sex and in the wrong race. She should have been born a white man, so that she could have become the Pope or Billy Graham. I toss aside the bedcovers and move to open the door, but pause when my sister adds her two cents' worth. If I live to be three hundred years old, I will still hold myself in utter contempt for my ghettorific reaction to Nicole's next words.

"No wonder Daniel got out of Dodge. I would have done the same if my wife was laid up like a beached whale."

The door seemed to open of its own accord. One minute I was facing off with the woman who had emerged from the same womb as I had nine years earlier, and the next we were on the floor, my hands clinched tightly around her neck while she thrashed frantically about like a fish out of water. I ignore Yvonne's pleas to let Nicole go. My own children, having heard the ruckus and raced upstairs, couldn't talk me into letting go. It took the petrified screams of a four- and five-year-old to pierce my armor of rage. It would take a lifetime for me to forgive myself the distraught look distorting my sister's crimson face just before she staggered to her feet, snatched up both her screaming babies, and ran as if the fires of hell were licking at her heels.

SANDRA FOY

~~~

"Your math teacher called today, Alex. Says you didn't return the algebra quiz she had you bring home for a parent's signature."

"I forgot."

"Forgot! You expect me to believe you forgot you made a fifty-six on your test or that you forgot to get it signed by a parent?"

"Both."

"Perhaps no football for a week will help your memory."

"What?"

"First your memory, now your hearing."

"Mom, I can't miss practice for a week. Mr. Fitzroy will put me on the bench."

"That's not my concern, Alex. You are learning that Education trumps everything else you got going on."

"I'm telling Dad."

"Tell your father any damn thing you want! And if he doesn't like my decision, have his ass come and see me about it!" Alex falls silent, but I can't leave well enough along.

"Something wrong with your potatoes, tattle-teller?" I say around a mouthful of peas. I know there isn't a damned thing wrong with Alex's food, but I'm fed up with watching him push it around his plate.

"Not a thang," he assures me. He even takes up a forkful and shoves it into his mouth to prove it.

"Save the Ebonics for your little friends, Alex. And don't stuff your mouth."

"You told me to eat um."

"That's eating them? And I didn't say eat, I asked why weren't you eating."

"Can I—make that, may I please, pretty please with sugar on top, be excused? I'm full."

"Go, Alex—wait. Did I get any phone calls this afternoon?"

"From who, Mom? Dad? Yvonne? Auntie Nicky? Yeah, right."

"Do you like having front teeth, Alexander Andrew Riley?"

"Yes, ma'am," he squeaks out. He not only looks contrite, he also looks quite scared.

"For your own health, remember that, Alex. Now get your lanky ass upstairs. And I'd better not hear any video games being played," I threaten, knowing how much he loves his new Spiderman game. He looks as though he'd like to protest his punishment, but his instinct for survival overrides his desire to challenge my authority. He departs, head hanging low and shoulders slumped.

I continue to eat long past the point of satisfying actual hunger. I gorge myself. I'm so stuffed now, when I yawn, it physically hurts my stuffed gut. My eyes happen to slide to my daughter, who is still eating ever so slowly. She is staring at me while she puts delicate bites of her dinner into her mouth without bothering to look at what she's eating.

"And you're staring because?" I say with a challenge in my voice.

"Nothing," she declares coolly, finally looking down at her plate.

"Well, it sure didn't look like nothing. It looked as if you had something on your mind."

"Nope. I mean, no ma'am."

I get the feeling she did that on purpose, and my next words convey as much. "I think it would be in your best interest to get on up to your room as well, Angela."

"What did I do?" she wails, her fork clanging against her plate as it falls from her long, graceful fingers.

"I'm not stupid, Angela, and best you remember, I wasn't always your mother. I was a wiseass thirteen-year-old once upon a time myself. I got the marks to prove it. Now get upstairs!"

"Can I call Daddy?"

"Not unless you wanna walk with a limp."

"I miss him! When can we call him?"

"When I say so. Bye, Angela." She wants to say more, but my dictatorial behavior succeeds in suppressing any further dialogue, and she quickly exits the dining room pretty much as her brother had. I continue with my-life-is-over behavior until that Friday when I get an unexpected moral boost—the Discreet Detective Agency calls me.

"Mrs. Riley, this is Cheryl Peterson. I'm calling on behalf of Mr. Davis. I noticed you didn't keep your appointment yesterday." She pauses, waiting, I suspect, to give me a chance to make my excuses.

"That's true," I confirm, allowing an awkward moment to pass.

"Well, Mrs. Riley, I'm calling to see if we can still be of service to you." The young voice rallies and succeeds in sounding upbeat.

"I don't think so. Not at this time, anyway."

"Okay, but if at any time in the future you feel you have need of the type of service we offer, please don't hesitate to call us back. You take care, Mrs. Riley."

"Good-bye, dear." I hang up. My spirits are lifted a tad. It's a struggle, but I manage not to call Nicole or Yvonne. But I need to speak with an adult who cares about my well-being. I call my mother, but after about fifteen minutes of listening to how good retirement life is and how stress-free they both feel, I discover I haven't the heart to visit my self-made suffering on them. I hang up on a pretend happy note. About an hour later I decide to tackle the mountain of mail that I've foolishly allowed to accumulate. A letter with my office logo in the upper left-hand corner snags my attention.

CHAPTER 7

"Mom?"

"What is it, Alex?" I ask moodily, without looking up from the letter I've been unable to open for the past hour.

"The cable's not working."

"That's the least of my worries right about now, Alex," I reply distantly, unconcerned with my son's dilemma.

"I was watching something and it just blanked out. Can you call them before I miss the rest of 'Gladiator Challenge'?"

"Out, Alex!" Guilt makes me shout. The Oreo I pop into my mouth briefly lodges in my throat.

"We want Dad," my son says so softly that at first I'm not sure if I imagined it. My eyes go immediately to his face. One look into his wounded hazel eyes and I know he's spoken the words I've been quietly dreading.

"We?" I ask. Alex doesn't look at me now. Instead, he focuses on the floor. Because of his medium complexion, I can easily detect his flushed cheeks.

"Have my children been plotting behind my back?" I prod when he doesn't speak up or show any signs of answering me.

"Me and Angela—"

"Angela and I," I correct, not helping the current situation.

"We want to see Dad," he finishes.

"Your dad knows where he can find you guys. If and when he decides to, he'll call. In the meantime, there's no need to go crawling to him, begging him to give a damn."

"Why can't we call him?"

"Was I speaking French a second ago, Alex? The part about us not crawling to him—I mean it."

"You can't order me and Angela not to talk to him because you're mad at him," my son challenges. That's twice in one evening. "Auntie Nicky was right about you."

"Who are you talking to like that?"

I'm on him before he can answer me. "Go to bed now—now!" I order. My hand stings from the hard slap I deliver to his cheek. At first he stands there, cupping his crimson cheek and looking shocked, as though he can't believe I struck him. The truth is, I've never hit him before. I'm a secret card-carrying member of the "dialogue generation," though I can talk a good 'big, bad, black mama bluff' to my kids when necessary. Truthfully, I've been conditioned by a rigid society that deems it better to "spare the rod." The ass beatings Nicole and I endured almost on a weekly basis have not been passed down to the next generation. Whether that is for better or worse remains to be seen.

"I'm going to Grandma's house," Alex calmly states, as if that's the end if it.

"Over my dead or dying body. You can believe that," I say, taking up his challenge. His stance immediately crumbles.

"Goodnight, Alex," I say, not unkindly. I wait until I hear his door close before resuming my place in bed.

Feeling contrite over my treatment of Alex, I speed dial the cable company's twenty-four-hour hotline to let them know my cable has blacked out. I'm floored when the friendly voice on the other end informs me my service has been "temporarily disconnected due to non-payment." I rummage through the stack of mail until I locate the cable bill. A quick survey of my account shows an outstanding balance of two hundred and seventy-six dollars.

I can hear the cable representative call my name, but I can't answer—my throat has closed off. I distractedly place the receiver back on its base. Now I frantically shuffle through the mountain of mail. When at last I come upon the gas and electric bills, I tear them open like a madwoman. "That trickster," I hiss, seeing the outstanding balances. "I've been had." I reflexively dial Yvonne. At the same time she says hello, I realize we're not speaking. "Wrong number," I say, sounding like Barry White. I'm not even a little surprised when my phone rings less than a minute later. "Eve," I acknowledge, my eyes closed tightly in dread.

"First of all, Barry White doesn't have my home number, and second, I have caller ID."

"Modern technology; I miss the good old days when I could just crank-call until my fingers went numb."

"You're crazy, Kimi," Yvonne says matter-of-factly, then chuckles. "How have you been? We've been worried."

She doesn't have to be more specific. We both know I know who *we* are. "I can't remember when I've been this down, Eve. If not for the kids, I swear to God—"

"Don't allow yourself to think that way. God put breath in you and He's the only one who has the right to take it away. He will never allow your burden to become too much for you to bear."

"I don't know about that, Eve," I tell her, forcing back a sob. "I hit Alex tonight for being a smart-ass."

"So?"

"So, I shouldn't have reacted that way. Alex is never a smart-ass. I should have asked myself why he was behaving that way and addressed the problem."

"In a perfect world, you would have handled things differently, but right about now your world is anything but perfect. Go to Alex and tell him you're sorry. Explain yourself. Don't make excuses, but don't fill yourself up with guilt, either. You've been his mother for fourteen years and counting. He knows who you really are on the inside. He'll forgive you and think twice about being a smart guy. He's not blameless, either."

"You make it sound so easy."

"It is. You spend entirely too much time analyzing your dilemmas and not enough time reacting to them."

"Here it comes," I predict with dread, hastily wiping my watery eyes.

"You got that right," Yvonne confirms, not bothering to pretend she doesn't know what I'm referring to.

"Well. don't keep me in suspense, Eve, out with it."

"Where do I start? You're endangering your health. You strangled your sister—your flesh and blood, Kimi.

What are you going to do about Daniel? Have you heard any news from your job?"

"For someone who didn't know where to begin, you sure got your bearings quick enough," I grumble.

"Well?"

"Well what?"

"Kimi, you gonna answer the questions or play dense? If you plan on playing dense, I'm gonna have to cut this conversation short. I have a headache that's kicking my behind."

"You're a nurse. Don't you get free drugs for occasions like this?"

"I took a Motrin. It took the edge off."

"So what you complaining about?"

"I still have discomfort, you bootyhole."

"Wish all I had wrong was a freakin' headache."

"The grass looks greener in your neighbor's yard. It might seem sunny, but it's raining hard," Yvonne sings in a perfect soprano pitch into the receiver.

"What was that awful shrieking? Girl, you better change the channel on your phone. I heard somebody auditioning for 'American Idol' a moment ago."

"Funny, Kimi. Seriously though, what's going on? Did you go to that detective agency?"

"No, but they called me back."

"And?"

"And I told them thanks but no thanks."

"Good for you. Nothing good would come of your snooping around behind Daniel's back, anyway."

"You don't know that."

"Yeah, I do."

"No, you don't. How can you assuredly say that nothing good would come of it? You psychic?"

"Here we go."

"No, here you go, talking that know-it-all shit—"

"Stop right there! I will not sit through a swearing session. You can call Nicole for that. Good-bye."

I slam down the receiver so hard after Yvonne has hung up on me, I'm sure I broke something on my phone. I'm tempted to call Daniel's black behind and confront him about the bills, but decide a face-to-face confrontation would be better for me. My mind made up, I attack the mountain of mail with a vengeance. At around 2 A.M. I wake up face down, surrounded by opened and unopened letters. At first I'm not sure what woke me. I'm totally clueless as to what I'm doing here. I'm in the process of pushing the large assortment of papers aside when the cable bill catches my eye. My memory is successfully jogged. My throat starts to ache from the pain of restraint. I want so badly to scream my rage to the top of my lungs. My eyes begin to burn from being forced to remain open. I refuse to blink because I know the moisture filling them and causing my vision to blur will spill over if I give in to my natural inclination and close my eyes to the truth of Daniel's deception. In a moment of anger and self-pity, I swipe my hand across the mattress, sending the letters scattering in every direction.

The floor is now covered with the evidence of my venting. Needing to get away from the paper witnesses of

Daniel's dishonesty, I head for the door. I intend to grab a bite to eat and crash on the couch. Instead, I stop in front of Alex's door. I can't say for sure whether it's a need to set things right or parental intuition that spurs me forward. As my hand frantically glides along the wall in search of the light switch, I'm at a loss to explain my sudden need to assure myself Alex is where he's supposed to be. I'm already mentally chastising myself for worrying needlessly when light floods his room. My eyes go immediately to the empty bed. The X-Men comforter I teased Alex for picking out on his fourteenth birthday is in a heap in the center of the bed—an indication that at least he did occupy it at some point during the night.

"Alex?" I call lightly, not wanting to wake Angela next door. Remembering the incident of a week earlier, I check to see if he fell out of bed again. No sign of Alex. I hurriedly go back into the hallway. I approach the upstairs bathroom, he shares with his sister, with little enthusiasm. It's partly open and I can see the light is out. I turn the light on and venture a quick peek inside, anyway. No Alex.

I have no trouble seeing where I'm going. The entrance light is turned on three hundred and sixty-five days a year from sundown to sunup, a testament to the fact that I never outgrew my childhood fear of the dark. Despite the light and because of my haste, I half stumble down the stairs.

"Alex!" I call loudly now, wandering from room to room until I've searched everywhere downstairs. Still no sign of him. Tears are blurring my vision as I scramble back up the stairs.

"Angela, wake—Angela? Angela! Where are my god-damn kids?" I scream to my empty house as I hustle about, first collecting shoes and then my car keys. I'm out the door and scanning the surroundings without the slightest hesitation because of the time of night. After about a minute, I'm wishing I'd taken a second to grab a jacket. It's forty degrees at best.

"I had better call the police. No, I'll call Daniel first. They must be with him. Where else would they go? Why hasn't the fucker called to tell me my babies have run away? I know they're with Daniel," I ramble on, taking comfort in my hopeful guessing.

Realizing I've left my cellphone behind, I've no choice but to waste time retrieving it. I can't chance driving all the way to my mother-in-law's house and my kids not be there. I'm so winded by the time I get up to my bedroom I fall heavily upon the mattress. It's a full minute before I can get my labored breathing under control enough to pick up the phone on my nightstand. I'm bewildered to find there's no dial tone. No time to ponder what's wrong with my phone. I grab my cell-phone. When I turn it on, I'm surprised to see I have unheard messages. I don't take the time to listen to them. I immediately call my mother-in-law's house.

"Where the fuck have you been, Kimi? I've been calling for over two hours."

"What?"

"What, hell. Why you got my kids out on the streets of Boston by themselves after eleven fuckin' o'clock?"

"Thank you, Jesus."

"Thank Jesus, huh? You better thank your lucky stars nothing happened to my kids, Kimi, cause it would have been your ass."

"Who you threatenin', a-hole?"

"I'm letting you know what to expect if anything happens to my kids. They say you wouldn't let them call me. What kind of shit is that? They're going through enough without you being an ass."

"Call me that to my face. I'll show you who's an ass. You the reason they have to sneak out in the first place. You didn't call them once since you packed up and jetted on us."

"I been trying to get my life together—get a job, get my head straight."

"You don't need to give me those lame-ass excuses, Daniel. Tell that shit to the kids. I know better. I'll be over in a few minutes for my kids."

I hang up before he can say more. When I pull up to my mother-in-law's house, Daniel is waiting out front alone. I know his nosy mother is somewhere within earshot. That nosy old bat wouldn't miss this confrontation to save her life. A quick scan of the two-story structure and I'm convinced my kids are up as well. Every light in the freaking place appears to be on.

I approach Daniel with outward calm and determination. But on the inside, I'm as scared as a newborn baby just taken from his mother's womb.

"Where are they, Daniel?"

"You've wasted your time coming here, Kimi. The kids and I are staying here for a while."

"That is not gonna happen. You are not keeping my kids. Move!" I attempt to get past him, but it's useless. I'm no match for Daniel's strength and resolve to keep Alex and Angela with him.

"Go home, Kimi, before I call the police to come get you," he says, blocking my way.

"You might as well call the police because I'm not leaving without my kids. Alex! Angela! Get out here! It's time to go home!"

"You go home, Kimi." Daniel points a finger in my face and then turns to leave, as if I'll obey.

I charge him, knocking him into the side of the house. I enter while he's attempting to regain his balance. I don't see either one of my kids at first, but they appear after the third time I call their names. My mother-in-law is not far behind, and she has the nerve to roll her eyes before saying, "Kimi, you need to leave. You look a mess."

I ignore her. I'm about to order my kids to get into the car when Daniel grabs me about the waist from behind. I struggle so fiercely at first, I don't realize I have help.

"Let her go," I hear Alex say over the ruckus Daniel and I are making. My eyes latch on to him. He looks and sounds much older than the "Spudmuffin" I've known for fourteen years.

"That's enough of this mess," my Dennis Rodman look-alike mother-in-law says, now that her son is out-numbered.

"Oh, now that's enough, huh, Dennis?"

All eyes are suddenly on me. I read confusion in Daniel's mom's slightly hazy, dull hazel eyes. Alex and

Angela both miss my meaning; they're staring hard at me with different degrees of bafflement, as if the harder they concentrate on me the more likely I'll start making sense.

Daniel's eyes are narrowed to slits. I'm not surprised; I've called his mother Dennis Rodman in drag during several of our heated exchanges. I'm not worried about him retaliating with violence. He's never been violent.

"Get out of my mom's house, Kimi," Daniel orders through clenched teeth.

"That's right. Out!" his mom seconds.

"Not without my kids, I won't," I assure them both.

"We wanna stay for a while longer, Mom." Alex pipes up, coming toward me.

My chest deflates as if a hundred-pound weight has been dropped on it. It's Daniel's turn to look smug. I'm steaming, watching him pat the hand Angela is gripping his arm with.

"Alex—" I direct my appeal to him, because I know he is the spokesperson for the two of them.

"We wanna stay . . . just until . . . until things get sorted out at home."

"There, they don't want to live with you either. Are you satisfied?" Daniel says, sounding like a prosecutor presenting his star witness.

"She should just leave them be," his mother interjects. I notice she looks everywhere but directly at me.

I ignore her, and reach up to stroke Alex's cheek where I'd struck him earlier. I see the love reflecting in his eyes and know I'm forgiven.

"You want to stay?" I repeat, and then have to cover my mouth to keep my anguish from bursting free.

"Yep."

"I'm sorry I hit you . . ."

"It's not just that, mom."

"If this is about football practice, perhaps I was a bit harsh."

"Mom, it's not."

"Okay, Spudmuffin," I say, giving in. My words are barely audible. "And you, Angela?" I rally to ask a bit louder.

"I'm staying."

"I see," I tell my diva in the making. "Well, you'll need to come by the house and pick up some clothes and your books for school," I remind them, attempting to sound carefree.

"I'll take care of all that before Monday. Now get out my mama's house. You done being disrespectful, Kimi."

"That'll be for the best," his mother loudly agrees.

I've had it with her two cents' worth and move to address her directly. "I don't give a hot damn what—"

"Mom!" both my kids plead in unison.

"Okay!" I scream, and then I point first to Daniel and then to his mama. "But this ain't over. I promise on my dead grandma, Anna Lynn Hemphill." I'm damned near tears when I finish my threat, but I manage to walk out with my back straight and eyes dry.

It's not until I'm lying in bed at five do I remember I forgot to confront Daniel about the unpaid bills. When I attempt to call him the phone has no dial tone. I recall what he had said about not being able to reach me. I go in search of the problem. A quick check of the living room shows nothing amiss, but when I enter the kitchen I discover the receiver has been placed on the countertop. Alex's doing, I'm guessing. He wanted to delay his father's being able reach me. He didn't want to come back to the house of hell I'd created. I'm out of control.

My legs are suddenly weak, and I give in to the need to just let go of the burden of self and collapse. I cry until my eyes literally ache from the never-ending downpour. I'm not sure how long I lingered there in my private world of despair or how long I would have remained there if the rapping on my front door hadn't beckoned, its eager insistence quickly escalating into a hammering demand for entrance. I'm about to ask who's there when my sister begins shouting my name. I throw open the door and grab her; only this time, it's to embrace her. She hangs on for dear life. Her sobs merge with mine, until I'm not sure where I began and she ends.

"Forgive me, Nicky?" I beseech, my voice ragged.

"Anything," she says with such conviction I believe her.

"Where are the kids?" I ask, largely because I'm concerned for their welfare, but partly because I want to fill the awkward moments following our embrace. I can't believe I attacked my sister. I can't maintain eye contact. I can feel Nicole's brown eyes burning into me.

"Don't do it, Kimi," she orders sternly.

"What?" I ask, even though I'm pretty sure I know what she's demanding I not do.

"Don't make what happened between us bigger than it has to be."

"How can I make it up to you, Nicky?"

"There's nothing to make up to me. That's a perk that comes with the dirty job of being a sibling. You get to F-up royally, and forgiveness is a money-back guarantee. Besides, I used the tough-love approach a bit too toughly. And you—well, you didn't use enough self-control. Let us leave it at that. We're sisters—end of story."

"I don't know if I can."

"Well, I can. I refuse to allow what happened that night to become the defining moment of our journey together. I should have known better—you're a Gemini, for God's sake. I backed the meek, kindhearted twin side of your nature into a corner and got myself attacked by the aggressive, black-hearted side."

"What the hell are you talking about, Nicky?"

"You are the quintessential example of a true Gemini. Good girl, bad girl. It's your destiny to struggle with these dual personalities."

"I hate to poke holes into your obviously heartfelt belief, Nicky, but good moods and bad moods are not restricted to only those born during a certain month. The entire human race is subject to times of happiness as well as bouts of extreme unhappiness. Call it the circle of life—man's destiny—even the human condition, but please spare me your lopsided view that basic human states of emotion can be characterized and used to define a fraction of the population with any degree of accuracy whatsoever."

"Are you done?"

"Only if you are. Now close the door, please, and come upstairs with me—my room is a wreck. We'll talk while I straighten up. I've a million and one things to tell you."

I can't explain how or why. But having one of my verbal sparring partners back has given me back a certain energy—and purpose.

"You still haven't said where the kids are," I remind her.

"What's that old saying? If you can't say anything good—etcetera, etcetera."

"They still don't want to see their crazy auntie," I say, totally understanding.

"More like they just need time to get over what happened. Besides, I wasn't exactly sure how this meeting would go over."

"And you wanted to protect them. Say no more." I nod that I understand, but I'm hurting nonetheless.

"I'll bring them by real soon, Kimi, I promise. This is rich—think about it for a sec—you are actually missing those two Bébé-Bébé kids." Nicole laughs heartily. As much as I try to resist, I end up joining her.

"What brings you by to pound on my door like a madwoman so early in the morning?" I ask when my laughter dies down.

Nicole doesn't answer me right off. Clearing an area of the bed she plops herself down.

"I got a real bad feeling that you needed me. For what, don't ask me, but I couldn't shake it. So here I am." Nicole's tender brown eyes empathetically staring up at me turns me to mush, and I turn into a blubbering mess there in the center of my messy bedroom. It's a good ten minutes before I can calm myself enough to tell about the kids running away, along with Daniel's deception regarding the bills.

"We're not taking this shit lying down. We have to talk. But first you need some tissues. You're a mess. I'll be right back."

By the time Nicole has cleaned me up—she insisted—I'm feeling a small measure of confidence that things are going to work out.

"First, we deal with you," she tells me, and then pushes a light blue card into my hand.

"What's this, Nicky?" I ask, the name Athletic Place jumping out at me.

"Just what I said. First we deal with you. I've taken the liberty of signing you up."

"Signing me up for what?"

"Athletic Place, of course," Nicole says, tapping the card.

"What does that mean?"

"Exactly what you think it means, Kimi."

"I don't have time to waste at a gym—thank you very much. How much was it, and how the hell can you afford it? You still owe me money," I tell her none too nicely, holding the card out for her to take, but she shies away.

"I have my own. That's yours. Check out the back. It even has your name printed there, and it's only seven dollars a visit," Nicole explains.

I turn the card over only because Nicole's eyes are pleading.

"Nicky, that's just my name printed out on sticky tab. You can remove it easily enough—here."

"Come on, Kimi, you have to do this. I think it'll get you motivated to get the weight off."

"I'm not going, Nicky. A roomful of women built like Janet Jackson shaking their rock-hard glutes to the latest top ten on the pop chart is not my idea of motivation."

"That's not how it is, Kimi. Everybody there is just like you, trying to get in shape."

"Baloney! If I were stupid enough to go, I'd be the only overweight person there. I guarantee you that."

"Okay, I'll make a deal with you—"

"No."

"You don't even know what I'm about to propose."

"I'll bet my last bottle of Pepsi that you're planning on continuing to nag at me about Athletic Place," I say, shoving the card at Nicole. She again shies away from taking it.

"I hope that Pepsi is ice-cold. I like it slushy."

"We'll see, Nicky. Let's hear your proposal," I say, not worried in the least about forking over my last Pepsi.

"You and I will start a morning workout routine— not at Athletic Place, but right here, or my place, or in the park. It doesn't really matter where; what matters is we do it."

"That's easy for you to say, Slim Pickens. I'm *very* particular about where and when I embarrass my big ass."

We both laugh, and I'm almost convinced Nicole's idea has a bit of merit.

"You pick the place, then. I'm at your disposal."

"What about the kids? If we go out in the morning, somebody's going to have to keep an eye on them," I say, shamelessly hoping I've severed the lifeline of Nicole's plans.

"Not to worry. Mrs. Leigh's daughter Mildred—you remember big-boobed Mildred with the lazy eye? She got hair like silk."

"Yeah."

"She's back home. She's gonna come down and watch the kids whenever I need her. I'll give her whatever you can afford to pay her. So I won't be needing you to watch the kids for a while."

"You really think I'm a bank, don't you?"

"Is that a yes? You'll pay her, right?"

"I still don't see how this will work. Didn't she get married and have about three or four kids?"

"She married cross-eyed Jeff. You remember Jeffrey. He was in my art class in ninth grade. He sat in front of me. I used to complain that I hated sitting beside Mildred, because when he turned to talk to her I always felt I had to be a part of their conversation. His left eye was always roaming in my direction, as if to say, 'What's up, Nicole?' "

"You crazy, Nicky. God hears you making fun of that man's handicap."

"Yeah, and He sees you smirking."

"I don't know where Mama and Daddy got you. Where do you get the shit you say?"

"Anyway, Mildred has three kids, seven, eight, and nine, but she left them back in Ohio with Jeff. She wants them to finish the school year. Then Jeff will bring them here, and Mildred will take things from there."

"What are we going to do then? She won't be able to effectively watch five young kids."

"You don't know that. Besides, that's months away, Kimi. We'll cross that bridge when we get there. Stop throwing up roadblocks. Just suck it up and rise to the occasion."

"Was that supposed to move me?"

"Didn't it?"

"You better call Eve. She's bound to have a Bible verse or two she can lend you."

"I'll do that, but in the meantime, promise to think about it. Take the rest of the day if you have to."

"Ooh, so generous," I mock. "I'll let you know by the end of the next week, Nicky."

"Tomorrow morning. It's Saturday, and we can work out as long as we like."

"The end of next week, Nicky, or the answer is no."

"So you let me know by the end of next week, then."

"I wouldn't hold out a tremendous amount of hope that I'll say yes if I were you. I got bills to sort through, and the kids being with Daniel is worrying me to death. The likelihood of anything fitting on my plate is nil."

"If you don't take stock of yourself soon, the amount on your plate won't mean much to you because you won't be around to worry about it."

"I feel fine, Nicky. I look like hell—but I feel okay."

"Which is it, fine or okay?

"Take your pick, but stop nagging me, please."

"Okay, okay, let's drop it—for now."

"You got any idea about how I can go about getting my kids back?"

"A few."

"A few? I would have settled for one. I'll clean up later. Give me a minute to change and we can grab something to eat. You got time?"

"A bit, but I'll pass on the food. A nice cold Pepsi would sure hit the spot, though."

CHAPTER 8

My mother-in-law answers Nicole's pounding. I lag behind, embarrassment written all over my face. My kid sister is here to fight my battle. I've hit rock bottom.

"We want to see Daniel—now," Nicole grinds out.

"What's this about?"

"It's a family matter."

"Daniel's—"

"Inside. His car's parked in your driveway, Mrs. Riley. Could you send him out here, please? This won't take but a minute."

"What's this about, Kimberly?" my mother-in-law asks, looking over my sister's shoulder to where I'm cowering just off-stage. Nicole wastes no time in letting her know she's the star of the show.

"Never you mind what we want with Daniel. He's a big boy. You just send him on out."

"I don't think so."

"We're not leaving. We've got business with him."

"Kimberly—"

"Kimberly what?" Nicole interrupts, her tone daring my mother-in-law to finish what promises to be a negative remark.

"Junior!" she calls instead, and then issues a warning. "I'll call the police here at the first sign of trouble."

"You hear that, Kimi? If Danny boy gets physical, she'll have him arrested."

"I'm feeling safer already," I say without a trace of enthusiasm.

My husband shows up before his mother gets a chance to respond. She has to settle for shooting me an evil look.

"What's going on?" he asks, looking from me to Nicole. His gaze returns back to me and stays on me.

"You forgot these when you left Kimi's place." Nicole steps boldly up to him and shoves a bundle at him.

"What's this?" he asks lamely.

"The bills you were supposed to have paid."

Daniel stares at Nicole for a long moment. His gaze slides over to me, sending a wealth of contrition my way.

"You bring our private business to my mama's house—"

"You've got to be kidding," I say.

"And don't talk to my sister any kinda way around me, Daniel. You will get your feelings hurt," Nicole warns. I hold my breath, not sure how Daniel is going to react. He snatches the bundle Nicole is defiantly holding under his nose.

"Attaboy. Call Kimi when you've made arrangements with each person in that bundle."

"I can't—"

"Call Kimi or I'll be back. Now where are the kids? I wanna say hi."

"Upstairs. Why don't you go on up and spend some time," Daniel cagily offers.

"No, I'll wait out here with Kimi. You send them out," Nicole counter-offers. She's on to Daniel.

"Suit yourself, but don't say anything to upset them. They were so upset when they got here I thought they would never calm down."

"Well, seeing their mom will be good for them," Nicole says in support of me.

My mother-in-law snorts and rolls her eyes before reentering the house.

"Like I said, I don't want them upset."

"How about you save the drama for your mama and go get my sister's kids?"

"Be careful, Nicky. Be careful," Daniel warns, but his voice is syrupy sweet. Something is not right here.

"What was that?" I ask Nicole as soon as the door closes on Daniel.

"I'll tell you one day when it doesn't matter. Trust me, you don't wanna know now."

Nicole's emphasis on "now" causes me to hesitate. Her look of repulsion mixed with sorrow stops me cold. But I accept her mysterious answer with a nod. My kids soon join us, and Nicole's presence makes for a tension-free encounter.

We take the kids down to a track not far from my mother-in-law's house. I sit on the bleachers as my sister loses first to Alexander and then to Angela in a race around the quarter-mile track. She loses despite the fact that she tries to cheat by latching on to Alex's shirttail, then takes off before I can finish saying ready, get set, go. My chest tightens painfully as I watch their carefree antics. I'm suddenly filled with unbearable shame over my behavior toward my children during the past month. It's suddenly clear to me why they ran away. Any sane person would have done the same. Whether or not that includes Daniel, I'm not mentally able to contemplate just now.

—◆◆◆—

"Can you be ready by six tomorrow morning?" I ask, keeping my eyes on the road.

"I'll be on your doorstep promptly," Nicky assures me.

"Yeah, well, don't expect me to overdo it."

"I won't."

"The way you and the kids ran around that track would have killed me."

"We'll just walk—briskly."

"Not too briskly at first."

"Not too briskly, you got it."

"Something funny, Nicky?" I ask none too nicely. I sense humor bubbling just beneath the surface.

"Nope," she says.

"Looks like it! You look ready to pop your cork."

"The kids looked pretty good, don't you think?"

"Subtlety is not one of your virtues, Nicky. But, yes, as much as I hate to admit it, the kids looked happy for a change. I'm trying not to hate that fact. I shouldn't hate it. I should be happy for them; I'm their mother. I'm supposed to be happy that they're happy, right?"

"I'm not sure there is a law against you resenting Daniel stepping in and healing a hurt he caused in the first place."

"I could have handled things differently, Nicky. I should have handled things very differently."

"You know what they say about hindsight. Don't do it to yourself, big sister."

"I think I'll call my boss today. Put an end to this night once and for all."

"Whatever you think is best, Gemi."

"Gemi? Never mind, I don't want an explanation," I say in disgust. "Clearly you've been reading the zodiac again, right?"

"I've been studying your charts with my psychic. You should let her give you a reading. There's a lot going on with Mercury right now. That's why your world seems to be turned on its axis. It has been, literally."

"I'm going to stop by the store. I need milk. Do you have to get back?" I ask, striving to avoid an argument.

"I have time. About the readings—" Nicole presses.

"Nicky, another time. When I'm extremely desperate."

"Fine. You have a closed mind, anyway."

We are strolling towards the milk section when a thought comes to me and I stop dead in my tracks and turn to Nicole. "What is it costing you to visit your psychic?"

"None of—"

"My business? Wanna bet? I can't believe you."

"It costs next to nothing, considering the value of the information."

"That means it's expensive, doesn't it, Nicky?"

"I didn't say that."

"But you're hedging. That tells me everything I need to know. Don't ask for money if that's what you intend to do with it."

"It's none of your business how I spend the money I borrow."

"You borrow? Borrowing is defined as money received with the intention of returning it."

"As long as I owe you, you'll never be broke."

"Sillyhead. Let's get the milk. I've had enough of you for one day."

"I'm crushed."

"You're a merciless nag, but I love ya," I say, signaling a truce.

Nicole beams and starts off. I'm about to follow when a familiar voice snags my attention. There are several minutes of irksome frustration because I can't for the life of me put a face to the whimsical voice chattering non-stop about why Paris Hilton and Nicole Richie aren't friends anymore and speculating about whether they'll ever be friends again.

Sounds life a soap opera plotline to me. No sooner than the thought occurs to me and triggers my memory as to where I recognize the youthful voice, and I'm about to seek her out when she suddenly appears from around the corner I'm heading toward.

"Mrs. Riley, hi."

"Hello again, Ashley. How are ya?"

"Good. Where's Angela?" she says all in one breath. Her large baby-blue eyes are hopefully darting about.

"Well, hello there. Kimberly, right?" It's her movie-star handsome father.

"That's right. How are you?" I ask, smiling awkwardly.

I want out of here now. I'm a mess, in a large loose-fitting navy-blue jogging suit that makes me look at least a size bigger. My hair is still in desperate need of repair; the ponytail making it barely passable. He, on the other hand, is standing there without a dirty blond lock out of place. His loose-fitting kaki pants are a perfect length. The waist-fitted jacket is a similar shade and is open. His cream-colored shirt is neatly tucked into his pants. It's clear this dreamboat is no slacker when it comes to working out. His smile grows wider, revealing a dimple in his left cheek.

"How're you doing, madam? I'm Thomas Klein. This is my daughter, Ashley."

I'm confused until I belatedly notice Nicole has silently come to stand next to me.

"Nicole Blackmon. I'm Kimberly's sister. It's nice to meet you both. You and Kimberly known each other long?"

"No," we both say at once. His "no" is an even-toned answer to a casual inquiry, whereas mine is a frantic denial of an allegation.

"We've only met—seen each other—once before. Ashley knows Angela from school. If our daughters hadn't both tried out for the cheerleader squad, I seriously doubt we would have ever met."

"Okay," Nicole says slowly, giving me a wide-eyed stare that clearly asks if I've lost my mind. My frantic rush to distance myself from Mr. Handsome Thomas

Klein was obvious. The reason would have to wait until I got my sister alone.

"And if I'm caught or captured I, too, will disavow any knowledge of our acquaintance then and now," Klein jokingly adds.

Nicole laughs. His daughter Ashley laughs. I look around for the nearest exit.

"Ready, Nicky?"

"Yeah, but where's your milk?"

"It's all expired. Let's go." I latch on to her arm before she can ask more questions.

"I'm listening."

"I've got a real good reason for getting us the hell out of there," I assure my curious passenger.

"I'm all ears."

"That's Thomas Klein."

"Get out of town. *The* Thomas Klein! As in, I've no idea who the hell he is Thomas Klein," Nicole says with feigned excitement.

"You are so adopted, Nicky."

"After that wacky performance back in Grocery Mart, the possibility of being adopted gives me much-needed hope that my sanity won't suddenly go poof as well."

"The guy works for Cauplum."

"Cauplum?'

"Remember, I told you about some questionable accounting and marketing over at Cauplum?"

"This has to do with the account Katherine, what's her face, never sent over to them regarding Thomas Klein," Nicole finishes, her eyes huge now.

"But he can't be *that* Thomas Klein. You think?"

"He drives a 2008 Bentley. You've seen him, but you should see him all dolled up. He looks like a million, no, two million bucks. You think there are two Thomas Kleins in the Boston area living large?"

"Very likely," Nicole reasons, settling into the passenger seat of my minivan.

"What are the odds of that, Nicky?" I ask, giving the parking lot a nervous once-over, trying to spy on the man under discussion without his knowledge.

"I couldn't say what the chances are, but there's a chance it's not him, so calm down. Besides, it's not against the law to know him, is it?"

I spot father and daughter exiting the market and getting into the now familiar-Bentley. I'm hardly surprised to see a blonde on the passenger side. I am, however, taken aback by the familiar way in which she tosses her head and then runs a hand through her hair. I strain for a better look, but it's useless; she's facing the other way.

"You don't get it, Nicky. The accounts missing from Cauplum's audit were accounts concerning Mr. Klein's account regarding their Bronzen account. Accounts last in Katherine's possession."

"That's a mouthful," she says. I can tell she is trying to sort it all out.

"There they are, Nicky."

"They're leaving, Kimi. Nothing suspicious about it."

"Here's my chance to prove this is *the* Thomas Klein." I also wanna know who his blonde passenger is. I move to follow.

"Mind telling me how you're going to go about that, Mrs. Columbo?"

"If he lives on Dove Street in Canton, he's the Thomas Klein I think he is. And if that's Katherine on the passenger side, it would explain everything."

"This is crazy. What if they see us following?"

"I'll be careful."

"That's even crazier. Why can't you ask Angela where they live? Didn't you say the kid's a friend?"

"They only just met. She might not know. Even if she knows they live in Canton, I doubt she'll know the exact address. Without that, I'll always have doubts as to whether or not he is the one and the same Thomas Klein."

"If she says her friend lives in Canton, that would be good enough," Nicole suggests.

"I don't wanna ask Angela. What would I say?"

"Whatever it is, it's gotta be better than us pursuing these people."

I continue to follow the Bentley for another five minutes before intentionally falling farther behind.

"What are you going to do now?" Nicole asks when I take the next exit.

"I'll think of something else, scaredy-cat."

"Meow."

"Discreet Detective Agency. How may I help you?"

"I'd like you to confirm an address for me," I tell the familiar voice on the other end.

"Not a problem, but it would be a lot cheaper to just go to whitepages.com or just call information."

Integrity. I knew my instincts about her were right. "Actually I'm looking for a little more than confirmation of an address."

"Why don't I schedule you to come in? That way, you can explain in detail what you're looking for. And if we can be of service, we'll take it from there."

"That sounds reasonable, but I'll need an appointment right away," I tell her pushy-like.

"Not a problem. You can come in later today, say three?"

"I'll be there."

"You have a pleasant morning, Mrs. Riley. Bye now."

I stand there for several moments, startled and a bit embarrassed to hear that I was recognized. She probably has me pegged as a paranoid loser. I should cancel or, better yet, just not show up. But she'll call me back, just as before. I won't answer the phone.

I'm running from a strange voice over the phone. I *am* a paranoid loser.

CHAPTER 9

It takes all the courage I can muster to open the glass door with words "D.D. Agency" printed boldly across its center. A petite brunette sits behind the U-shaped desk, her welcoming dark-blue, almond-shaped eyes watching me approach, which does nothing to lessen my skittishness.

Just turn and walk out. She'll never be entirely sure it was you, a voice inside nudges me. At the exact moment I make up my mind to leave, she speaks up.

"Mrs. Riley, Mr. Davis is expecting you," she tells me, coming around the desk with her hand extended.

I've been told more times than I care to remember that you should always give a firm handshake. It conveys self-confidence or backbone. I try, but when our hands connect all I can think of is how soft hers feel and how delicate they look. I end up giving a shake that my three-year-old nephew could put to shame.

"I'll let Mr. Davis know you've made it. Take a seat. Don't go anywhere; I'll be right back."

Her voice is teasing, but I get the feeling she means exactly what she is saying. Less than half a minute later she comes back and ushers me into a neatly appointed office. A rather tall and rather handsome black man, in a well-fitting light-gray suit is standing behind a cluttered desk. He has warm dark-brown eyes, which peer directly into me—seeming to never blink. He gives me what is just short of a smile. He leans forward to extend a well-manicured hand in my direction and I'm ready for him. I make sure my grasp is sure and strong. I even hang on several seconds longer than what my comfort zone would allow, just to be sure not to expose my reluctance to be here.

"I see you and I hail from a similar boot camp. Louisiana, class of '89, student of Mr. Donald Davis Sr. Mr. Davis's class motto—"

"Motto?" I interrupt, confused.

"Strong handshake—you get an A-plus. Look 'em straight in the eye; I'd say strong B. Never let 'em see you sweat; I'm afraid I'm going to have to fail you."

"I'm have to be going now," I tell him, turning and heading for the door, wiping at my perspiring nose as I go.

"I can tell you where he lives. How long he's lived there, the name of the doctor who delivered him, and where he's been the thirty or so years since then. Please don't say who," this strange man orders.

"If not who, then surely I'm free to ask, what are you talking about?" I ask, playing dumb for now.

"Cheryl says you were pressed for time. If we agree to be honest with each other, I can guarantee you the information you seek, in half the time," he says with complete confidence. He reminds me of Nicole suddenly.

"His name is Thomas Klein, K-L-E-I-N. He's about your age, I would guess. I want to confirm where he lives—I think Canton—where he works, Cauplum, an accounting firm, and who he's dating." I don't mention my suspicion about Katherine. If this guy is as good as he is carrying on, I'll know if it's her soon enough.

"Okay," he says confidently.

"Okay?" I ask, surprised by his unwavering self-assurance.

"Is it okay by you, Mrs. Riley?"

"Sure, I mean, that will be fine. How will I get the information from you?"

"Cheryl will call you at the number we have, unless that's not good for you."

"No, no, that'll be fine"

"You should hear from us by the end of next week."

"Next week?"

"We'll need time to confirm what we find out, Mrs. Riley."

"You misunderstand, Mr. Davis. I wasn't expecting to find out so fast."

"Careful, Mrs. Riley. Too much flattery and my price might just go up," he says, but his friendly wink tells me he's just joking. I smile, starting to relax.

"What's something like this going to cost me, anyway?"

"It varies. You sound like you want us to scratch the surface—get his address, where he works, who he's keeping company with—canceling a couple of trips out to dinner will cover it. You want to know where he hails from and how long he's been where he is now? His boss's name, and what he calls his secretary? What he usually has for lunch? Does he prefer boxers or briefs? Cancel any plans to go to Disney World."

"That won't be necessary."

"I'll have Cheryl draw up an agreement. Come by Monday. You can look it over."

"You're not going to ask me why I want the information on Thomas Klein?"

"No one is paying me to. Besides, I don't need to know that to do my job, Mrs. Riley."

"I suppose you're right."

"That's usually the case."

"Good day, Mr. Davis," I say, not unpleasantly.

My mind is racing, so when we shake hands, I'm not really paying attention to the act. I give him a normal unembellished handshake. His faint smile brings me back to the present, but it's now too late to correct my blunder. He's already releasing his grip on my hand. I'm halfway out the door when a comeback hits me.

"One more thing, Mr. Davis." He arches one thick eyebrow. "I never got below an A minus in any subject, and 'never let them see you sweat' was never a motto of mine."

"Good day, Mrs. Riley."

"You were always a morning person. I hate you," I tell my sister between gasps for air.

"Once more around the block, Kimi, and we'll call it a day," she tells me in an even, crisp tone.

"I can't believe I let you talk me into this shit. I think I'm dying. I can't catch my breath. You're pushing me too hard."

"Stop complaining. You'll conserve energy."

"Don't pretend to care now, Nicky. I've seen your true colors."

"Kimi, we've been walking for a good ten minutes; that's hardly overdoing it."

"Ten minutes? You sure?"

"I checked my watch when we started."

"Seems as though we've been at it for at least half an hour," I say, disappointed.

True to her word, Nicole had shown up on my doorstep at six sharp. One look at her trim, fit body encased in a fitted sweat suit and skin-tight spandex and I wanted to slam the door in her face. She had pulled back her hair in a loose ponytail.

"This is only the first day, Kimi. It's natural to feel exhausted, beat, like you can't go on, like big—"

"I wouldn't finish that thought if I were you," I warn her.

"Okay, fine. Let's talk about something else. It'll take your mind off what you're doing." I doubt that, but I don't tell Nicole that.

"I tried to call you last night. Where were you, Nicky?"

"Me and a couple of my girlfriends went clubbing."

"Since when do you go clubbing?"

"Earth to Kimi. I have needs that don't fall into the category of kids, work, or school, big sister. Every blue moon or so, I answer a call from my feminine urgings."

"Feminine urgings?"

"Yes, a need for male companionship."

"Make sure he likes kids," I advise.

"Why?"

"Why?"

"Yeah, why? I'm not looking for a father for my kids, Kimi. I'm looking for a virile male to scratch me wherever it itches."

"What about commitment?"

"I'll let the forty-and-over crowd worry about commitment, for a change. For once, I'm just thinking about the fuck aspect. I don't want a relationship per se."

"That's just an excuse to fuck without having your conscience enter into it."

"My conscience plays a large part in my decision to please thyself. It wants me to get my groove on, Kimi. That little voice is egging me on, actually: Nicky, go fuck somebody, anybody," she says eerily, as if she's telling a ghost story.

"Mama dropped you on your head at an early age, Nicky."

"Enough about me. Let's talk about Thomas Klein. What did you find out?"

"Well, I called the private dick. I went to see him, and if all goes well, I'll hire him to do the job for me."

"Were you trying for a sexual undertone, or am I that horny?"

"It's you; you're nasty like that."

"Nope, it was the part about private dick doing the job for you."

"Are you done?"

"Go on."

"Anyway, his fee is reasonable, and I've got a good feeling about this guy."

"Good feeling as in attraction?"

"No, desperate and dickless. Good as in he can get the job done. Find out who Thomas Klein is, and if he's dating Katherine."

"What happens when he does find out who Thomas Klein is? And it's Katherine?"

"If he's the Thomas Klein and it was Katherine I saw him with, I expose them."

"What!"

"You heard me. I'll redeem myself. Ted will beg me to come back, of course. I'll refuse, maybe."

"Listen, Nancy Drew, what you're talking about could have dangerous repercussions," my sister warns, pulling me to a stop. "This isn't TV or some novel where you can save the good guys with the stroke of a pen or click of a few computer keys. If this guy is stealing money from a big corporation, he must be educated and making a lot of money."

"So?"

"So he's not going down without a fight. What if he finds out about you and tries to kill your nosy ass?"

"Look at you, all worried—your eyes extra moist."

"Go to hell, Kimi. Hit the showers before you hit the ground. We're done for the day."

"Bless you, but aren't you coming by the house for a few?" I ask, not ready to part company.

"Don't try to use me as a substitute for—" she stops, but I know what she was going to say, anyway.

"I'm okay about Alex and Angela now that I've seen that they're fine. I'll even admit that they're better off right now, anyway, without me."

"I wouldn't go that far," Nicole says in my defense.

"Loyal to a fault. I like that," I tease.

"Bye," Nicole grumbles and heads toward the T station. I watch her until she enters and then stroll the twenty or so feet to my house.

By about five o'clock I've picked up and put down the phone about twenty times. I want to call and check on the kids, but I don't want to upset them by pressuring them to come home, and I know if I call I'll do just that. It's become second nature for me to have them here. I can't remember the last time I went a whole day without breaking up one of their spats. I actually miss yelling for one or the other to turn down BET or MTV. I miss hearing the weird sound effects of Alex's video games when I pass his room. Finding my headbands in my room instead of in Angela's doesn't have the pleasing effect I thought it would. What I wouldn't give to find a half empty cup of milk in the living room or a Snickers wrapper carelessly discarded on the sofa. I never envisioned the day when my kids' annoying habits would become precious memories. That I would one day yearn for their familiar disruption was as foreign to me as the English shores.

The doorbell is a welcome distraction. That it should be Daniel standing on the other side looking very annoyed seems fitting.

"I'm here to pick up the kids' school stuff."

"Where are they?" I had to ask; I'm a mother. The hurt that resonates through my limbs because of the gloating mask my soon-to-be ex-husband is wearing is a small price to pay. It's worth any price, even holding a civil conversation with Daniel.

"They're great. Better than they've been in a long time."

"They told you that, did they?" I ask sarcastically. I don't believe a word of it.

"They show me that," Daniel claims.

"They show you. Yeah, right," I scoff.

"Anyone who isn't legally blind or deluding herself can see it. Look, Kimi, I've been up all night. I'm beat. Can I just get the kids' stuff so I can go?"

"Like I care. Stay there, I'll get their stuff."

"It's gotta be thirty degrees out here," he complains.

"Thirty-eight," I say, slamming the door in his face. I get Alex's book bag and suitcase and then Angela's. Daniel is not at the door when I return. He's in his car. He revs the engine when he sees me approaching. It's clear the man would like nothing more than to run me over. Nearly twenty years of togetherness and we have been reduced to barely containable hostility. I approach with Alex's things but Daniel makes no move to get out and help me. He sees me struggling, the bum. I ignore his scowling regard and place the things in the trunk.

"Is that it?" he calls out gruffly.

"No!" I shout with open hostility.

When I return with Angela's bundle, I'm practically running. I'm not dressed properly, so I'm now chilled to the bone. My plush house shoes are hardly adequate to keep out the moisture from stray pieces of ice littering my driveway. I successfully maneuver around as much of it as possible and put Angela's bags into the trunk. But when I slam the trunk and turn in a rush to get inside, I slip, ending up flat on my back behind Daniel's car. I immediately scramble to my knees, embarrassed and not wanting Daniel to see. When I place my hand on Daniel's car for support, I'm surprised to feel it push against my hand.

I realize I'm in danger of being run down, and I scream my head off. The force of the car pushes me backwards on my butt before it comes to a sudden halt. I hear footsteps running toward me from a different direction, but I'm no longer embarrassed. I'm scared, and I'm pissed.

"Kimi! My God. Baby, you all right?"

"What the fuck, Daniel! You knew I was loading the trunk! Why the hell would you back up?" I'm yelling at the top of my lungs, all the while fighting the hands that are trying to assist me.

"I must've dozed off, baby. I heard a slam and thought you had gone back inside."

"Is she all right?" one of my neighbors asks Daniel. From what I can see, there are about seven, maybe eight, people in my driveway now.

"I'm fine. Show's over. Good-bye," I tell the small, concerned crowd ungraciously.

"She's shook up, but she'll be okay. Thanks for coming over to check. When I looked back and she wasn't standing there, I thought she'd gone back inside. I stopped the car as soon as I heard her screaming. I don't think I hurt her. She's just frightened."

"What, you filling out a police report or something, Daniel?"

"Calm down, Kimi. You're making a fool of yourself." I've often imagined what the parting of the Red Sea would have felt like in person. When I start to stand up, everyone—including Daniel—as if by an unspoken command, makes haste to get out of my way. I'm halfway to my front door before conversation commences. The last words I hear before slamming the front door shut are, "It was an accident, I swear!"

———— ∾∾∾ ————

"The bastard tried to run me down, Eve."

"Calm down, Kimi. You said yourself you didn't see which way he was looking before he started backing up. Sounds like he was careless, I'll give you that, but it is possible he thought you had gone back inside."
"How, by clicking my heels together?"

"As I said, he was careless."

"Whose side are you on? No, let me rephrase that. Whose best friend are you, Eve?"

"One has nothing to do with the other." I'm wishing I hadn't called Yvonne; she can be so middle of the road. Makes me want to pull my hair out. I should've called Nicole. "I wish I'd called Nicky," I'm mad enough to taunt.

"No, you don't. Because you know she would be in jail right now. She would've gone over, sliced and diced Daniel and worried about the consequences—never."

"True," I admit softly, calmed by the reminder of Nicole's willingness to forsake everything for love of me.

"I, on the other hand, put all things in God's unchanging hands," Yvonne continues. "If Daniel intentionally tried to hurt you, which I seriously doubt, God will deal with him one-on-one. And He'll do a much better job than you or I or even a vigilante kid sister can. I know you're angry, and rightly so, but you're gonna have to admit sooner or later that it was most likely an accident."

"I don't know why I called to make up with the likes of you, Eve."

"You called because you needed to share something very terrifying with a friend. As for apologizing, I'm still waiting."

"And I hope you're holding your breath."

"For you to admit you were in the wrong? Hardly."

"You know me so well," I own up.

"Hmmm," is all she says, but I can still detect the smugness years of our close friendship has afforded her.

I can't resist piercing her armored certainty. "Seeing that you know me so well, you won't be surprised to hear I went to see the detective I told you about."

"Surprised, no; disappointed, yes."

"Why?"

"Because."

"Because, why?"

"Because no good will come of it, Kimi. No good can."

"So you don't have a legitimate argument to present?"

"Be careful looking into Daniel's every move, Kimi. You might just find all you're looking for."

"Ooh, I'm so scared," I say sardonically.

"No, you're not. You haven't the sense to be. Taunt me now, but you're going to need me later to pick up the pieces."

"You can't scare me, Eve. You can't change my mind with biblical quotes or sinister predictions. All you can do is support me on this."

"Fine. What do you hope to do with the information from the detective? Use it in court against your husband, the father of your two beautiful kids, who probably loves them just as much as you do?"

"Now that's the good old support I'm talking about."

"Any time."

"For your info, Mrs. Negativity, I didn't hire him to investigate Daniel. I hired him to investigate one Thomas Klein."

"You did what?"

"There's something not right with the whole Cauplum business, and I'm going to prove it."

"Crazy, crazy, crazy!" Yvonne says, her voice rising with each declaration.

"Thanks for all the love and support, Eve. Bye." I hang up, not the slightest bit perturbed.

CHAPTER 10

I start an outline six times before I get a paragraph arranged to my satisfaction. But instead of getting frustrated, I'm giddy. I've been at it since two in the morning and it's now six twenty, and the sun has been up for a while now. But I'm not feeling the smallest twinge of fatigue. I've decided to base my current literary endeavor on my own life. Unlike my other countless unfinished attempts at storytelling—which I pulled out of a hat, so to speak—this story is largely already written. I'm well into page nine when my phone rings.

I'm more than a little surprised to hear Mildred's chipper voice saying, "Hold for an important call."

Seconds later, a familiar voice says, "Kimberly, how are you?"

"Recovering, keeping the faith, hanging in there, keeping my chin up. Take your pick, Mr. Stevens." He clears his throat several times. "I've spoken with human resources, and I'm told they've prepared a rather generous package. Have you responded to their correspondence?"

"Not as yet."

"I'd strongly advise you to consider doing so, Kimberly."

"Believe me, Mr. Stevens, I'm taking the matter quite seriously," I respond, intentionally not revealing a thing.

"Glad to hear it. There is one other matter I'd like to mention while I have you on the phone."

"I'm listening."

"There remain a few loose ends concerning Cauplum."

"Okay," I say slowly. My brain is racing to figure out his angle before it's too late and I'm hoodwinked.

"Kimberly, I'd like to send over a messenger with several documents that require your signature. Nothing out of the ordinary; just your basic housekeeping."

"Mr. Stevens, you're the chief financial officer; you can sign by proxy," I say, pointing out the obvious.

"That is true. However, Jeremy feels—and I concur—it would be most effective, considering the current economic climate at Cauplum Industries, if you were to sign the documents with which you were primarily involved."

What a bunch of bullshit.

"I see. Okay, Mr. Stevens, send the messenger over."

"Terrific. And, *Kim*, if it's okay with you, I'll instruct him to hang around until you've signed the documents. I've had the appropriate sections highlighted for you. It'll save time."

"How thoughtful is that? I'll be here. Good-bye, *Ted*." I hang up without giving the worm a chance to say more.

They must have FedExd the guy over, because about ten minutes later he was standing on my doorstep. "Mrs. Kimberly Riley?"

"Yours truly," I confirm, pleasantly for now.

"I've been instructed to deliver this envelope and to await your reply," the young pup tells me, very businesslike.

He looks exactly how I picture a business gofer should look—eager to please, unwavering stare, a cropped haircut, not a strand out of place. His dark blue-suit has the look of good quality at a reasonable price all over it. He's trying so hard to exude confidence, but he doesn't even come close. I've been around the block a time or two. I know a new kid when I see one. I imagine if I took the envelope and threw it over his shoulder, he'd immediately fetch it back—as any eager-to-please pup would.

"That won't be necessary." Once the package is in my possession, I say "Good day" and shut the door before he can get another word out.

"Mrs. Riley, please," he pleads through the door.

"Go away," I call out, opening the legal-size manila packet.

"I'm supposed to wait for those documents, Mrs. Riley. Open up," he orders.

I pivot and return to the door, opening it so fast the red-faced young man, who was leaning against it, almost falls on his face. He quickly catches his balance, though. "What did you just order me to do?" I ask indignantly, looking him up and down.

"Please, Mrs. Riley, this is only my second week."

"Well, then, you're not attached yet. Step back."

"What should I tell them?"

"Oh, I don't know—surprise me."

"If you're not going to sign, Mrs. Riley, I'll take them back and tell them you refused," he offers, scrambling for a solution to his dilemma.

"I'm going to give you to the count of ten to get out of my driveway, and then I'm calling the cops," I threaten. "Now step back!"

He wisely and hastily moves. I close the door on him with more force this time.

"Can I get you some coffee, Kimi?" Yvonne offers, moving to get it before I can answer one way or the other—leaving Mike and me alone on the sofa with her abandoned space between us.

"Did you read this?" Mike asks without looking up from the documents in question.

"Every word," I answer. "From your tone and expression, I think my interpretation is right on the money," I say with rising dread.

"They plan on sending you down the river, all right," Michael tells me without mincing words.

"Don't say it like that, Michael," Yvonne scolds. "You sound so matter-of-fact. Show a little empathy."

"I'm a lawyer, Yvonne. I'm supposed to tell her straight. If she'd wanted coddling she would have called you. Besides, Kimberly already had it figured out. I'm just confirming it for her."

"That may be true, but still."

SANDRA FOY

"It's okay, Eve. Mike's right; I came here for straight talk," I say, wanting to quash their disagreement before it gathers steam.

"What exactly are they accusing her of?" Yvonne asks, passing me a cup.

"Well, to sum it all up, Thature Mathematics is saying that Kimberly, and Kimberly alone, is responsible for Cauplum not having pertinent documents that Thature Mathematics assured would be ready for an audit Cauplum had scheduled months ago."

"Bullshit! I'm just an employee. There were at least four, no, five people over me who have to give an account of their actions."

"Not if they are all united and pointing a finger at you," Mike says, playing devil's advocate.

"Are you saying they can pin this on Kimi and get away with it?"

"They can sure as hell give it a good try."

"You have to do something, Michael. She's my best friend. Make this go away!" Yvonne says, resuming her seat.

"Calm down, honey," Mike says.

"Not until you fix this!" Yvonne says. For once her voice is raised.

"God is going to send us the answer, Eve," I say awkwardly, just to calm her.

"He already did. He sent us Michael."

"True that." I smile and hug her close. "Listen you, guys, I've gotta get going. I wanna call Nicky. I need some of that coddling Mike mentioned earlier."

"You can get that right here, from me," Yvonne offers, holding on.

"Yvonne, please let her go. She wants to be with her family now."

"I don't know about you, but I'm family."

"I meant—"

"I know what you meant, Mike, and it's true. Eve, try to understand."

"I do, but I'm here anytime—you know that."

"I know that."

———✺———

"Just a little farther, Kimi. You're doing much better. Look at you, girl. I swear you look ten pounds lighter already."

"There's a fine line between empathy and condescension, Nicky. You mind stepping back across it?"

"Sorry."

"Don't mention it," I say, picking up the pace. We've been meeting to work out for five consecutive days and, to my amazement, each day I've felt more motivated than the day before.

"How's the book coming?"

"Smooth, Nicky, real smooth."

"How about you give me a break here; I'm trying."

"That's the problem. I don't need you trying. Just be Nicky. Can you do that?"

"Mom called last night. I think I did a great job. She didn't suspect a thing, though I felt like crap after I hung up. She says you haven't called recently. It's one thing to keep this from them, but shutting them off—"

"Shutting them off? You know Mom overreacts when she doesn't hear from us every other day."

"Then you need to call every other day. You have free long distance on your cell just as I do."

"Okay, fine, I'll call today. Happy?"

"Mom will be—"

"Are we done here? I need to hit the shower. My head is about to explode." After a quick glance at her watch, Nicole nods her okay. She's pissed.

"I'll see you in the morning, Kimi."

"I was thinking we'd try the gym. That is, if you haven't canceled the membership."

"The gym it is. But they don't open until seven-thirty in the morning—that'll make me late dropping off Nat."

"We can try the night class," I say, being more flexible. "Eight?"

"Pick me up around seven-thirty," Nicole readily offers.

———∞———

My key is in the lock when I hear my phone ringing. I hurry and manage to pick it up before my answering service does. It's Mr. Davis.

"Mrs. Riley?"

"This is Mrs. Riley."

"Mrs. Kimberly Riley?"

"Mr. Davis, it's me."

"I have the information you asked for."

I'm speechless for a full ten seconds.

"Mrs. Riley, are you still there?"

"Yes, I'm here."

"Are you okay?"

"Sure. When can I get it?"

"Well, I've several items I'm working on today. I could drop by your place, say tomorrow tonight around eight?"

"Oh."

"If that's no good, we could make it later."

"It's just that—well, to tell you the truth, Mr. Davis, nine-thirty would be better for me."

"Nine thirty it is."

"Thank you."

"All in a day's work, Mrs. Riley. Bye."

———∞∞∞———

"I'm not stripping down in front of these people, Nicky. I know they have private changing rooms."

"You're lookin' at it. Come on, Kimi, nobody's paying you no mind."

"I'm paying myself mind. If I had known the setup, I would not have come."

"We're all women here. All sizes and, might I add, we all have two tits and a coochy. Why are you trippin'?"

"I'm trippin' because I'm particular about who sees my out-of-shape tits and coochy."

"Fine, go change in the bathroom."

"I will. And don't leave me," I say in a hard whisper before moving off. I try to ignore the fit, naked bodies strolling casually about. With great effort, I manage to squelch the lump of envy festering in the pit of my stomach.

"What took you so long?" Nicky asks when I reappear.

"I lingered," I boldly admit.

"Excuse me?" Nicole responds, with the outrage I expected.

"I ling-er-ed," I repeat in a way suggesting she's dense. I'm secretly wishing we'll fall out so I can walk out.

"What did you do that for?" Nicole persists, playing into my hand.

"I did it because I felt like it, Nicky. Let's do this thing before I change my mind."

She must have sensed I was seriously itching to get the hell out of this place, because she exits the locker room without another word.

"What do you wanna do first?" Nicole asks, not looking at me.

"I was thinking I'd start out on the bike."

"Excellent choice. Let's hit it," she says, sounding pepped up but looking anything but.

"What's wrong?" I ask, getting on the first available machine.

"Nothing," Nicole says unconvincingly.

"Liar. You're angry, Nicky. And I don't think it's totally about my baiting you in the locker room. Otherwise, I'd be on my way home."

"Yvonne called me."

"She shouldn't have done that."

"She wanted to share her concerns with someone. She knows I love you as much as she does. The truth is she assumed you'd told me about the messenger. You said you would."

"You have enough going on, Nicky—the kids, school, and now you're helping me with this workout business. Just how thin do you think you can stretch yourself?"

"You let me worry about that. You're my sister."

"Okay, okay. I'll keep you updated. Now, can you please get the stick out of your ass?"

"Humph."

Stationary bikes have come a long way since I last ventured into a gym. Back in my heyday the only gadgets attached were the timer and the odometer. This bike has an estimated fifteen settings, all of which light up at once when I start to pedal.

"What the freak?"

"What's wrong?" Nicole wants to know, looking at the flashing console.

"I need a user's manual to operate this thing," I tell her, randomly pressing buttons.

"You're over-exaggerating, Kimi. Just start with the first button and work your way across. Better yet—read the directions."

"How about I just look at my watch. In fifteen minutes I'll get off."

"That'll work," Nicole says.

"But it is unnecessary," a new voice butts in. "Just hold down the timer—like so—it starts to blink—like so—and then you *simply* punch in the numbers that corresponds with the amount of time you wish to work out for. The machine will buzz you when you're done—*simplicity*."

"Do we know you?" Nicole asks the perfectly proportioned redhead, who looks about Nicky's age and has positioned herself on the bike beside me.

"I was only making a suggestion," the redhead claims. "Just trying to be of help."

"Well we got this." Nicky.

"Forget I said anything," the redhead says, averting her eyes and hunching her bony shoulders before starting to pedal as if she really expects to go somewhere on that thing.

"I will be glad to *forget it*, because it sounded a lot like mockery to me." Nicky complains and positions herself on the bike to my left and starts pedaling toward the same unreachable goal the redhead is aiming for. "Did it sound like mockery to you, Kimi?"

"Mockery, condescension—it's hard to say which," I offer absently, busily pressing one button after another. "None of which matter, Nicky, cause I didn't come here to exercise my mouth." And then, like a fool, I attempt to follow them. About five minutes later, I'm sweating profusely, and the pain in my lower leg is so bad I can't think a complete thought—including how to stop my insane ride. A hand on my upper arm shocks and relieves me. I have an excuse to bail out of this silent race, and I gladly take it.

I can only imagine what I must look like to the petite Asian lady who is staring up at me with visible concern. The large Athletic Place logo on her white T-shirt tells me she works here, even before she confirms it.

"Madam, I'm one of the health coordinators here, and part of my job is to keep an eye on the people working out. You look a bit distressed. Are you okay?"

"I'm fine," I stoutly maintain. But my throat is burning, and I can't catch my breath.

"I'd like you to take about ten minutes to really get your breath under control. Do you mind if I take your pulse?" She takes hold of my wrist before she is done asking permission. I don't take her to task; not so much because I realize it's her job but because I suddenly realize all the eyes are on me. It seems all thirty or so gym-goers are also concerned about my big sweaty ass. Even Nicole and the redhead stop the madness to take notice.

"Kimi, are you all right?"

"Yeah, never better," I huff, trying my utmost to sound but failing.

"Well, your pulse is a bit higher than we like, but you'll live," the pint-sized coordinator says, the worry lines in her face no longer visible. I'm about to relax, thinking one of my most embarrassing moments is about to end, when I glimpse two other T-shirt-clad female staffers walking purposely toward me. Damn Nicole and her bright ideas!

"What did they say?" Nicole asks as soon as I emerge from the gym office.

"They wanted to offer me a lifetime membership. What the hell you think happened, Nicky? They want a medical waiver, stating I'm physically able to participate in strenuous exercise—after which we would be delighted to have you back, Mrs. Riley," I say, mimicking the gym director's tone perfectly.

"What type of shit is that? Look at you. Can't they see you need this? I'm going to have a talk with somebody."

I stop my determined sister by pulling her back with a hard jerk on her arm.

"No way! I don't need a serving of humiliation to go with the generous helping of embarrassment I've already received. Let's just discreetly get out of here."

"We will take our business elsewhere!" Nicole suddenly shouts.

"That a girl, Nicky, discreetly," I reprimand, while pulling her in the direction of the door.

"After all the trouble and effort to get you here."

"Let's just go, Nicky," I say, trying my best not to run off ahead of her because of all her carrying on with the lip smacking and arm flailing.

On the way home, I tell Nicole everything going on with Thature Mathematics. I also inform her of my planned meeting with Mr. Davis. Her insistence on accompanying me home has me regretting opening my mouth. We've been inside for a good fifteen minutes when the doorbell rings. When I answer it, Nicole is off raiding the refrigerator.

"If you have any questions about the information or photos feel free to call my office in the morning," Mr. Davis is saying when Nicole reenters the living room; some protector she is. The man could have had me twenty ways to Sunday by now if he had been so inclined. "Mr. Davis, I'd like you to meet my sister, Nicole Blackmon."

"Hello," they say in unison. They then fall silent, their eyes locking.

"Well, I'd better be going. I've got a busy day ahead of me." Mr. Davis finally announces, but he doesn't budge. I say goodnight and shove a check in his direction.

"Me, too," Nicole echoes, clearing her throat. The little hot tamale; could she be any more obvious?

"Nicky, just give me a minute, and I'll drive you home," I offer because I'm expected to. I know she doesn't want me to drive her home.

"Don't be silly, Kimi, I'll take the train. I'll be home in no time."

What a liar. We all know what public transportation is like at this hour.

"Perhaps I could give you a lift. That is, if you don't have any objections to Busta."

"Busta?"

"My dog. He's had a bad reaction to wool, of all things. Anyway, I just picked him up from a two-day stay at the vet's."

"Oh, that's too bad," I say happily. "Nicky, you're wearing a wool vest."

"That's because I thought I would be taking the train, but since this nice gentleman has offered me a ride, I'll just leave it with you, big sister. That is, if Mr. Davis is sure I'm not putting him out."

"It's no trouble at all," he assures her with a smile. He even helps her out of her vest.

"Nicole lives in Roxbury," I toss out. "Roxbury, that's nowhere from here by car," Mr. Davis responds.

"I'll get my things and meet you out front," Nicole says before I can think of another subtle objection.

"Great," Mr. Davis says and heads out.

"What do you think you're doing? He's a stranger, Nicky!" I shout as soon as the door closes behind the detective.

"What does it look like I'm doing? He seems like a nice guy. And I wouldn't mind seeing how nice of a guy. Why didn't you tell me he was so good-looking?"

"Because—well, I didn't think to, actually."

"Well, I'm gonna get going. Call me after you've read his report. Bye."

I spend the next three hours reading and rereading Mr. Davis's report. It doesn't seem real. It feels like a bad dream. Hungry and exhausted, I turn out the light, deciding to attempt sleep. "I will not cheat on my diet!" I shout out loud. It seems to strengthen my resolve. Half an hour later, I'm at my computer adding the last turn of events to my story. The ringing phone abruptly awakens me to a new day. I've fallen asleep at my computer. I wonder why my answering machine doesn't pick up; it does. Nicole's voice calling my name is a mixture of annoyance and excitement, mingled-together. I have a pretty good guess why. I bet she can't wait to spill all her secrets regarding Mr. Davis. I rush downstairs, click off the machine, and make a mental note to move it upstairs at the first opportunity.

"Hello, nasty girl," I sing into the receiver.

"Call me what you want, but I got the digits," Nicole says, unrepentantly.

"Is that all you got from Mr. Davis, Nicky?"

"That's Donald Douglas Davis, to be exact. Donald to his friends and family."

"Oh, and what do you call him?"

"Donald for now. But I'm looking forward to calling him Big D."

"Please spare me. Big D?"

"Get your mind out of the gutter, big sis."

"Yeah, you know you being a wiseass."

"I like the sound of it, actually."

"From the look of it, you like a lot about Mr. Davis, excuse me, Donald. I should call him Donald, now that you're a hop, skip and jump from hookin' up with him."

"Kimi, Kimi, Kimi. Ye of little faith. Give me a little credit for having some dignity, restraint, self-control—"

"You're trying not to scare him off."

"Exactly." I can't help chuckling. My sister is a character. "All jokes aside, Nicky, I wish you the best. He seems nice."

"He's got a master's degree from Louisiana State, loves kids and animals. He has the sexiest laugh you ever heard, and he says he'd like to get to know me better. Asked me out to dinner tomorrow night. And the best part is he's a Capricorn, the intellectual ruler of the Zodiac, thank you very much."

"You went and landed the perfect male right on my doorstep."

That sounded spiteful, and the truth of the matter is I didn't intend it to. But I guess it must have been lingering in my subconscious.

"Nicky?"

"I'm here."

"I don't know where that shit sprung from. You gotta believe me, I'm happy for you."

"You don't have feelings for Donald, do you?" she asks belatedly. "I mean, if I've stepped in on something between you two—"

"No, no! Absolutely not. Trust me. I think Donald is hot and all. But no, I've never thought of him the way you obviously do. The truth is, he made me think of you when I first met him. But your age difference—"

"He's only thirty-six, Kimi."

"True that. Look at you, defending him already. In the words of Martin Lawrence, 'You go, girl.' "

"Whatever."

"Bet you blushing."

"Bite me, Kimi."

"Get your new man to do it."

"Crazy."

"Yeah, but enough about you. I wanna tell you what was in Mr. Davis's report."

"Donald."

"He's Mr. Davis, until he tells me otherwise. He didn't tell you what was in the report, did he?"

"He's a professional, Kimi. Of course he didn't tell me anything."

"But you asked."

"He didn't tell."

"Nosy-ass."

"I'm all ears."

"Anyway, the Mr. Thomas Klein from the market is indeed the same Mr. Klein employed by Cauplum Enterprises."

"Get out."

"The address and the place of employment are a match."

"What about Katherine Rings. Is he dating her?"

"Afraid not, at least not as far as Donald could tell. Mr. Klein has been keeping company with several ladies, including two blondes. Both turned out to be dead ends."

"No connection to Thature or Cauplum?"

"None that Donald could find."

"What now?"

"Well, to tell you the truth, I'm not sure. I was positive Mr. Davis would confirm my suspicion that the lady in Mr. Klein's car was Katherine. She tossed her hair the same way Katherine does."

"Do you know how many blondes in Boston have perfected the head toss?"

"Yeah, you're right, but still, Katherine has a unique toss. Sort of a Marilyn Monroe thing going on."

"Marilyn Monroe?"

"Like in the clip when Marilyn sang happy birthday to JFK. Everyone over twenty has seen it at least fifty times."

"Yeah, that one I know."

"Good. Remember how she moves, gesturing all seductively?"

"Uh huh."

"That's how Katherine is, only not the least bit seductive. She's always messing up her damned head so she can toss it like there's a camera nearby. I've seen her. I've upchucked my lunch more than once witnessing her obnoxious performance."

Nicky chuckles and then asks me to hold because her other line is ringing. While holding, I hear my front door being opened. I hang up and go to investigate. I'm surprised to see Angela coming over the threshold.

"Angela, what are you doing here? You should be at school."

"I wanted to get my compass."

"Come again?"

"Mom," she says in a small voice and looks down at her shoes.

"Get over here, and give me a hug or something." Angela does as ordered and I crumble. I know I'm probably squeezing her too hard, but I can't help it. I've missed this soaring beauty.

"How you been, baby?"

"Okay."

"How's Alex?"

"Good, I guess. Why haven't you called? Don't you want us back?"

"Baby, I never wanted you to leave in the first place. But I know now that I left you no real choice, and I'm so sorry," I admit, dropping my guard and baring my soul to this thirteen-year-old child.

"I wanna come home."

"I'll pick you up from school. Do you think Alex wants to come back?" I ask hesitantly.

"He does. He told me he couldn't stand Dad's—"

"Dad's what?"

"Nothing."

"No, it's obviously something, honey."

"I don't want to say."

"Okay. I'll ask Daddy," I threaten. Angela's horrified response has me immediately regretting my bluff.

"No!" she shrieks, grabbing on to my arm for dear life. "Mommy, please, I promised Dad I wouldn't say anything."

"And you haven't. Believe me, I'm clueless," I assure her.

Relief washes over her and her grip becomes bearable.

"You better get going before you're late for school, and Dad is late for—work."

"Dad didn't bring me."

"What? Then who did? I know you didn't come alone."

"No, Ashley's dad gave me a lift."

"Ashley's dad?" I rush to the door, fumbling with the tie to my robe, crack it open to get a peek of the Bentley parked in my driveway.

"Stranger danger, Angela. Remember that?"

"Mom, Mr. Klein isn't a stranger. I've been to his house, like, three times already."

"In Canton?"

"Yep."

"We have an awful lot of catching up to do. How long were you at your grandma's?" I ask, as if I don't know.

"Barely ten days, Mom."

"Well, it's fine and dandy you don't count every minute. I personally counted every second you and Alex were away."

Angela beams.

"Forget I admitted that."

"Nope, and I'm telling Alex."

"You do, you forfeit the Beyonce CD you've been drooling over."

"Mom, not fair."

"Whatever, the point remains the same. Blab and you don't get jack. So zip it."

"Mom—"

"Shh. He's getting out of the car. Are you sure this guy is okay? I mean, he takes you straight to school, right?"

"He's no pervert, Mom. If he were, I'd do the move Dad taught me."

"The move Dad taught you?"

"He showed me how to kick 'em, where it counts. Just in case Mr. Klein was—you know."

"We'll discuss your violent tendencies later. Get going before Mr. Klein gets up the nerve to venture to the door. Oh shoot! It's too late to slip you out without having to speak to him. He just got his nerve."

Taking in a deep breath and exhaling slowly, I regain my composure and open the door. With some effort, I manage to upturn the corners of my mouth. His smile appears natural, the genuine kind that only babies and old people have these days.

"Hello, Kimberly."

"Thomas," I respond, hoping that it came out as casual as I was trying to make it for Angela's sake.

"I'm almost ready, Mr. Klein. I just need to get my compass from my room. That reminds me. Mom, my math teacher says I need a scientific calculator by Monday or I can't do next week's assignment."

"How long have you known this, missy? Don't answer that. We've kept Mr. Klein waiting too long already. Get moving."

"Where do I sign up to learn skills like those?" Thomas asks after Angela runs off.

"Excuse me?"

"It would have taken me at least another twenty minutes of bickering to get Ashley to do as she's told."

"It's all in your tone," I explain, relaxing a little.

"Tone, huh?"

"Absolutely. Sort of like music."

"Music?" he muses, folding his arms across his chest. His smile takes me to a warm fuzzy place I haven't been in a long time.

"You have your sweet alto, almost pleading—honey, could you please turn off the television and start your homework?"

"That's me," Thomas claims. "Funny, I never thought of myself as an alto-type guy."

"Don't take it so hard. I use to be an alto myself. But with endless practice I've blossomed into the very effective 'don't make me tell you twice' baritone I'm today."

"Can I be so forward as to ask for a lesson or two?"

"You, sir, are an optimist. A lesson or two wouldn't even get you attention, never mind obedience."

He gives me that genuine smile again. But this time he chuckles. It's a deep, truly masculine sound, which makes the hairs on my arm stand up.

"Mom, I can't find my compass. I'll need a new one. So that's two things I need, okay?"

"That's one and a maybe. I'll look for the compass myself. Now get going."

I'm glad for the distraction though. I'm keenly aware that Mr. Klein hasn't taken his eyes off me.

"Take care, Kimberly," he says.

"You, too," I murmur. That had to be the longest five minutes of my life.

CHAPTER 11

"I think Daniel has a lady friend already." I can't keep the hurt out of my voice.

"You haven't been separated that long, Kimi."

"Can you get any more naïve, Eve?" I say, my hurt and anger seeping out.

"What makes you think he has a girlfriend?"

"Angela let it slip."

"When did you see Angela?"

"She came by the house this morning. She said Alex couldn't stand Dad's—"

"Dad's what?"

"She wouldn't tell me, partly I think because she didn't want to hurt me by revealing Daniel has a girl-friend, and partly because she promised her dad she wouldn't."

"You don't know for sure it's another woman. Call Daniel and ask him. That's the only way to be certain."

"He tried to run me over on the sly. I'm not asking him a damn thing. Pardon my French."

"You need prayer."

"And you need to put Mike on the phone."

"He had an early deposition to prepare for. He already left. But I know he spent the better part of last night working on your problem."

"Great, I'll call you later on and thank him personally."

"No need. I spent an hour and a half this morning thanking him for you."

"Shit, it's me you're talking to, Eve. I know your minuteman hasn't suddenly turned into the long ranger."

"Forget you, Kimi," she says, raising her voice so it could be heard over my laughter. "Mike is quick only when he gets too excited."

"Hmmm, tell it to the hand, Eve, tell it to the hand. You said Mike was quick to draw and even quicker to fire. Pow! Game over."

"Better to get it quick then not at all."

"Anyways . . ."

"Yeah, I thought as much."

"Look at the time. I gotta get going. I need to call Nicky for a sec, and there are a few money matters I have to attend to, and then I have to work out."

"Did you say work out?"

"Yes, I did."

"Since when?"

"Since Nicky browbeat me into it. Now I'm on a roll."

"How long have you been at it?"

"Just about a week."

"That's great. In no time at all you'll have the weight off. How's your appetite?"

"Manageable."

"Let me know if you notice you're having a hard time staying out of the kitchen. Mike was using this pill called the Appetite Eliminator. He dropped the ten pounds he wanted to lose in one week. I kid you not. Said he had to leave himself a message in order to remember to eat. It's that good."

"I don't know, Eve. It sounds, I don't know, scary comes to mind."

"What's scary about having no desire to overeat? Mike has lost the unwanted weight and gone on with his life."

"I'll get back to you, Eve. I wanna try dieting the natural way first."

"You been there, done that a million times."

"So a million and one won't kill me, but your Appetite Eliminator pill just might."

"Suit yourself."

"Bye, Eve."

"Wait, call me tomorrow if you work out in the a.m. I'm off the clock. I wanna come along."

"I'll think about it. You might slow me down."

"Girl, please, there are athletes competing in the Olympics who wish they were in as good a shape as me."

"Just because you're a toothpick, Eve, doesn't mean you're necessarily in good shape. What's your cholesterol like? How about your blood pressure?"

"Call me, Kimi. I mean it."

The call to human resources to sort through the procedure of withdrawing funds from my 401K retirement savings lasts an hour. But in the end, it's worth it. The paperwork to start the process is on its way. After the incident with the messenger, I'm pretty sure I'll need it. By the time I throw on my burgundy jogging suit and grab my water bottle, I'm revving to go, so much so I actually bump into the hefty fellow poised to knock on my door.

"Pardon me, ma'am, this is for you."

Caught off guard, I automatically reach out and take the flat legal-size white envelope he is holding out. My name is typed on a label in the center of the envelope, and the company's logo is stamped in the upper left-hand corner. Afraid of what's inside, I hesitate before opening it. In the end I manage to shore up my flagging courage and open the package.

I half expect to find a pink slip inside. I don't, but the two-page document might as well be a pink slip; it informs me in no uncertain terms I've been terminated. I retreat back into my house. I'm on autopilot now. Raid is the only word to describe my attack on the refrigerator. I devour a slice of cold lasagna, leftover chicken salad, a baloney and cheese sandwich with way too much mayonnaise and a granola bar and wash it all down with a Pepsi.

Ashamed and defeated, I withdraw to my room. After closing the blinds and drawing the curtains, I collapse onto the bed, curling up into a ball—actually, my best simulation of one. If my cellphone had not gone off I might have stayed there indefinitely.

"Kimi?" Nicole asks, not sure if the lackluster voice saying hello is me.

"I don't feel like talking, Nicky. I'll call you later."

"What? Wait! Where are you, Kimi? It's after two. I know Alex *always* has football *torture*, but, unless cheerleader practice has already started, shouldn't you be on your way to pick Angela up right about now? This morning you called shouting the roof down about them coming home today."

"Oh, my God—yes. Are you sure it's after two?" I ask, scrambling out of bed—trying to focus on my watch at the same time.

"I'm sure. I'm looking at my watch right now."

"I must have fallen asleep," I explain.

"You want me to pick up Ang?"

Nicole surprises me by offering.

"You?" I scoff. "No way. I can get there quicker driving."

"And how do you know I'm not driving, too?"

"Because you don't own a car."

"My new man does."

"Nicky, stop playin' and say whatever it is you're dying to say."

"Donald let me borrow his car today."

"Why?"

"We had lunch, if you must know."

"Cut the shit, Nicky. You're bursting at the seams to get it out, so tell me already," I say, my impatience showing.

Nicole's quick "no" does not surprise.

"Why not?" I ask, pretending not to know my impatience has turned her off.

"You don't sound as though you care to hear the ins and outs. So, no, I don't want to talk about it anymore."

"Fine, Nicky, suit yourself."

"So should I pick up Ang or not?"

"How is your driving these days? It's been more than a minute since you've been behind the wheel."

"That's because Daddy is the only one who knows what a good driver I'm. He always used to say, 'Nicky, you can drive me anywhere anytime.' "

"Now that's a parent's love."

"So it's settled, I'll pick up Ang."

"Hold up, hold up. The truth is, I'm thinking about sending her back to her grandma's house."

"What! Why?"

"Because last time I checked I was her mother and you were not!"

"I'm picking up Ang. Bye!"

Half an later, before I hear the sounds of muffled voices below.

Nicole yells out, "We're here."

I make no move to vacate the oversized chair I'm slumped in. Less than five minutes later, Nicole is outside my bedroom door calling my name. I don't answer. I hear the door creak slightly.

"Kimi?"

"Go away, Nicky."

"Why you sitting in here with the curtain drawn like you're in mourning? What happened? Is it Daniel?"

"Daniel, you, me, my job. Take your pick!"

"Shh! Nat and Nick are downstairs. I wanted to surprise you."

"Well, you did. Happy?"

"Okay, what the heck happened? When we talked this morning, you were a totally different person."

"Reality happened, Nicky. Reality happened to your big sis. I mean the last literally, by the way."

"You fell off the diet wagon," Nicole guesses.

"None of your business!" I shout, hating her powers of deduction right now.

"That wasn't a question, Kimi," she says me kindly.

"I can't see anybody right now, Nicky. I screwed up once; I don't want to do it again. Please take the kids and go—Angela, too."

"Nope."

"Fine, stay. Get out of my room, please. Now."

"I'm staying and the kids are staying."

"Tell me something, Nicky, why is it I did everything right—marriage, school, kids, nice job—yet my life is shit? You, on the other hand—"

"Careful, Kimi."

"You did exactly whatever the fuck you wanted, when you fucking wanted, and you're living the life of Riley—excuse my pun. You even have a guy you just met giving you the keys to his car."

"Everything I have, I have because you and Mom and Dad love me enough to want it for me. The kids and I would be who knows where if you didn't give a damn, Kimi. I'm getting my college degree because you're making it possible. I'm not just talking about the money and minding the kids for me. I'm talking about your faith in me. It boosts my self-esteem, you know. Hell, if it weren't for you, I wouldn't even have met Donald. So if you are experiencing some kind of jealous thing and thinking my life is somehow better than yours, don't make me your punching bag. Give yourself a couple of knocks upside the head for stupidity, because you make my life work."

By the time Nicole finishes, I'm slobbering all over myself. And when she kneels down in front of my chair and takes me into her arms, I slobber all over her nice leather jacket.

"Nicky?"

"Yes?"

"When did you get the money for this nice expensive jacket?"

She releases me and stands up, moving towards the door.

"It was on sale at Filene's, Kimi."

"When did you get it?"

"Does it matter?"

"Damn right it does. If you got it recently, that means my fifty bucks helped pay for it."

"I can't wear my wool one anymore—Busta's allergic."

"I don't give a—"

"Shh. Remember the kids. You don't want to upset the kids again, do you?"

"I was fired today, Nicky. Fired."

"You should've told me. Why didn't you tell me that when I called?"

"Because—I don't know, Nicky."

"We should go. I'll take Ang and Alex with us. They don't need to see you like this their first night home."

"Alex? You have Alex with you, too?"

"Yep, stopped by the football field and wrestled him from the coach. And he was all for coming back, Kimi. They've missed you."

"Give me ten, no, fifteen minutes to get it together, and I'll be down. Can you stay for dinner?"

"Are we going to discuss my jacket?"

"If not tonight, then we'll do it the next time Big D is around."

"I'll be downstairs— turning them all against you."

I end up taking close to half an hour to muster the nerve to face the victims of my misplaced wrath. I spend part of that time on my computer working on my book, which is the only thing going well. I'm heading downstairs when I hear familiar zapping coming from Alex's room, zapping I've yearned for over the past week. The door to his room is slightly ajar. I hesitantly push it open.

"Alex," I say, my voice low and uncertain.

"Hi, Mom, you're up. Aunty Nicky said you were napping. Is everything okay?"

"Now that my kids are home—yes."

Alex looks at me thoughtfully and nods.

"I straightened up in here; let me know if you can't find something."

"Yeah, okay."

"Yeah, well, what's funny?" I want to know why my son is suddenly wearing a Kool-Aid grin.

"Nothin', Mom. It's nice to see the old you again, that's all. The lady that was here impersonating you before I let this place go to pot."

"Hey, no mentioning me and old in the same breath. You haven't been gone that long," I tease, relaxing a little. "And as for letting this place go to pot, try not to let it happen again." Alex grins and nods slightly. His approval encourages me to be myself with him.

I leave Alex's room and head downstairs to face the last hurdle—my niece and nephew. I find them in the kitchen, along with Angela and Nicole, who is giving out snacks.

"There you are, Kimi. I was just suggesting I try my hand at beef stroganoff. I've a real good recipe from the net. You have all the ingredients I need. I checked."

"Sounds like a plan to me," I readily agree, my eyes on my niece and nephew, who in turn are purposely ignoring the person who attacked their mother.

"Well, now that that's decided, why don't you take the kids out for a bit, Kimi?"

"I don't wanna go," Natasha says anxiously.

"Me either," little Nicolas says, moving to latch onto his mother's leg.

"Well, it's good I didn't ask you or you. Now get your jackets on. Ang, you mind helping them?"

"Not a problem. Come on, you two. You're used to my mom. Come on." Angela's mixture of cajoling and commanding gets the desired result.

"I don't wanna force them, Nicky. They'll come around—I hope."

"A little push in the right direction never hurt anybody."

"Are we still talking about the kids?"

"What do you think?"

"I think you've made your point."

"Good. You better get a jacket. It was nippy when we came in."

"Speaking of going out, what were you thinking volunteering me to go out again with your hyperactive kids? They're like the Duracell bunny—going and going."

"Perfect, that's just what you need after your overindulgence, humpty butt."

I would have loved to give Nicky a piece of my mind, but her kids reappeared, and from their frenzied movements, I easily deduce they were in a hurry to get back to the kitchen. And I'd bet a year's supply of chilled Pepsi it wasn't the thought of accompanying me that put the extra pep in their step. It's concern for their mother that has them arriving wide-eyed and in different stages of dishevelment in my kitchen doorway.

"I'll get a jacket and meet the kids out front in a minute," I say, straining to make my words sound carefree. Afraid my facade won't hold up, I don't wait for confirmation, ignoring the way they both wrap themselves around my sister.

"Who wants to feed the ducks?" Dead silence. My two reluctant companions have been lagging five paces behind since we left my house, and clinging to each other as if they were born that way.

"I want to feed them," Angela claims with dubious interest when it becomes apparent I've missed my intended targets.

I give her a brief thank-you hug, the kind that doesn't require words to explain. For about ten minutes, Angela and I act as though feeding a steadily growing flock of waddling, loudly quacking, intimidating creatures is akin to winning a trip to Disney World. After no show of the slightest interest by either my niece or nephew, who have moved to a nearby bench, I give up and shamelessly abandon Angela to the mob of ducks.

"That goes against the mother protecting her off-spring to the death rule, doesn't it?"

I know it's him before I turn and see him standing about ten paces away, his hands on his narrow hips.

"Every woman for herself, I'm afraid," I respond, walking toward this man of mystery.

"In that case, I won't feel so guilty the next time I abandon Ashley to her own mysterious pursuits."

"So do you come here to the pond often?" I'm more than a little surprised by his presence here of all places.

"Not lately. Afraid all I've had time for lately is work. But weather permitting, I'm starting to make time for some of life's more enjoyable pursuits."

Now why did that comment make me blush and look away?

"Well, good for you. I'd better get a move on. This outing is supposed to be a combination of pleasure and pain."

"Oh?"

"I'm supposed to be working out," I admit.

"Well, you've picked the best season for it."

"Why do you say that?"

I want to step the hell away from this man and what he makes me feel, but I'm curious to hear what he thinks. If I were to leave without knowing the rhyme to his reasoning, I would kick myself for the rest of the evening.

"Come spring, when everyone else is peeling off layers of clothing and moaning about the fall and winter pounds they've piled on, you'll be gliding about like a runway model."

"Who says I wanna look like a runway model?" I pounce. I'm offended by his insight.

"Pardon me, I didn't intend to offend. But most women I know are striving to be a size zero," he says, and then smiles. Could the man get anymore handsome?

"Well, that explains your reasoning, I'm not a woman you know."

"I'd like the opportunity to rectify that," he says, his expression completely devoid of humor now. His come hither blue eyes are looking down on me, heating me from the inside out. I feel my nose starting to perspire and I know, without a doubt, I need to get away from this mesmerizing man before I do something foolish—like invite him to dinner.

"I'd better get going. The kids—"

"Are having a great time," he interrupts before I finish formulating an excuse.

I look at the bench my niece and nephew had occupied a short time ago. It's now empty. I locate them a little ways down the trail. Angela has somehow managed to arouse their interest. They are now running to her for chunks of bread to throw at the ducks. When the ducks get too close for comfort, they make a mad dash to take cover behind Angela's long slender legs. Their faces are beaming.

"Well, will you look at that? Five minutes ago they were like bumps on a log. I couldn't get them to move anywhere near the ducks."

"I've learned the hard way not to force a difficult situation. It's best to allow it to resolve naturally. Everyone involved is better for it."

Now why don't I think he is no longer talking about the kids and ducks?

"Uh, well, I'll remember that. I gotta get going."

"Why?"

"Excuse me?"

"Why do you have to get going, Kimberly Riley?"

"Because I do, Thomas Klein," I grumble, only because his playful sort of flirtatious behavior is turning me on and I'm not prepared for it.

It's been eons since Daniel said anything remotely sexually stimulating to me. Plus the extra weight I've packed on over the years has been an unwelcome deterrent for any would-be admirers. Which brings me to the core of my misgivings in regards to this gorgeous man's intentions.

His movie-star looks guarantee him the pick of the litter, so to speak. Why in the name of sanity is he displaying interest in me? What do I have to offer him, after all? Not that I don't have it going on when it comes to brains and looks—I do. I immodestly acknowledge that I have smarts and that my face is put together extremely well. My body is another matter altogether. A man this gorgeous wouldn't dream of settling for two out of three. He doesn't have to.

"How about dinner tomorrow night?"

"I'm married." My words are indignant, but my soul is soaring. He wants me!

"In name only," he says softly, reaching a hand toward my face. I react by leaping back as if he were fire licking at me. "Our girls talk."

I look around to see if what if we've attracted an audience. No one seems to be paying us the least bit of mind so I return my attention to the man of mystery standing before me.

"I gotta go."

"I'm sorry, I didn't mean to—"

"Good-bye, Mr. Klein."

I can tell he wants to say more, but I walk away before he does.

CHAPTER 12

"He actually said 'in name only'?"

"Yep."

"I hope you told Mr. Suave where to go," Yvonne declares.

I don't answer right away.

"Well?"

"I didn't say much, Eve," I admit.

"Why not? You're not falling for him, are you?"

"What? No! No, I'm not falling for him."

"Which one of us are you trying to convince?"

"Forget I called, Eve. Forget I told you anything about Thomas. Just forget it."

"No, I won't be forgetting Thomas. I'll be fasting and praying you forget about him."

"Why do you have to trip, Eve, and bring God into every little thing?"

"Because He belongs in every little thing. That's your biggest problem, Kimi. You need to allow God in. Make Him your center, and He'll bring balance to your rocky world."

"Hallelujah, sister!" I shout into the receiver.

"Make fun if you want, but I'm living proof he's the answer."

"My other line is beeping, and it's coming up unknown. You holding on?"

"Yes, I am."

"Fine," I say and click over.

"Hello?"

"Kimberly?"

"Who's calling, please?" I ask the vaguely familiar soprano voice.

"It's me, Christine."

"Christine, hello."

"Hi, I got your number from the office database. I know I'm not supposed to call you at home with personal matters, but I needed to talk to you. I'd wanted to talk to you before you left the office, but I didn't get a chance."

"That's okay. Besides, I don't think my escorts would have allowed it."

"I still can't believe they had security put you out."

"Yeah, well, believe it."

"I'm calling because you've been on my mind, and I just want to say that I wanted to speak up for you during the meeting that day."

"But what?"

"My husband had just gotten downsized the week before, and I can't pay my mortgage with two unemployment checks."

"I can respect that, Christine."

"Thank you, but what I really called for was to give you a heads-up."

"About what?"

"I overheard Katherine saying that getting fired is the least of your problems."

"What is that supposed to mean?

"She was on the phone."

"So it was a one-sided conversation?"

"Yep, 'fraid so."

"What else did you hear?"

"Look, the rest of it was just Katherine being Katherine."

"Noted. What did she say?"

"That if you'd put as much energy into the Bronzen account as you did into overeating, you wouldn't have screwed up."

"What else?"

"Something about you trying to lose weight and it being a joke."

"Where did she get that?"

"I've no idea. Damn, I think I hear my husband pulling up and I promised him I'd stay out of this. I gotta go. Good luck, Kimberly."

I click over and tell Eve word for word what Christine told me. "That doesn't prove she's in cahoots with Thomas, Kimi."

"Definitively, no, but it is mighty suspicious. Don't you think?"

"I'm afraid to agree for fear of fueling your obsession with this Katherine person."

"Fine, where were we?"

"I was telling you God is the answer."

"For you, Eve—He's the answer for you. For me, I'm not totally sure. See, I don't have that unfailing, unwavering belief thing you got going."

"You should call Pastor Roland; he'll counsel you. It'll be good for you."

"Maybe. Look, Eve, it's after ten and I wanted to get some writing done before I call it a night. We'll talk, okay?"

"You can run, girlfriend, but you can't hide. Remember that. Goodnight."

Two hours later, Yvonne's words are still blasting in my head, causing me to lose concentration every five minutes or so despite the fact my novel is coming along nicely.

I sign off my computer, giving up for the night. By the time I check the locks downstairs and look in on the kids, I'm looking forward to claiming my own bed. I'm turning down the sound on my television when the phone rings.

"Kimberly?"

"Who is this?" I ask in a small voice.

"It's Thomas."

"Thomas," I repeat, panic temporarily causing my mind to go blank. I couldn't think of anything else to say.

"Were you sleeping, Kimberly?"

"No, I was just settling down, though. How did you get my number?" I can't resist asking, struggling to put it together.

"From Ashley. I hope you don't mind. I wanted to apologize for my behavior at the pond today. I don't know what got into me."

"Your male hormones outran your brain."

"Ouch."

"You deserved that," I tell him unapologetically, and smile to myself. I snuggle further under the covers, feeling oh so good. Male company feels good right about now.

"You're right, I did. I didn't mean to come on like gangbusters. I saw a beautiful lady I'd love to get to know better, and I let my male hormones get the best of me."

"You're forgiven," I tell him, flattered despite my resolve not to be.

"Thank you," he says, sounding genuinely relieved. "Can we start over?"

"I'd like that, Thomas," I say encouragingly, trying out his name in a soft tone.

"Perhaps we can go to dinner and a movie Saturday evening— if you're free," he adds quickly, as if he's afraid I'll take offense at his presuming I'd be free on Saturday night.

"I'd like that," I tell him putting extra cheer into my voice in a bid to put his mind at ease. "I've been meaning to catch that new James Bond movie."

"You're kidding. You actually like action movies?"

"I like a handsome man in a tux, actually," I say teasingly.

"Here I thought I had finally met a female who could appreciate the artistry involved in maintaining a degree of realism so essential to successfully bringing a big-budget action adventure to the silver screen. Someone who shares the raw adrenaline rush when the hero's futuristic sports car weaves in and out of traffic on a congested highway, at about a hundred twenty miles per hour, without receiving so much as a nick on its immaculate exterior."

"Eloquently put, but you neglected to mention the eye candy."

"Eye candy?"

"The damsels in distress—the Bond girl types, all of whom leave nothing to the imagination."

"Unnecessary attempts at stimulating the male viewer," he claims.

"Unnecessary, huh?"

"Absolutely. Give me half a dozen how-did-they-do-that explosions, believable gun battles and a hero who barely walks the line between good and evil, and I'm hooked."

"And half-naked babes have nothing to do with your enjoyment?" I ask, pressing on.

"I don't need eye candy to enjoy myself, Kimberly. At the movies or anywhere else, for that matter."

"Good answer." I'm shamelessly attracted to Thomas Klein.

"I'm glad you think so," he responds. I believe him.

"I better go. I'll talk with you soon, Thomas."

"Wait."

"Yes?"

"Is there a restaurant you'd prefer? I'd like to make reservations."

"I'm not particular. You pick."

"Okay then. Tomorrow, Kimberly. Goodnight."

I carefully place the receiver back on its base; I want to make sure it is hung up. I fall back on my bed and let out a hoot of laughter. I immediately cover my mouth because my laughter seems overly loud in the quiet of the house this time of night. I'm on the threshold of uncon-sciousness when the phone rings again. "Hello," I say, half awake.

"Kimi."

"What?" I ask my estranged husband, none too kindly.

"I'm calling to check on the kids. I want to make sure they got settled."

"You're about five—no, six—hours too late. They're sleeping. Call 'em tomorrow. Bye."

About half a minute later, the phone rings again.

"Kimi, we need to talk."

"About?"

"About a lot of stuff. By the way, I've made arrange-ments to pay those bills. Cable will be back on tomorrow."

"About time."

"I got a good job."

"That's not any of my business. As long as I start get-ting money for the kids, I don't care if you're working in the pit of hell, just so long as you work."

He sighs loudly.

"Anyway, I get paid on Thursdays. They hold back a week, so—"

"So what are you saying? Tell the kids to ignore their growling bellies until your ship comes in? What else is new?"

"You're exaggerating, Kimi. There's money in the sav-ings account."

"For emergencies," I say emphatically.

"If our kids' bellies start to growl, that would be an emergency, right?"

"Anything else, smart guy?"

"I want to apologize for taking that money without checking with you."

"So do it."

"I'm sorry I took the money, and I'm sorry I lied about paying those bills. Hell, I'm sorry about a lot of stuff. Anyway, I put the three hundred back into savings. You can check tomorrow."

"Where did you get the money—your mama?" I ask, refusing to acknowledge his apology.

"No, I didn't get money from my mother. I won five hundred off a scratch ticket. Now you answer something for me. Why do you always manage to make my mama's name sound like a curse word?"

"Thanks for putting the money back where it belongs and for straightening out the mess you made of the bills. As far as your *mama* is concerned, I don't know what you're talking about."

"Yeah, right."

"Bye, Daniel."

"Hold up—one more thing, Kimi."

"Make it quick."

"I want to come home and make love to my wife."

"A booty call? You can forget that," I say, sounding real tough. I'm melting on the inside.

"I miss you, girl."

"You still can't come over, Daniel."

I know this sweet-talking heartthrob. Romance is the one area where my husband still has more cunning than a hungry tiger stalking its prey. Daniel Riley could charm the panties off an eighty-year-old nun if he wanted to.

"Don't you miss making love?" he asks, managing to sound hurt.

"Who says I've been going without?" I ask.

"Kimi," he warns.

"Daniel," I mimic.

"Why you playing games when you see I'm horny?"

"That's not my concern anymore."

"You're still my wife."

"Now you remember. Bye, Daniel."

This time I hang up and immediately take the handset off the base, just in case he decides to try again.

"Earth to Kimi, holla back," Yvonne taunts after I miss another easy serve.

"I'm sorry, guys, I've got things on my mind today."

"That's an understatement. You've been preoccupied to the point where I've had to hold your hand crossing the street twice this morning," Nicky claims.

I'm not sure whether or not she's exaggerating. I've truly been out of it since leaving home this morning to join her and Yvonne for an early tennis match. Thoughts of Daniel and nervous anticipation of Saturday's date with Thomas Klein have my stomach in knots.

"Is it Daniel? Has he come back?" Nicole asks, her expression hardening.

"No, he hasn't, knock on wood," I declare, reaching over and lightly tapping her forehead.

They both chuckle.

"It's not the kids. You said the reunion could not have gone better."

Yvonne deuces, coming close to the net separating her from Nicky and me. Her skin looks ashen and ailing instead of its usual dark and lovely. She's winded, I notice, though we've only been playing for twenty minutes. I smile briefly and squeeze her nose.

"Stop that—you gonna make me lose consciousness," she says seriously, backing away. Nicole and I laugh ourselves silly. "Girl, I'm serious. I saw stars when you did that."

"Try standing in one place as Kimi does and only hit the balls that come directly to you. Or, you should breathe through your mouth," Nicky suggests, still laughing.

"I'm breathing out my mouth and my nose, and it still isn't enough. This two-against-one stuff, *even with Kimi's scarce contribution*, isn't necessary anymore. I've lost my edge," Yvonne complains.

"That puts to rest any lingering question about whether you could have gone pro, girly girl," I taunt her without mercy.

"Yvonne, a pro tennis player?" Nicky asks, looking from me to Yvonne and then back to me.

"Eve considered pro tennis, but love shelved those plans."

"You used to be able to keep a secret, big mouth," Yvonne admonishes, moving in to intentionally bump shoulders.

"I never knew that, Yvonne." Nicky says. "You're good; don't get me wrong. But I just never imagined . . . I'm impressed."

"And I didn't know it was top secret, Eve," I say, defending myself. "You never once said I couldn't repeat it. Besides, what's the big to-do? So you've given up a dream in the name of love."

"Kimi, if it wasn't six in the morning, I'd think you were drunk airing people's dirty laundry like you crazy," Nicky says assuming a serious tone, but she's sort of smirking. "My brain's misfiring because it's freezing out here this morning." I say. "Try running for the ball for a change, Big sis, it'll help."

We're moving back into position to play again when Nicky adds, "While we're on the subject of dreams, Kimi, let's talk about the biggest single most regretful sacrifice you've made in the name of love."

"I can't think of—"

"Careful, remember you're talking to the two people who know you best," Yvonne warns, firing off a ball in my direction.

I don't even try to return her serve; I just get the hell out of its way.

"Oh, it's that way, huh?" I say, sending back my best serve.

Yvonne easily returns it. Nicky gets in on the action. After about a minute of continuous play, Eve says, "We're waiting to hear about your sacrifice, the one you can't think of."

"I don't consider marrying and starting a family a sacrifice, Eve. I managed to fit college into the mix. If I'd wanted to at the time I could have selfishly continued struggling to carve out a writing career. I chose to give it up. Both Daniel and I pursuing our individual dreams at the same time would have been disastrous. I did the sensible thing—accounting."

"You say it so proudly, Kimi, as if you're announcing that you discovered life on Mars or a cure for the common cold. I could barely detect the underlying defensiveness," Nicole puts in, nearly missing a return serve.

"I'm proud of planning my life, Nicky, no matter how it turned out. Allowing life to just happen can be a big mistake. But you know all about that."

"And you know what you can do with your uppity-ass viewpoint," Nicole says, steaming now.

"Careful, Kimi, you'll turn her against you, and then you'll be against the master all by yourself," Yvonne inserts.

"By telling it like it is? I don't think so."

"There's always a polite way to say anything, my friend. You just have to care enough to find it," Yvonne informs me, clearly not pleased with me.

"There's also the time when blunt honesty is all that will do, as Nicky demonstrated not too long ago—remember, Nicky?"

"How can I forget? You almost dismembered me for it. As for carefully planning out life, I say to each his or her own. When Mom had you, she says they were between a rock and a hard place. She wasn't sure where their next meal was coming from. Faith and determination brought them through, not some infallible scheme."

"That was our parents, Nicky, a different world ago. The goal, if you haven't been told, is to do better, to save for our children's future so they won't have our struggle, so they won't have to give up a dream. That starts with education and creating a traditional family unit in which children can flourish emotionally and financially."

"And what are you, the fountain of wisdom spouting popular crowd-pleasing jargon? Most of which, I might add, would be hypocritical if Daniel hadn't married you when he knocked you up," Nicky muses aloud, while effortlessly sending a powerhouse serve back in Yvonne's direction.

Yvonne is as shocked as I am by the terrific serve. All she can do is get out of its way.

"Oh, shit! Where were you hiding that all the times we've lost to Eve in the past?" I ask.

"I wish I knew," Nicole says, looking genuinely surprised. From the perplexed look on her face, I see she is sincere.

"I think we'd better call it a day before I—before someone gets hurt. Too much misplaced emotion going on here, I tell you," Yvonne complains, running forward to shake first Nicole's hand, then mine, as is her custom. We're all struggling for breath now, so we crash on the nearest bench.

"A couple of months of that, and I'll be back in shape in no time," I announce when I can speak again.

"You're looking thinner already," Yvonne says, eyeing me up and down.

"You can tell that even though I'm wearing a frumpy sweat suit?" I ask, skeptical of her positive assessment.

"Girl, just take the compliment and move on. Black people—I tell you."

"You sure you alright, Eve?" I ask, leaning closer. Her excessive sweating and panting alarms me. "You don't look right and you don't sound right."

"Nothing wrong that a little more physical activity won't cure. What time is it?"

"Quarter past seven," I tell her, running my hand across her still perspiring forehead.

"Doggone it, I better get going. I told Mike I'd be no later than seven thirty. We're having dinner with his parents, God help me. I need to spend some time reminding him what he stands to lose if he doesn't stand up to his mama.

"I have a date," I blurt out as we are nearing my driveway.

"What?" both my companions ask in union.

"You heard me," I say in a tough-guy-tone.

"Coward. Saving the topic for the last possible second," Yvonne charges.

"Guilty as charged," I confess, without a trace of regret.

"Who is it?" Nicole asks suspiciously, as if she thinks she knows who it might be.

"Thomas Klein, and it's not what you think," I divulge—after I've opened my front door.

"Are you crazy?" Yvonne shouts.

"She's crazy," Nicole answers, starting forward. I put up a hand to stop her.

"Don't bother coming in if your intent is to talk me out of going."

"Yeah, right. Move it or lose it, sister." Nicole doesn't wait for me to comply; she shoves her way past me into the house. Yvonne just stands there, looking up at me.

"What you smirking about?" I ask.

"Because it's two against one. Good will triumph over evil."

"Shouldn't you be home on all fours servicing Mikey Mike?"

My laughter aborts any comeback Yvonne might attempt—to ensure I have the last words that matter, I soundly close the door,

"You shouldn't talk like that to Eve, you know," Nicole scolds me as soon as I turn around. "She's really religious."

"Girl, please, Eve's probably freakier than you and I put together."

"Maybe she is, maybe she ain't. It still doesn't mean she wants to go there with you."

"I'm her best friend, Nicky. Plus, I'm grown, so mind your business."

"You'd love for me to get mad and leave, wouldn't you, Kimi? That way you carry out your immoral plans in peace. But that is not going to happen."

"Immoral plans? Girl, please, we're going to the movies. It can't get more innocent than that."

"What about your marriage?"

"It looks over. What else is there to know about it?"

"This isn't like you to go against what would be socially acceptable. You're going on a date, and your divorce papers haven't even been filed."

"Totally anti-Gemini behavior, huh?"

"Not totally; it's your flip side. Your other half is somewhat flighty and yearns to be free—promiscuous, even. It appears that side of you has emerged."

"Bout time, I'd say."

"Are you definitely divorcing Daniel then?"

"That's the usual conclusion to the course we're on, Nicky."

"There's always a chance of reconciliation."

"What's wrong with you, Nicky? You gone and put rubber bands around your legs to hold up your socks again—cutting off the blood circulation to your brain?"

"Why you gotta bring up the past, Kimi? I was ten—"

"Eleven and a half."

"Ten, eleven. I was young."

"Old enough to know better, according to your own momma."

"Whatever, okay. You're going off on a whole other subject, anyway. I'm just trying to establish that you are serious. Your mind can't be changed? You are divorcing your husband of umpteen years?"

"Must you remind me how many years I've wasted on that nigga?" I ask, starting up the stairs.

"Sorry, I know this can't be easy. Hell, look at my situation with Robby. Now you know that was one no-good nigga there."

"That's the truth," I agree.

"But still I stayed, hanging on for dear life, like he was some lifeline I couldn't live without. Lord knows, I should have ditched that deadweight years earlier."

I stop and turn to get a good look at Nicole.

"What's your point?"

"Don't play dumb, Kimi, you know what I'm getting at."

"That's your story, your life, your bad choices."

"Yeah, but I'm hardly the first, nor will I be the last, woman to stay in a bad relationship."

"Well, you're looking at one less sucker here, so stop worrying," I assure her. "What's the matter?" I ask, seeing that her expression had devolved from mere concern into heart-wrenching dread. Her eyes fill with tears. "Nicky, tell me what's wrong. I know you're not upset over this Thomas Klein thing."

"It's about Daniel."

"I don't want to know," I say calmly but sternly, no longer anxious to know what's wrong. If something about Daniel has her this much of a wreck, then it doesn't leave much hope that I will fare any better.

"But, Kimi—"

"I said—"

"It happened a long time ago."

"All the more reason I don't wanna know. All water under the bridge."

"I promised myself I'd tell you when it no longer mattered. When it couldn't hurt you. I can't take it to my grave, Kimi. I couldn't rest in peace."

"Nicky, I'd say it's a safe bet you have a few more years, at least, before taking it to your grave is any real concern."

"Can you be serious?"

"Can you just drop it, please? Whatever Daniel did that has you this upset, I don't want to know—ever."

"When you were in New York at that computer training in '01, me and my friend Chantel spent the weekend to help look after the kids, because you didn't trust Daniel to take care of them for a whole weekend by himself—"

"I said I don't want to hear this!"

"Kimi, please."

"I said no!"

"I have to explain what happened," Nicole pleads, starting to cry.

"If you want our relationship to continue, you'll shut up now, Nicky. I mean it. Besides, do you think I was blind all those years ago—do you think I was blind?"

"He'd been drinking," she sobs.

"Don't you dare make excuses!" I scream.

I start back down the stairs but stop myself, afraid of what I'll do if I get too close to my sister right now.

"Get out of my house, Nicky."

"I wanted to tell you, Kimi, but I didn't know how to go about it. Then Daniel swore nothing—"

"Daniel swore? Who cares what Daniel swore? What about you, Nicky, what did you swear—to keep your mouth shut?" I scream.

"I swore on our dead grandparents' grave that if I saw him so much as smile at another woman again I'd gut him. I swear, Kimi, I wanted to tell you, but I couldn't get the words out. I felt so guilty, because Chantel was my friend. Then the years started zooming by, and it became less and less of an issue."

"Your friend sleeps with my husband and you think time diminishes the severity of the offense?"

"Sleep with your husband? Hold up. Are you crazy? Hello! I'm your sister! I caught Chantel creeping and I followed her into your bedroom. I hid out to see what was what. Daniel seemed down with her seduction attempt. It could have been me, just seeing what I wanted to see. I was young and prone to exaggeration. But that's when I stepped to them and broke things up. I told Daniel where he'd better keep it, and I put Chantel's whorish ass out. I'm sorry for never having the courage to tell you before now. I knew what time it was. I could have stopped Chantel before she climbed into your bed, but—"

"You were curious as to whether or not Daniel would take what she was offering," I finish for her.

"That's not all—"

"What else?" I ask, curious now.

"Jealousy. I wanted the pleasure of catching him trying. I was so angry over the beat-down Daniel had given Robby. How foolish was I? I'm so sorry, Kimi. I was young and jealous and stupid. I think part of me wanted to see your perfect world fall apart," she confesses. Her face is now covered with tears, and her nose is running unchecked. "You're my sister. How could I have done that—how could I have wished that on you?"

"You were young and jealous and stupid. I would've been devastated had I known when it mattered."

I can tell from the relief that floods her face before I pull her into an embrace that she has picked up on my choice of words, and she knows my use of her own words is intentional.

"And don't tell Daniel you know, or we won't have any more leverage," she mutters into my shoulder.

"Blackmail," I ponder aloud. "I like it," I admit, and kiss my sister tenderly on the side of the head.

———◈———

"I'm begging you to reconsider this, Kimi. Let Mike handle this Cauplum business in court," Yvonne pleads for the hundredth time.

"No! This is my life. It's time I took control of it. Now are you gonna help me dress or keep pestering me? If you're only here to pester, you can leave. I'll dress myself."

"How many times you gonna change your clothes, anyway? That dress looks as good as these other three did," Yvonne complains, bending to retrieve the dresses I've carelessly discarded on my bedroom floor. She doesn't mention Thomas again—for the moment. I'm not convinced she's done trying to talk me out of going on this date.

"That's the problem, Eve, this dress looks no better than the others. I'm trying to beguile the man so that he will tell me everything I wanna know. Oh, hell. Look at my stomach, just sitting there mocking me. I hate my pear-shaped body. I'm up to a hundred sit-ups a day, and this sack of potatoes hasn't shrunk an ounce. Why is that, huh?" I shriek in anguish while clutching the excess fat around my navel. "I need a tummy tuck and an ass lift. I will settle for a girdle," I decide suddenly, turning to face Yvonne.

"Don't look at me. I don't own one," Yvonne says, throwing up her hands.

"What time is it?" I ask, reaching for the phone.

"Six o'clock. Relax, that gives you about an hour before Mr. Wrong is on your doorstep."

"Shit, answer the phone, Nicky," I say into the receiver.

"I thought you said she took all the kids out for pizza, and then to Video Mania afterwards."

"Cellphone, Eve, ever heard of them? I can actually reach her—if she answers the freaking phone."

"What are you bothering her for? I've volunteered to be at your disposal. Just tell me what you need."

"A girdle, Eve. Look at me. I need a girdle! How can I seduce this man into telling me anything with this pouch thing hanging there? It'll distract him. Hell, it's distracting me and I'm used to it."

"Okay, calm yourself. Jesus, help me. For someone who has ulterior motives, you're stressing out as if you want to impress this Romeo," Yvonne observes.

"I haven't been on a date in more than eighteen years, Eve. Stressful is putting it mildly."

"You look good, Kimi. I like your hair long. It's grown so much," Yvonne relents enough to say.

"Was that a reality check?"

"Absolutely," Yvonne says shamelessly.

"Thanks, I needed that. I spent the better part of yesterday getting the braids taken out. It was worth it."

"Look, I can zoom over to Kmart and try and find a girdle. What size do you need?"

"Look at my stomach, Eve. I'm guessing a large."

"You're being cynical. A medium should do the trick. Don't you think?"

"We've been down this road, Eve. All I know for sure is the last time I tried to look sexy, I didn't need any extra support."

"I'll be back in half an hour or less."

When the doorbell rings, thinking it's Eve, I grab my robe and rush downstairs. I should have known better. That would have been too easy. The handsome man standing on the threshold takes my breath away. His masculine scent surrounds me. The dark-blue single-breasted suit appears to be tailored to fit and is set off by a tasteful two-tone tie. His hair seems a bit shorter. It has a healthy-looking shine to it and is neatly combed, as usual. I see I'm not the only one who paid a visit to the hairdresser. I'm pleased.

"You're early," I say.

"I apologize for that. I had business in the area that finished up earlier than I anticipated. I didn't want to risk driving all the way back to Canton so here I am. I could wait in the car if—"

"No, no, don't be silly. It's just that, as you can see, I'm not altogether ready," I say, self-consciously pulling my robe closer to my body.

"You look all together to me," he claims. His eyes sweep up and down my body before returning to collide boldly with mine. I clear my throat and look away.

"Won't you come in? Make yourself comfortable in the living room. I'll be down shortly."

I don't give the answer to all my male fantasies a chance to say anything else; I dash off, practically running up the stairs. I will never be entirely certain, but I could have sworn I heard him chuckle. I want to crawl under something until he goes away. I've been prowling about my room for thirty or so minutes when I hear the doorbell. I'm so pissed I'm tempted to not even open it.

"Should I get that?" a masculine voice calls out.

"If you don't mind, Thomas, that would be great," I call down in my best cultured tone. I wait a full five minutes before poking my head into the hall. What the hell is keeping Yvonne's ass down there? I'll bet my last dollar she's cornered Thomas with a barrage of questions that are none of her business.

"Yvonne, honey?" I call down with syrupy sweetness. "I'm coming."

"What took you so freakin' long?" I demand, snatching the Kmart bag from her hand and rushing off to the bathroom.

"You're welcome!" Yvonne shouts after me.

I return a few minutes later, wearing only my bra and the girdle.

"What do you think?" I ask, turning around in a slow circle.

"You look like Kimi, wearing a girdle."

"Forget you, Eve," I say disappointed.

"What do you want me to say? You look fine, with or without the girdle."

"Just forget it. Help me get the red dress on. I think I liked it the best."

"I think you're right. It does look better with the girdle," Yvonne says, stepping back to give me a once-over.

"Told you. But it sure doesn't feel better," I say, examining myself in the mirror. "Feels like somebody's squeezing me extra tight and won't let go."

"Well, look at it this way, it's only temporary. Another month or so of serious dieting and exercise and you can burn that thing," Yvonne says, trying to be positive.

"Looking on the bright side won't help the here and now, Eve," I say, turning about in front of the mirror to get a look at myself from all angles.

"You're only interested in this guy to clear your name, right?"

"That's right," I'm quick to confirm. Yvonne looks relieved, if not convinced.

"What did you think of Thomas?" I ask suddenly, catching her off guard. Our eyes meet in the mirror, mine measuring, hers apprehensive.

"That bad, huh?" I ask, chucking awkwardly.

"No, that good," she says, confusing the hell out of me.

"Can I get that translated into plain English, please?"

"Kimi, he's great looking. From the short conversation I had with him, he seems well-versed."

"He's the stuff dreams are made of," I finish for her.

"Exactly."

"So what does he see in me, right?"

"You're beautiful, Kimi, you know that. "

"But you don't think he's sincerely interested in my black ass."

"I didn't say that."

"Don't go all around the block, Yvonne. Save it for your patients or some stranger on the street. I'm your best friend. I'll take the unfiltered, unedited truth, if you please."

"Fine, I don't think he's interested in you, not seriously. He looks like Prince Charming."

"Then why is he pursuing me?"

"Maybe he wants to take a walk on the black side. Maybe he's between relationships. Maybe—"

"Maybe you don't know what you're talking about," I interrupt, not liking her frank answer after all.

"Maybe I don't know what I'm talking about in this instance, but there is one thing I'm sure of."

"What's that?" I ask, turning to face her.

"I'm sure that you're not gonna drop this dress and let Prince Charming in on this little secret," Yvonne predicts, pulling the elastic on the waist of my girdle, and then letting it snap back into place.

"You're a fool, Eve. A darn fool."

I try not to laugh, but her laughter is contagious and I end up joining in.

"I better get going before Prince Charming gets tired of waiting and moves on to find his Nubian princess."

CHAPTER 13

"Would you like to go somewhere else, Kimberly?" Thomas asks.

"Why? Do you want to leave?" I ask, without answering his question.

"No, actually, Masacci's is one of my favorite places to dine. You, on the other hand, seem a bit, well, uncomfortable comes to mind."

"Well, I'm not," I lie, not willing to admit I regret not accepting his offer to let me choose the restaurant. I couldn't have known the man would choose an Italian restaurant all the way up in Mansfield. I'm the only black face out of a good sixty patrons, give or take. I've looked the room over three times.

"Can I take your orders?" a twenty-something lollipop-shaped waitress asks. With growing annoyance, I notice she only has eyes for Thomas.

"Would you like me to order for you, Kimberly?"

"No, I would not," I assure him, coolly. "Thank you," I belatedly add.

He looks sort of hurt. Recovering quickly he puts up his hands, signaling he's backing off. He studies his menu for several long seconds and then orders in Italian. He returns his menu to the waitress. I realize belatedly I've been staring at him the entire time.

"I would have never guessed you had such a fluent grasp of the Italian language," I admit. Who the hell is this mysterious man? I keep that question to myself. "I am impressed, though I must confess I haven't the faintest idea what you just said."

"There are many Italian words I could teach you—if you like," he says and winks.

The waitress politely clears her throat, drawing my attention.

"Would you like some help, dear?" she asks with arched brows. I glance at my menu. I become flustered when I see the entire menu is in Italian.

"I'll have a Caesar salad with a glass of white wine," I manage after clearing my throat several times.

As soon as the waitress leaves Thomas starts up again.

"You look beautiful tonight, Kimberly," he says, smiling.

"Thank you again, Thomas," I say, stressing *again*.

He's told me I'm beautiful three times already, and I'm still not convinced he means it. By the third time, it sounds as if he's trying too hard to convince one of us, and I'm not sure which.

"I'm sorry. I'm making you uncomfortable."

"Something like that," I admit.

"I'm glad you agreed to come, Kimberly."

"Why is that?" I ask, boldly searching his eyes for some insight into this man's motives.

"Because from the first moment I laid eyes on you, I knew I had to get to know you better."

"Why is that?" I repeat, refusing to be satisfied with a wordy answer that could mean anything.

"Why not?" he asks, refusing to be dissected.

"I'm married, Thomas."

"But are you happily married, Kimberly?"

"I have two children."

"I love kids."

"And I'm black."

"And you could be green with pink spots and I'd still have asked you out."

"Handsome *and* a way with words. You, Thomas Klein, are deadly."

"Only if you resist," he assures me with a sexy smile.

Goose bumps are forming on my upper arms. Our drinks arrive, and I attempt to defuse my unease by drinking up.

"Tell me about yourself," he says.

"You mean what you haven't milked Ashley for," I suggest.

"Guilty," he confesses.

"I don't think there's much more to know," I tell him, being evasive.

"Don't be modest. I'm sure the details behind the vital statistics are the stuff movies are made of."

I'm flattered by his assumption, but I cover up well. "Certainly not in the tradition of James Bond," I joke, hoping to lessen the intensity of the mood.

"I like a good family epic every once in a while."

He is good at this. Practice makes perfect, I'll bet.

"Okay, here goes," I say, feeling cornered in. "I'm originally from Georgia—"

"Home of the Atlanta Falcons. They're doing pretty good this season," Thomas interrupts.

"Can I continue?" I ask, mildly irritated.

"Sorry, please do," he urges.

"My family moved to Boston when I was quite young. I married much too young to know any better. I have two terrific kids. My son, Alex, is fourteen and plays football. You know my daughter Angela."

"That I do. She's a beauty, just like her mother."

"Thank you—again."

"So are you a stay-at-home mom, Kimberly?"

"No, yes, I'm a stay-at-home mom at the moment. I'm an aspiring writer. Until that bears fruit, I'm moon-lighting as an accountant. Until recently I worked for Thature Mathematics. It's a private auditing firm. Ever hear of them?"

The food arrives, but not soon enough to sufficiently cover the telling silence following my unanticipated inquiry.

"I work for Cauplum Enterprises. I'm a stock analyst and, yes, I've heard of Thature Mathematics. What exactly did you do there?" he asks casually.

"I'm a CPA," I reply.

"Thature is a large auditing house. They do the books for dozens of corporations—"

"Including Cauplum Enterprises," I say, bringing a quick end to his fishing, though I know I don't really need to.

"Including Cauplum Enterprises," he repeats matter-of-factly, his beautiful blue eyes locking with mine but revealing nothing. Instinctively I know we've both shown as much of our hands as we dare—for now.

"If we're going to make the show, we'd better eat up," I suggest, calling a ceasefire—for now.

———— ·∾· ————

"Tell me that wasn't the best James Bond to date. An excellent balance of action and dialogue," Thomas enthuses as we make our way back to his car. The parking lot of the theatre is mobbed with all the cars seemingly trying to exit at once. I move to open my door, but Thomas beats me to it. It's been a long time since I've had that pleasure.

"The movie was well paced," I allow, when he gets into the car.

"Does that mean you liked it or you didn't hate it?"

I look over to see he's smiling at me. I swear, the heat radiating from the man's eyes could melt ice at the North Pole.

"It was a good movie," I finally concede. "Are you happy?"

"Extremely," he claims. "Was it really as hard as it looked for you to admit you enjoyed the movie, or was it admitting you enjoyed yourself that you find hard?"

"I'll get back to you on that," I say, refusing to answer either part of his question.

While Thomas adjusts the heat and gets himself situated, I'm allowing his luxurious Bentley to lull me into semi-consciousness. Suddenly the theme from Charlie's

Angels snaps me back. The sound is coming from Thomas waist.

"Sorry, I meant to set my phone to vibrate," he quickly apologizes.

I nod my understanding and pretend to be interested in the view outside my window. I'm extremely curious as to who is trying to reach him at eleven on a Saturday night. I surmise from Thomas's end of the conversation that some documents hadn't arrived at their expected destination, and whoever is on the other end really wants them tonight. Thomas repeatedly asks if first thing in the morning would work, but I gather from his frustrated sigh that the answer is no. He hangs up the phone and immediately apologizes again, but not for the interruption this time.

"Sorry about that Charlie's Angels stuff. Ashley must have been playing around with my phone when she used it earlier today."

"No need to make excuses, Thomas. If you're a fan—you're a fan. I won't hold it against you," I say in a light, teasing tone.

"I'm not responsible for that—Ashley is."

"Sure, sure. But I'm curious, are we talking the Farrah Fawcett *Freeze or I'll hit you with my big hair* Angels, or the Cameron Diaz *Freeze before I drop kick your ass* Angels?"

"I'm not into either," he insists between bouts of laughter.

"Okay, Thomas, just forget I asked."

"You're funny, Kimberly Riley."

"I know it. In another life I would be a comedian."

"I believe it."

He sends me another one of those sincere smiles, accompanied by a wink this time. I'm convinced he knows how emotionally lethal he is to the female species.

"Do you have to get home right away?"

I'm debating my answer when Thomas, who is still in the process of attempting to back out of the parking space, suddenly slams on the brakes. Thanks to my seatbelt I mainly stay put, except for being slammed back into the plush seat. Thomas bolts from the car. I follow at a much slower pace. He makes sure the young couple he'd apparently nearly collided with are okay, and insists on exchanging registration information—just in case. We then return to his car and manage to exit the parking lot without further incident.

"So, do you have to get home right away?" he asks again.

"Not *right* away," I say cautiously.

I'm not sure why he's asking the question, so I wisely give myself wiggle room just in case he has something in mind that is out of the question.

"I have some computer graphic work that I need to send over to this fellow who is updating my website. I needed it done by yesterday, and he's booked on an early-morning flight to China, believe it or not. If I don't get the changes to him tonight he won't do them until he lands in China."

"So, what do you need exactly?" I ask, still not committing.

"I'd like to stop by my house for half an hour, an hour tops. I have to get the information to him and give him time to get the new version up and running, and then I'll take you straight home."

"This isn't the 2008 version of I've run out of gas, is it?"

He looks confused for a second, and then he smiles and shakes his head. "I promise this isn't a ploy to get you all alone, though I find the idea appealing. I really do have to get this graphic business taken care of."

"Put that way, how can I object?"

Thomas makes the mistake of asking me about my book writing. His prompting questions about editors and publishing houses seduces me into giving my tongue free reign, and I ramble on endlessly about my dreams and aspirations of one day seeing my work in print.

The ride to his house takes about half an hour.

"This is it," Thomas says, pulling up to an imposing two-story dwelling.

"Very nice," I comment lightly.

The truth is I'm drooling on the inside. The house is painted in my favorite shade—flaxen. Daniel and I could never agree on a color when we bought our house, so we ended up compromising on a nondescript shade of gray—timber wolf, the painter called it. We've repainted the house twice since we bought it, and both times we've ended up with the same lackluster shade, again, because we could not agree on a new shade. If I told him this soft-yellow house with gold trim is my dream house, I doubt he'd believe the coincidence.

The interior of the house leaves me awestruck. His entranceway pops in quilt gold and dazzles with a sparkling crystal chandelier hanging from its soaring ceiling with eye-catching semi-glossed crown molding carrying out the effect. Gleaming, dark bamboo flooring runs the length of the downstairs. To the right of the entranceway, bamboo flooring continues up the polished Victorian banister staircase with grand, white newel at the top and bottom.

We pass a door that is ajar and I slip a peek inside. It is overflowing with medium-sized boxes. The name Cauplum Enterprises is in large bold print on the sides of the ones closest to the door.

"Are you moving?" I ask, though I seriously doubt that he is.

"Not even close."

"What then?" I ask

"Let's just say I'm doing some overdue house-keeping," Thomas explains and closes the door. I'm about to probe further, but something, I'm not sure what, stops me.

"Good luck," I end up saying. I honestly can't think of anything else, as I decide not to ask the question that is really on my mind. Why does it look as if he has moved his office into his house?

"Come on in and make yourself comfortable."

I follow Thomas into a spacious living room with bay windows. It is painted husky orange and decorated in a complementing blend of neutral browns and ambers. An inviting honey brown marble fireplace is the focal point of the room. To the left of the living room is a huge archway leading into a roomy and spotless kitchen. It's my dream kitchen, with granite countertops, an island, and stainless steel appliances.

"This is nice, Thomas. I must have the name of your decorator—along with your charge card," I say.

He chuckles.

"Can I get you something to drink, Kimberly?"

"No, I'm fine," I assure him, making myself at home on a plush high-back loveseat.

"I'll be upstairs. My office is the first door on the right. If you want to pop in and say hi, or maybe check out my CD collection, feel free to come on up."

"I might just do that," I say, returning his infectious smile.

As soon as his footsteps peter out, I'm on my feet and tiptoeing back to the door that contained the boxes. I attack the closest box marked Cauplum and proceed to rummage through its contents. It contains documents that look to be businesses owned by Cauplum. A quick scanning shows Cauplum's dealings with a number of different companies; I'm familiar with one. I take note of what seems to be Thomas' signature on a number of documents. I hear movement coming from above stairs, so I scramble to set things back the way I found them and then tiptoe back to the living room.

My heart is racing. I hear him on the stairs now.

"It shouldn't be much longer, Kimberly. I'm sending the needed files over even as I speak," Thomas assures me as he enters the room. He is minus his suit coat and tie, and the first three buttons on his dress shirt are now undone. "Is something wrong, Kimberly? You seem distracted."

"Nope, nothing is wrong. I have a lot on my mind these days, that's all."

"Anything you care to talk about?" Thomas asks, joining me on the loveseat.

"How about we pick up where we left off in the restaurant?" I suggest, managing to sound calm. "Cauplum."

"I finally meet someone I'm seriously interested in getting to know better, and not only is she married, but she's connected with Cauplum—my Achilles' heel."

"We know nothing about one another."

"I know my life will never be the same now that I've kissed you."

"You haven't kissed me," I remind him, unaware I was being duped until he spoke again.

"Allow me to correct my oversight."

I have plenty of opportunity to turn away from him, as his motion is unhurried. But don't move a muscle. My eyes lock on his lips, and I am spellbound watching as they approach mine. His lips are warm and slightly moist. At first he delivers only tantalizing pecks, but as soon as I peck back, his lips part as if I've answered some unspoken question. He suckles first my top lip then my bottom before kissing them deeply in unison.

Thomas doesn't attempt to thrust his tongue into my mouth, and I'm grateful. I don't think my palpitating heart and overstimulated senses could handle more without wanting a whole lot more than mere kisses. I'm bringing my arm up to wrap around his neck when his phone rings.

"I better get that. It could be Ashley," he says.

I want to believe the breakneck break with which he gets to the phone is the result of an innate parental need to assure himself that his child is safe. After that toe-curling kiss, I really, really want to believe it's another female causing him to answer his phone with discernible apprehension. I'm still holding on to a slim bit of hope when Thomas turns and points to the phone at his ear and then toward the stairs, indicating he needed to take the call in private.

Thomas returns some fifteen minutes later, and I am steaming. If I weren't using him to get to the bottom of the Cauplum matter, I'd walk the hell out the front door. I got cab fare; my mama taught me that.

"Where were we?" Thomas asks, rushing back into the room. Is he serious?

"You were just about to tell me why Cauplum is your Achilles' heel and why you have a room filled with company property," I toss out. My words are just as casual as his had been.

"Excuse me?"

"While you're busy getting your story straight, let me enlighten you about a few things. I saw you two together at Grocery Mart, and I know it's because of you Katherine didn't send Thature's findings regarding Bronzen," I lie convincingly.

"That is one far-fetched assumption. Have you repeated it? " he asks, coming toward me.

I stand up. I feel a tad better standing—less defenseless.

"Wrong answer, Thomas. The right answer for the game and a taste of my kitty cat was, Katherine who?" I reply.

"Maybe we should start over," he suggests.

"No, thank you. I'm fine right where we are. Where we should have been to begin with."

"Meaning?" he asks, stepping closer to me. I will be eternally grateful to the person who chose that moment to ring Thomas's doorbell. Something—perhaps desperation—had come into Thomas's eyes when I made my accusation.

"You better get that," I recommend, stepping aside to put space between us. For the first time since I met him, his smile is forced.

"Don't go away," he orders, trying to sound playful. He fails. He walks briskly toward the door. I grab my jacket and I'm fast on his heels, though I go to great efforts to be sly about it. Whoever is at the door is my ticket out of this place.

"I believe you have someone here who belongs to me," I hear a familiar voice say.

Any other time I would have been totally offended, and would have told him where to stick his male chauvinistic posture, but not in this moment of panic. I quickly move to where I can be seen.

"What are you doing here, Daniel?" I ask, pushing past Thomas and out the door.

I don't give either man time to say anything, because I'm making a beeline to my husband's Beamer before they can string two words together. By the time Daniel joins me, I've locked my door and secured my seatbelt.

"Aren't you going to ask me how I found out where you were?" he asks, after we've been on the road for several minutes.

"Thanks for coming to get me," I say suddenly.

By the look on my husband's face, I'm not the only one shocked by my admission. I hadn't meant to admit I needed rescuing.

"Yeah," he says just before giving his undivided attention to the road.

"The kids are staying over at Nicky's tonight," I say, sounding lame. We're at the house now.

Daniel doesn't ask to come in; in fact, he uses his own key to let us in, and turns his anger on me as soon as I cross the threshold.

"I know where my kids are, Kimi. What I'd like to know is what my wife was thinking of playing detective?"

"I wasn't—"

"I've spoken with Yvonne and Nicky, so don't lie to me!"

"Don't lie? You first," I shoot back.

"Let's stay on this subject for now, please."

"Fine. They had no business telling you, of all people, my personal business."

"I'm your husband," he says, his hands going to his lean hips. He's looking fit—as always.

I start up the stairs, wanting to end this confrontation before it gets really heated. I'm suddenly feeling drained.

"Funny—you haven't acted the part in so long, I had begun to stop thinking of you that way."

He looks away and I slowly mount the stairs. My knight in shining armor.

My first order of business when I reach my room is to rid myself of the restricting girdle. I've just sent my dress and bra the way of the offending girdle when the bedroom door opens.

"What?" I ask in a hard tone, because I'm embarrassed to have him staring intently at my naked imperfect body. I we haven't lain as husband and wife in a long time.

"I'm about to leave; we'll talk tomorrow."

"Fine—tomorrow," I agree, not giving an inch. I know he wants me. His eyes are all over me, and when they dart to mine briefly they're shooting flames of unspent desire my way.

"Did you want to sleep with him, Kimi?" Daniel asks, surprising me, not by the question but by the unmistakable hurt it contains.

"I was totally attracted, but I couldn't sleep with him—tonight," I add the last, refusing to relieve my husband's mind totally. He doesn't deserve to have peace of mind right now. He accepts my challenge and comes farther into the room.

"Why you got to get smart, huh?"

"Because that's what you deserve." He's standing directly in front of me now.

"Give me a kiss, Kimi."

"No."

"Can I give you one?" He's lowering his head before I can get a word out. "Forget I asked," he says before he captures my lips. I'm in heaven. These skilled, warm, sensual lips are like mom's homemade apple pie—uniquely delicious and completely satisfying. I'm returning his kiss, and within seconds I am eagerly pulling at his clothes. He doesn't help me, his hands are busy roaming all over me— my back, my butt, my thighs, around to my breast, along a path to my protruding stomach, finally stopping at the juncture of my privates. His loud moan of delight signifies that he has reached some goal he had set for himself.

I'm quivering all over. His skillful fingers learned the location of my G-spot eons ago. A vaguely familiar euphoria builds in the region of my woman's core. When it hits me, I'm about to climax—I am climaxing. I grab on to my husband's neck for dear life, and ride one of the most spectacular waves of ecstasy I've ever experienced. Every time I feel the wondrous sensation ebbing, Daniel increases the back and forth motion his fingers are applying to my G-spot, and I'm right back where I started in the mist of a sensational, unforgettable ride of wondrous proportions. By the time Daniel shows mercy and slows down his sensual assault, I've collapsed on him and moaning like a wounded animal.

"You all right?" he asks, in a tone that sounds suspiciously like mockery.

"Whatever, Daniel, let me go." I'm not surprised my soft and whiny request is denied.

"We're just getting started, baby," Daniel informs me, his words determined and self-assured.

I lean away so I can see into his eyes, which areas determined as his words. Before I know it, I'm on the bed and Daniel's bearing down on me. I can't help myself; I reach up and kiss his beautiful lips.

"I missed you, girl."

"Whose fault is that?"

"The demons that were riding my ass."

"Good answer," I say, laughing, while at the same time opening my legs to accommodate my husband, who is wiggling around on top of me.

I feel the cold metal of his belt buckle as he settles partly on me. I can feel his hand fumbling with the button of his jeans, and I smile secretly because I can tell he wants me bad. My secret smile turns to a wide one of sweet satisfaction a moment later when Daniel fills me with his member.

I'm reminded of the first time we made love. We were much too young to be French kissing, let alone having sex. But Daniel made my first time special and unforgettable. He was gentle, attentive and unbelievably uninhibited. Not even the hundred-degree heat of mid-July or the fact that we were cramped in the back of his airless '72 Volkswagen Beetle could lessen the sweet memories I still carry to this day with regards to our first time. Over the years Daniel has taught me to be just as uninhibited in bed as he is. I offer him my breast and watch in elation as he eagerly takes the nipple into his mouth and suckles it. I reach down and squeeze both of his muscular buttocks in silent praise of his actions.

"We're off our rhythm schedule, Daniel," I say between moans.

"You got a towel handy?" Daniel releases my breast and asks as if he is in pain.

"Why would I? I wasn't expecting to be lying under my husband tonight," I remind him, rotating my hips before pulling down on his buttocks. I smile widely when my gesture causes him to gasp in pleasure.

"Keep it up and baby makes three," he threatens.

"Use your shirt," I suggest.

"It's a new shirt, Kimi."

"Oh, well, then get up," I say, releasing my hold on him.

"Okay, okay, but you're cold, baby. After you get yours, you get all indifferent," Daniel complains, hastily removing his shirt.

"You call this indifference?" I ask, rotating my hips again.

"You shouldn't feel this good. You use it as a weapon," he tells me grudgingly. I'm enjoying myself too much to respond. Way too soon, Daniel is pulling out of me and spilling his seed onto his new shirt.

"You shouldn't feel this damn good after all these years. And don't say 'whatever, Daniel.' "

I would have said just that if he hadn't pressed two fingers to my lips. I settled for loudly kissing the offending fingers instead. Reality can be a very cruel and embarrassing thing, I reflect several hours later. Daniel is leaning over me, his expression a mixture of impatience and superiority.

"What, Daniel?"

"You tell me."

"Tell you what?"

"Everything you've been up to with that Thomas Klein guy."

"I believe my backstabbing sister and best friend already did that."

"Humor me."

"I think not. I'm thirsty. I'm getting a drink."

I slip out of bed and into the bathroom. I'm not looking forward to discussing my scheme to expose Thomas and Katherine with Daniel, of all people. He'd just love a chance to laugh in my face for what he would term a wacky plan.

"Kimi," Daniel says as soon as I come out of the bathroom.

I blow him off. "I'm extremely agitated right now, Daniel, and not with you. Don't get in my face right now, please!"

He wisely allows me to get into bed without another word. Content, I sleep instantly.

I wake and go down to the kitchen, and I'm pouring a glass of water. It ends up all over the floor, thanks to Daniel. Startled by his sudden appearance, I jump a foot into the air.

"What are you doing down here, following me?"

"I'm setting the record straight, that's what I'm doing."

"What are you talking about?" I ask from my new position on the floor, where I'm cleaning up the water spill.

"The day I hit you with the Beamer. I had dozed off—I'd been up all night the night before."

Daniel joins me on the floor, and takes the paper towels from my limp hand and picks up where I left off.

"When I heard the bang, I woke up, thinking you had returned to the house."

"I had closed the trunk."

"I know that now. When I glanced back—and I did glance back—there was no one in sight."

"So you didn't try to kill me on the sly. I still have enough grievous acts done to me by you to last a lifetime."

"Such as?"

"What do you mean 'such as?' You were there every time."

"Just so that we're clear, I'd like you to spell them out for me—the most grievous ones, that is."

"Who you playing with, Daniel?" I challenge with open disdain, because I detect laughter in his unblinking gaze.

"I'm totally serious, baby. I want to know from your lips to my ears how I've hurt you. Seriously. I've seen a counselor, and he tells me that's the best place to start."

"Yeah, right. That's why your eyes are laughing at me."

I'm out of the kitchen and heading for the stairs when Daniel catches up to me. "Hold up, hold up. Kimi, baby. Baby, come on," he pleads, latching onto my wrist. "Forget my damn laughing eyes. Baby, I can't help it. We just made the kind of love we haven't made in years. Shit, my eyes might never stop laughing."

"Try," I say, not willing to dismiss his claims when I feel the same way about what happened upstairs between us.

"Now tell me, how have I hurt you?"

"Where do I start? Your insensitivity about my weight, your unfaithfulness, your lies about bills, your

selfishness when it comes to keeping a job, your unwill-
ingness to put this marriage first?"

"You're talking about my mom there at the end?"

"Yes, your mama!"

"No need to yell. I was only asking for clarification."

"See yourself out. I'm going to bed—alone."

"You can go to bed alone, but I'm not leaving. I
should never have walked out that door. I'll be down here
thinking," he calls after me. I close my bedroom door
without another word between us.

———

After about the gazillionth ring, I realize the annoying
sound isn't a part of my dream. It's the phone on my
nightstand.

"Hello?" I grumble into the receiver.

"Kimi?"

"Et tu, Brute?" I say.

My sister sucks her teeth loudly.

"Yvonne is on three-way. We just wanted to see how
last night unfolded."

"And you honestly expect an accounting from me? I
still have the knife protruding from my back. Can you
two get any more shameless?"

"I prayed all night," Yvonne interjects softly.

"And I had your chart done, girl. You are in way over
your head," Nicky declares dramatically.

"Thanks for the prayer, Eve. I welcome prayer any
day. Nicky, you and your psychic friend, however, can go
to—"

"Lord, have mercy on her, please," Yvonne interrupts, luckily for Nicole.

"I second that, Sister Yvonne," Nicole claims.

"Yeah, yeah, praise the Lord, the Son, and the Holy Spirit. Do you two want to hear what happened or have church?"

"What happened?" they ask at once.

———

"I thought you would be gone by now, Daniel."

"I don't know what gave you that idea. I thought I was pretty clear when I said I'd be down here thinking."

"Yeah, well, I'd appreciate it greatly if you'd go think at your mama's house or whatever house you're residing these days."

"Angela," Daniels says, coming to his feet. He's wearing nothing but a pair of black spandex boxers, and he looks damn good.

"What about Angela?" I ask, playing dumb to protect Angela's slip of the lip.

"You don't do dumb very well, Kimi. It's the fire in your eyes that gives you away."

"I want your house keys," I demand, as if I really expect Daniel to hand them over. Men of Daniel's macho caliber don't just hand over their property on demand without darn good incentive. An angry spouse isn't a darn good reason.

"What you got, Kimi, a severe cold, the flu, loss of memory? I live here! Why would I hand over my keys? I was stupid to up and leave like that. I was childish, inconsiderate—"

"Keep 'em coming," I tell him, not budging from my unforgiving stance.

"I'm still your husband."

"That's the best you got?"

"I'm getting dressed, and then I'm arranging to have *our* things returned to *our* home, after that, I'm going to pick up *our* kids from your sister's and take them for breakfast. You coming?"

"Only if you promise to choke!"

"And here I was under the misconception that you wanted me around. The way you were wiggling your ass all over me, I thought you'd tear my skin off if I'd tried to leave."

"Self-flattery is so despicable, Daniel."

"And denial of the obvious is so pointless."

"What's the obvious, Daniel?"

"You're no more ready to dismiss me than I am to dismiss you."

"You must be suffering from amnesia, because you dismissed me pretty easily."

"You wanted me out, Kimi."

"Did I say that?"

"Baby, you didn't have to say the words, they were all over your face every time you looked at me."

"From amnesia to mind reader, I'm impressed—not!"

I storm off in the direction of the kitchen.

"So should I wait for you or not, Kimi?" Daniel calls after me.

I silently hope he's holding his breath for an answer.

CHAPTER 14

"You did the nasty!" is the first thing Nicole says when we meet on the tennis court. Yvonne smiles broadly at me before taking up a position on the opposite side of the net.

"I don't know where you get that idea from," I deny weakly.

"I overheard Daniel telling the kids he was back home."

"Overheard, my ass. Knowing you, you had your ear stuck to the other side of the door."

"That is beside the point. So he stayed the night. And if he stayed the night—you two did the nasty. So you worked things out."

"Not even close. He's home, but there is much too much water on the bridge. We couldn't possibly muddle through to work things out."

"But you're under the same roof—that's a huge step in the right direction," Yvonne puts in. She's looking too thin to me.

"True that," I allow.

"How was it?" Nicky shamelessly asks.

"How do you think it was?"

"Let's see, an estranged husband charges in and stops his wife, who has never slept with another man, from committing one of the biggest transgressions of matrimony. I'd say it was downright earth shattering."

"I wouldn't go that far."

"Of course, you wouldn't—Gemi. Your bleak, pessimistic side is outmaneuvering the upbeat optimistic side of your nature."

"Come again?"

"What Nicky is saying is you've been hurt by Daniel, so you've got your guard up against him," Yvonne translates before firing a ball our way.

About five minutes into the game, Nicole pipes up again.

"Speaking of Thomas Klein—"

"No one's speaking of him," I point out the obvious.

"Well, I was thinking of him. That's like the same thing. Anyway, Dougie says he can put a tail on him if you want him to. He has connections at the Area E detective unit, girl."

"Dougie?" I repeat.

"I wanted to call him Big D but it embarrasses him in public, so we compromised with Dougie."

"I think Donald got the bad end of the compromise."

"He doesn't think so," Nicky brags, rolling her hips.

"Nasty girl," I tease.

"Break!" Yvonne calls suddenly, getting our attention.

"Eve, you don't look so good. What gives, girlfriend?" I ask in all seriousness.

"Nothing, I'm just tired from entertaining Mrs. Holier-Than-Thou last night. My mother-in-law is as close as you can get to Satan and still be alive. Believe that."

"I don't see how one night can run you down like this. You look wiped out." I push the issue, not at all appeased by Yvonne's explanation.

"Then it must be from all the jumping and shouting I did at church. You should try it."

"I'm guessing you jump and shout every Sunday, but I've never seen you looking like this," I say, still not buying her explanation.

"I don't know what else to tell you, Kimi. Look, I've gotta go. You gonna be at home later?"

"Yeah, why?"

"Mike's got something he wants to talk with you about. I tried to get it out of him, but he wouldn't budge. He takes the lawyer-client privilege stuff seriously. I trust you'll tell me whatever he tells you."

"You know I will."

"Good. Later, guys."

"Something is wrong with her," I say with certainty, watching Yvonne rush off.

"Yvonne's a Taurus, right?"

"Don't start, Nicky. I'm seriously worried about her."

"And I'm seriously trying to help."

"By reading the stars?"

"Don't knock what you won't bother to try and understand."

"Fine, she's a Taurus. What does your infinite zodiac wisdom say about that?"

"She feels that her stability, security, and material comforts are at stake. Those are the only things that really scare a Taurus—mind, man, and money."

"I'm not buying that—your average Taurus maybe, but not Eve. She's too much a believer in the big guy to let a man or money become her focus. As for her mind, Eve is as sound as they come."

"So she's perfect, you're saying?"

"On that ridiculous note, Nicky, darling, I'll say, see yah."

———

"One hundred ninety pounds. I don't believe it. I'm down eighteen pounds. Go, Kimi; go, Kimi—it's your birthday; it's your birthday."

"Good news?"

Damn. Is it just me, or is Daniel doggin' my steps? Ever since I got home from the tennis court, and he with the kids, he has popped up wherever I am.

"Do you mind? I'd like a little privacy. That's why I'm in the bathroom."

"Sorry, didn't mean to bother you. You've got a call. Mike says it's important."

"I didn't hear the phone ring."

"I was talking to my boss. She wants me to bring in more of my artwork tomorrow. She's seriously considering giving me a shot at a showing."

"Good for you."

"If it happens, it'll be good for us."

"If you say so."

"Kimi," Daniel says and sighs heavily.

"Daniel," I mock perfectly.

"How do you do that?" After all these years, he still marvels at ability to mimic just about anyone.

"No time for chitchat; my future is hanging in the balance."

I'm only half joking. I'm wishing I hadn't said a word, because Daniel follows me back into the bedroom and openly listens to my every word. Soon he loses interest and abandons me. I don't allow myself more than a heart-beat of hurt over his apparent lack of concern, because Mike's news has flooded me.

"A criminal matter?" I say.

"According to my source at the U.S. Attorney General—"

"You have a snitch at the U.S. Attorney General?" I ask and Mike nods.

"According to my *source*, Thature Mathematics blew the whistle on Cauplum, accusing them of round-tripping. Cauplum allowed money to flow out through a middleman. Those very same funds come back, and Cauplum claims it as revenue. The transaction has no real economic impact on the company, and the bogus numbers substantially improves Cauplum's financial statement."

"I understand round-tripping, Mike."

"Sorry."

"How much money are we talking about?" I ask.

"About $67 million, give or take a hundred thousand, according to my source. "

"Oh, shit."

"You can say that again."

"And the middleman?"

"That's where it gets really messy. Thomas Klein is being fingered as the mastermind behind a deal between Cauplum and Bronzen to inflate Cauplum's financial outlook in order to appease anxious shareholders."

"What's in it for Bronzen?"

"Word is Cauplums's sister company Birkwirth—"

"Birkwirth, the big art gallery?"

"And upstart cable-provider. Anyway, Birthwirth has a joint venture with Bronzen to provide cable service to about thirty states."

"Sounds ambitious, but innocent enough," I say, not seeing a problem so far.

"Birkwirth agreed to allow Bronzen to show a book profit before there were any actual profits."

"How much?"

"Something in the neighborhood of $67 million."

"You scratch my back and I'll scratch yours."

"Exactly."

"How does this involve me?"

"When Thature checked the books for Cauplum, the scam was discovered, but Thature claims someone on the inside attempted to conceal it from the Cauplum auditors. According to my source, Thature is fingering you as the likely culprit."

"Oh, my God! Oh, my God. I'm involved in a corporate scandal!"

"Calm down, Kimberly."

"Oh, my God."

Mike continued talking, but I couldn't for the life of me repeat or remember anything he said after his revelation that I was in major trouble. My next conscious memory is of a hand on my shoulder. Daniel has reentered the bedroom. His expression is a mixture of empathy and strength; I see that he is on the downstairs cordless phone.

"Mike, Kimi is going to have to call you back. She needs to get her bearings before she can digest any more of this."

I thank God for Daniel in that moment of personal crisis. I'm sure I would have crumbled to the floor if he hadn't stepped forward and wrapped his arms around me.

"Should I apologize for listening in?"

"No."

"I didn't think so."

I run until my chest hurts, and the muscles in the back of my legs are so tight I'm sure my circulation is on its last leg, too. I can barely catch my breath. The gentle breeze on this pleasant spring-like day does not cool me down. I'm steaming on the outside but cooking on the inside. I would kick my own self in the behind if it were possible. Only a yes-man or yes-woman could find himself or herself in my predicament—accused of misdeeds involving millions of dollar yet have not a penny of the millions to show for the trouble. I collapse heavily on the first bench I come to. I've managed to run to the quarter-mile mark around the two mile pond. I can think of a time when such an accomplishment would have left me swollen with pride—not today. I'm bereft of spirit. The voice hesitantly calling my name surprises and angers me at the same time.

"I hadn't truly expected to run into you here—again." I manage, struggling for breath.

"Jogging. It's hardly an original idea, Kimberly."

"Traveling twenty miles from Norfolk County to Suffolk County for a two-mile jog *is* an original idea. If I didn't know better, I'd say you were following me."

"Not that the idea of following you doesn't interest me, but it *is* a ritual of mine, running here at least three times a week, weather permitting, dating back to the days when I lived in the area and grew fun of the pond. But I can't deny I'm glad I ran into you."

"Oh yeah, why?"

"Now I can apologize for last night in person."

"Last night is the least of my concerns, Thomas."

"I hope I didn't cause you any difficulty."

"Nothing that I couldn't explain my way out of."

"Good, that's good. Your husband appeared upset catching us like that. I was really worried."

"Well, it's all good. So I'll be seeing you around, Thomas."

My words are purposely dismissive. I want no part of this criminal mastermind.

"Wait, Kimberly. When can I see you again?"

"Never. My husband is back home, and we're working things out."

I hate having to explain myself to this stranger, but I've led him on, so I haven't a choice.

"Can I at least call you again? I really liked the time I've spent with you. I got the impression you felt the same way."

"Look, Thomas—"

"Don't do this, Kimberly," he interrupts, gripping my arm. His grip is painful.

"Have you lost your—"

"I'm sorry. I didn't mean to frighten you. I just don't want us to end like this."

"Us? There is no us, Thomas."

"That's not the impression I got when we were kissing last night."

"Good-bye, Thomas, and good luck."

That's as close to a warning as I dare give him. I turn on my heels and get the hell out of Dodge. That had to be the weirdest conversation I've had with anyone since, well, forever.

—∞—

I give up trying to sleep. I've been tossing and turning for over an hour. It is now past midnight.

"Do you wanna talk about it?" Daniel asks.

"No," I say.

"I'm here."

"Thanks for sharing. Goodnight, Daniel!"

"Where are you going, Kimi?"

"Last time I checked, I was still a free woman. Free to come and go as I please."

"I didn't say you couldn't come and go as you please. I just asked where you're going, if you please."

"Funny, you're real funny, Daniel. Let's see how funny you can be when you have to tell the kids mommy's in jail."

"I won't let that happen."

"I feel better already. I'm going downstairs. I'm hungry."

"You sure that's a good idea? It's after midnight."

"Look here, Daniel, I appreciate your attempt to morph into a caring husband, I really do, believe me. But I've got too much going on to play along."

"Fine, I'll come with you," Daniel declares, surprising me with his thick skin. This is a side I've never seen of my husband.

"Well, you going or what?" he asks when I just stand there staring up at him—trying to figure him out.

"Nope, I've changed my mind."

I climb back under the covers, leaving him standing in the middle of the floor.

"Goodnight, Kimi," he says, getting back into bed.

"Yeah, goodnight," I grudgingly reply, moving as far away from him as possible.

Daniel moves in on me and meshes his long muscular frame to mine from behind.

"I'm gonna fall on the floor," I gripe.

"Sorry, baby," he says, with what I'm sure is phony contrition.

He then secures a hold on me with one strong arm. He feels so good I have to bite down on my bottom lip to stifle a moan—truly. I manage to conceal the heavenly feel of him behind a faux sigh of frustration.

"You comfortable?" he asks.

"What do you think?" I snap.

"You ready to talk?" he asks, ignoring my snippy response.

"At almost one in the morning?"

"You can't sleep anyway—we might as well talk. We need to clear something up."

"You know something, Daniel, that might be better than counting sheep."

"Must you always be flip with me?"

"What you wanna talk about?" I ask.

"First, can you turn and face me?"

"I'm quite comfortable as I am. Thanks for caring."

"I'm supposed to pour out my heart to your stiff back?"

"Take it or leave it," I tell him with a dismissive yawn.

"I'll leave it—for now," he says with surprising patience, snuggling closer and sighing contentedly into the side of my neck.

I manage not to do the same, just barely.

—◦◦◦—

"I could teach you how to get the most out of stomach crunches if you'd like," Daniel offers. I was hoping to be done before he woke his ass up.

"Not interested," I say, struggling with my forth setup.

"You're using your upper body to pull yourself up when you should be allowing your abdominal muscles to do all the work. Resist the urge to use your shoulders," he says, crouching down beside me. God, help me ignore this fine-ass man.

"I don't have abdominal muscles, Daniel."

"Baby, everybody got ab muscles. It just seems like you don't because—"

"Because what?" I dare him to finish.

"Because you haven't been using them to their fullest potential."

"Yeah, right," I say, pushing his hand off of my thick middle.

"I've got this under control, Daniel," I assure him, but he doesn't budge. He just adjusts himself on his hunches and stares me down. Not a mean or intimidating stare, but soft, almost caressing. It definitely has an 'I want to make things right' quality to it.

I'm up and out of there before I do something stupid—like fall under Daniel's hypnotic spell.

—∾∾—

"Kimi, think you can come and take a look at my paintings later?"

"Excuse me?" I say, stalling because Daniel has just sprung this on me in front of the kids. Now they're looking at me with pleading eyes.

"You haven't shared your paintings with me since the Ma Riley incident."

"I was wrong, Kimi.

"Well, I've a lot going on. I have to meet Mike later on," I tell him, managing to conceal my deep regret.

"Maybe tomorrow?" Daniel persists, but there is hurt in his eyes. I'm sure he won't ask me again.

"Maybe," I agree for the kids' sake.

"You two better finish your breakfast instead of wasting your time staring at me," I remind my two little defectors.

"Here, Kimi—my business card. The gallery's address and phone number are there. It even has my e-mail address."

Daniel's words seem to be coming from a great distance and seem to echo in my head. I take the card and look at. The name Birkwirth Gallery, in bold letters, jumps out at me.

"What's wrong?" Daniel asks, as confused as I am transfixed on the card.

"This can't be. You work for Birkwirth Gallery?"

"I told you that."

"No, you didn't tell me that."

"I told you, babe."

"No, you didn't!"

"Calm down, Kimi."

"NO! I won't calm down!"

"Okay, guys, get your things together so I can drop you off," Daniel tells the kids, dismissing my outburst for the moment.

Instantly contrite, I wisely wait for the kids to leave.

"They've been through enough, Kimi, they don't need to see you blow your stack," Daniel tells me sharply. His newly minted cool has somewhat evaporated.

"Whose fault is that, Daniel?"

"Largely mine."

His admission shocks me, so much so all I can do is look away.

"Don't you remember the night I called you and told you I had a job?"

"You didn't say where, Daniel. I would have remembered if you had."

"You kept interrupting me. Why are you acting like I'm working at Three Mile Island?"

"Because Birthwirth may very well be the equivalent for me."

"Come again?"

"Birthwirth is the sister company to—"

"Cauplum. I heard Mike tell you, remember?"

"Then you know what it means? You're working there?"

"No, I don't know."

"Daniel, they're doing illegal things there."

"That doesn't have jack to do with me."

"How can you say that?"

"Because my hands are clean. I just want to display my art."

"That's crazy talk."

"I'm just a brother trying to catch a break."

"That's even crazier talk, Daniel!"

"Crazy or not, I'm taking some more of my paintings in to my boss. If she likes them, I'm in business."

"You can't do that. You have to quit—today."

"And give up the opportunity I've hungered for as long as I can remember, just like that?" he says, snapping his fingers.

I vigorously nod yes.

"You're out of your mind, Kimi. I put up with way too much crap to get where I am. I'm working in one of the top art galleries in the nation—finally I'll be mingling with artists who have connections, artists I would have no chance of meeting otherwise. This could be—no, this *is* the break I've been waiting for."

"No, I don't believe that. Fate wouldn't be that cruel."

"What about all the other people who work there? Should they quit, too?"

"I don't care what they do, just so long as you do."

"No, I won't do it."

"Then we're done here."

"Meaning, you want me out again?"

"Do you wanna get out—again?" I toss out.

"This sounds and feels too much like déjà vu. I've gotta go to work. I'll see you later."

CHAPTER 15

"Are you Kimberly Riley?" I'm tempted to ask who wants to know, but the two serious-faced men in trench coats have an air of authority. I nod and they flash a couple of authentic-looking badges at me and identify themselves as U.S. Marshals. I can honesty say that the time between opening my front door and my sitting in an interrogation room of the Federal Bureau Of Investigations—the FBI—is all but a complete blank to me. I didn't even know there was an FBI office in downtown Boston.

One minute the U.S. Marshals take possession of me; the next, I'm being escorted downtown in an unmarked car and delivered into the hands of two FBI agents who fingerprint me and handle me in the good cop; bad cop tradition. Sometime during this surreal ordeal I must have asked for a lawyer, because Mike is here and interrupts just as the FBI agent playing bad agent asks how long I've been having an affair with Thomas Klein.

"Mrs. Riley is happily married with two beautiful children. Next question," Mike says briskly.

"That's not what we hear," bad agent smirks.

"We're not here to answer to rumors," Mike says sternly, his expression sour. "So unless you are prepared to charge my client with something, we're leaving."

"Mrs. Riley, did you know it's considered corporate fraud to falsify financial information?"

"You don't have to answer that, Kimberly," Mike tells me, and I keep my mouth shut.

The frowning agent is not deterred.

"Do you know you're facing felony charges that carry with it stiff fines and imprisonment?"

"Mrs. Riley has done nothing wrong. She was only a lowly accountant for Thature Mathematics—nothing more."

"Our sources say differently."

"Whoever is saying differently is lying," Mike says, his tone mater-of-fact.

It is good agent who engages him this time.

"There are always three sides to every story that comes through those doors—yours, theirs, and the truth. The job of the federal government, however unpleasant for your client, is seeing that the truth prevails."

I look at good agent. I run his sympathetically delivered declaration through my thought processes a couple of times, and suddenly I'm no longer scared of being here. I'm pissed. They actually think I'm a sucker. And they're intent on playing me along just as I've seen on television. And I'm sitting here wringing my hands in petrified fear and allowing someone else to stand up for me. But who better to stand up for me than me? More so than well-meaning Mike, I've a vested interest in seeing me cleared.

"I never took so much as a paperclip from Thature without permission. Any case I was given to assist in auditing, I did my portion of the work to the best of my ability—no exceptions. Ever!"

The three men are staring at me with different levels of startlement on their faces. That's when I realized I've literally stood up and shouted my innocence.

"Take a seat, Mrs. Riley," bad agent barks.

"No!" I shout defiantly, though I've no idea where I go from here.

"Kimberly, please, sit down. Getting angry will accomplish nothing," Mike says coaxing. But I'm having none of it.

"Speak for yourself, Mike. Standing up for myself accomplishes a great deal in here, where it counts," I tell him, patting my chest.

"I want to hear them say what they *think* they have on me specifically—no more guessing, no more innuendoes. Can you do that?" I ask, gesturing to bad agent.

"That's Agent Sumptshon, and to be *specific* you're involved in fraudulent transactions involving several multimillion-dollar accounts, lady."

Agent Sumptshon goes on to paint a picture similar to the one Mike had outlined for me concerning Cauplum, Bronzen and Birthwirth. Thanks to Mike's snitch, the Cauplum-Bronzen-Birthwirth triangle is all old news to me. I wisely don't let on to that fact. I'm just starting to feel smug, listening to bad agent rattle off what he obviously thinks are shocking revelations. When he says something that deflates and shocks.

"Mr. Klein has been most cooperative in this matter, Mrs. Riley. I'd strongly advise you to do the same. It's every man for himself now."

"Meaning?" Mike beats me to the bait.

"Meaning Klein has given us pertinent documents bearing fingerprints which match your client's, as well as this tape, which raises a good deal of suspicion as to the truth of your cries of innocence, Mrs. Riley," bad agent says smugly, placing a small pocket-size recorder on the table.

I slowly sit down. I listen in astonishment as the last conversation I had with Thomas in the park fills the room. I don't know how a mostly innocent encounter could come across so . . . so dirty, but it does.

"I want a minute in private with my client," Mike says stiffly when bad agent turns off the recorder.

"This is insane! He had no right to record that. Is that even legal?"

"That's the least of your worries, ma'am," good agent says with a hint of empathy.

"No, Kimberly, it's not legal in Massachusetts and they know it," Mike informs me. His words are accusatory, and I get the feeling his condemnation includes me.

"We can sit here and split hairs on whether the tape is legal or not for the next five hours—when my shift ends, by the way—but the fact remains, your client is looking at a serious criminal charge unless we get some satisfactory answers."

"Such as?" I quickly ask, his last words giving me hope that I just might get out of this room without handcuffs after all.

"Kimberly, I must advise you to limit your responses until we've had time to talk," Mike sternly reminds me.

"It sounds like your client is interested in cooperating and you're hampering a Federal investigation," good agent tells him.

"Get real," Mike scoffs, clearly not intimidated in the least. "My client will cooperate, but not at the risk of forfeiting her right to protect herself. The Fifth Amendment—ever heard of it?"

"She cooperates fully, or I read her her rights!" says bad agent.

"Mike—"

"It's okay, Kimberly," Mike says soothingly. "So far, all they've proved is they're good at spreading gossip. But I suspect they haven't shown their hand yet."

"We have evidence that a crime has been committed," good agent says, picking up from bad agent. "There is a lot of evidence pointing to your client. Mr. Klein states that she was his contact at Thature Mathematics—"

"That's a lie!"

"There are witnesses—reliable witnesses—who place you on numerous dates with Mr. Klein."

"Bullshit! He set me up!" I charge. I strain to recall who these reliable witnesses who saw me with Thomas might possibly be: the stranger from the park, the girl at the restaurant, the young man from the movie theatre parking lot—they all come to mind.

"Kimberly, please," Mike cautions. I don't heed his pleas. "There were never numerous dates. I had dinner with Mr. Klein once. And that was only to get to the bottom of his dealings with Bronzen. It was never romantic. And the kiss he's referring to was—was nothing."

"That clears up a lot, Mrs. Riley," good agent says sarcastically.

"Thomas kissed me—we kissed each other, okay—it was an isolated incident. My marriage is—was on the rocks. I allowed things to go a bit further than I'd planned with Thomas, but the kiss was it."

"Tell it to Mr. Riley," bad agent chimes in.

"Forget you!" I rail at him with unconcealed loathing.

"We have witnesses who place you two together on Jamaica Pond, at the movies, out to dinner—"

"That's no surprise, since we were not trying to hide anything. Look, I'm one among many who went over the Cauplum accounts. Why am I your only suspect?"

"You're the one Klein named as his contact at Thature," good agent says casually.

"What! He said that?"

"We have no reason—or proof—to believe otherwise."

"At last, a glimpse at the hand you're playing," says Mike.

I'm on my feet again, but this time I start for the door. Mike's hand on my elbow stops me.

"I want to go. I want out of here, Mike!" my words are frantic.

"Okay, we're going. Just sit tight for one minute, please," he beseeches me when it's clear I have no intention of remaining there. I don't respond but do take my seat—slowly.

"What kind of deal are you cutting Mr. Klein for his false statements regarding my client?" Mike asks without preamble.

"Spell out what you want, Agent Whalen?" Mike asks, cutting to the chase.

"Your client's full cooperation in this matter," he says, smiling engagingly at me, the kind of smile my momma always told me to be wary of.

"I've already done that," I say firmly.

"You've given us some food for thought, Mrs. Riley. But—"

"But?"

"But the fact remains—you still appear entangled rather deeply in criminal misconduct."

"What do I have to say that I haven't already said to untangle myself?"

"The question isn't what you have to say, Kimberly," Mike says, his expression grim. "The question is what does the FBI want you to do?"

Agent Whalen sighs.

"We have an idea who Klein's contact at Thature really is."

"Good for you. Arrest them. Let's go, Kimberly."

Mike doesn't wait for my voluntary compliance; he practically drags me toward the door. Agent Whalen's next words stop us cold.

"I can't do that. We have no hard evidence tying the individual to Klein."

"That didn't stop you from dragging my client in here."

"In Mrs. Riley's case, we have circumstantial evidence and Klein's confession," he claims, joining us near the door.

"Not a shred of which will hold up under cross-examination," Mike shoots back.

"Off the record?" Whalen asks softly.

"Off the record," Mike agrees.

"We want to recover the money Klein is hiding, along with his cohort. But we can't drag our feet."

"Because it's an election year," Mike says, filling in the blank.

"If your client is all we've got when this goes public, she's all we've got."

"What do you people want from me?" I ask, frustrated. My head is suddenly throbbing.

"Help us get a confession out of Klein."

"Absolutely not! Get one of your guys—they've trained for years to risk their necks to do it!" Mike thunders before I can say anything.

"There's not enough time for a plan. It can take a month to establish the type of relationship we're talking about. Klein is not just going to spill his guts to a total stranger. Mrs. Riley is the best we've got right now."

"What about the deal you made with Thomas?" I want to know.

"It stands—for now."

"As a fallback," says Mike.

"He can't know we suspect he's duping us," says Agent Whalen.

"There has got to be another—"

"None that we have time to put in the works," Agent Whalen says, not backing down.

"I don't believe that," Mike snaps.

"I am offering your client the only possible way out."

"First you have your agents work my client over, then you stroll in with your one-sided deal."

"I suggest you take it."

"Thanks, but if you don't mind, we'd like a second opinion."

"Be my guest, but time is running out, counselor."

CHAPTER 16

It's about eight now. We've had a quick meal, and the kids are all upstairs— Nicole's and mine. Five minutes have passed since Mike's retelling of what happened with the FBI, and no one has said a word. We are all seated at my large kitchen table: Nicole and Yvonne on either side of me. Daniel is across from me, and Mike seated to Yvonne's right.

"It's got to be Katherine!" I declare, pounding a fist on the kitchen table, earning looks ranging from concern to doubt from everyone at the table.

Nicole pipes up, "Katherine . . . do you really think so?"

"Yes, Katherine Rings. Nicky, you remember her from the market. She was in the car waiting for Thomas," I remind her, rising and going toward the refrigerator. Nicole and Eve follow.

"We never saw her face, Kimi. For all we know that could have been anybody," she says, rushing ahead and silently blocking my path to the refrigerator.

"It was Katherine!" I maintain, giving my sister a taste of my evil eye.

"Anything is possible," Yvonne allows, pulling me back towards my chair where her and Nicole surround me—again.

"Mike, surely the *FBI* can get a copy of Thomas's phone records. That'll prove whether or not he's connected to Katherine," I say, sending Nicole and Yvonne 'I'll get you later' looks.

Mike sighs. "If the FBI has shown probable cause—which I'm sure they have—and obtained the phone records and can establish Klein's connection to Katherine, they are probably reluctant to show their hand."

"Why not?" Daniel asks.

"Klein is their ace in the hole. If they can't nail him, they at least need his cooperation."

"Are you saying the FBI would really look the other way regarding that swine Klein?" Yvonne asks incredulously.

"I'm saying they want everybody involved, but in the end will settle for whoever they can get."

"Meaning they will cover their eyes when it comes to Klein's lies about me if necessary," I interject.

"If necessary," Mike confirms. "If Klein says you're his accomplice at Thature, and the FBI can't prove otherwise, rather then ask a jury to believe only part of Klein's tale, they will peg you as Klein's accomplice. You're going to have to prove otherwise."

"That's outrageous!" Nicole says loudly. "I'm going down to the *FBI* and giving them a piece of my damn mind," she vows.

The idea is ludicrous, but so sweet. I can't help but hug her close.

"Sillyhead," I tenderly whisper in her ear, before turning back to face the others.

"They have you on tape admitting to kissing him," Daniel says, deliberately repeating the charges. His hazel eyes are ablaze with anger and burning into mine.

"This is hardly the time to discuss a meaningless kiss," I respond softly, looking away.

"Right now works for me," he fires back.

"You're hardly in a position to throw stones," Nicole reminds him, coming to my defense.

"I've had all I'm going to take of your butting in, Nicky. You look at me like I'm a walking disease. One, I used the money to take art classes, instead of paying the bills. Kimi was watching every penny so tightly and I wasn't working steadily. I know she would have said no if I had asked to put money into my craft. I know that's no excuse, but it's all I got. As for your friend—I didn't sleep with her, I didn't even kiss her. You got so bent out of shape when you saw us—screaming your fool head off— I just let you say your piece."

"You two were in my sister's bed getting chummy," Nicole says, refusing to back off.

"She came on to me. I won't deny I was flattered to have a young, attractive woman coming on to me, but—"

"She had her hands all over you, and you were doing absolutely nada to try and stop her," Nicole charges. "If I hadn't burst in on you, I can only imagine how 'flattered' you would have ended up being!"

"I've never slept around on your sister. I wasn't about to start with your little girlfriend—believe that."

"You just enjoyed your share of foreplay."

"That's a lie!" Daniel counters.

"I was half asleep and half dreaming when she came at me!"

"What about the woman you had over at your mama's house?" Yvonne asks, getting in on the interrogation.

"Yvonne," Mike says chidingly, "that's not for you to ask. This whole conversation is inappropriate. What happened or didn't happen is between Daniel and Kimberly."

"Wrong. He causes my sister to be unhappy, his actions become my business," Nicole butts in.

"The day you came over, Bobby had brought a girl by my mama's house, Kimi," Daniel admits. Whether he *wants* to come clean or is wilting under the pressure from my two guardians, I'm not sure. "I had no idea he was gonna do it. He knew we'd been having problems—I didn't think you'd believe I had nothing to do with it. I—"

"I don't wanna hear your excuses, Daniel Riley," I say, cutting him off.

"But I'm explaining."

"No, you're cleaning up your mess. The kids saw you with a woman at your mama's. Probably the same hoochie Bobby hooked you up with."

"No, that was the daughter of one of Mama's bingo partners."

"What?" I screech.

"That's more than I needed to know," Mike says, hastily exiting the room.

"Dennis hooked you up, knowing you got a wife and two kids you had just walked out on!"

"Kimi, you know how Mama is."

"Yeah, I know. I know if she was any kind of woman she wouldn't do half the shit she does."

"Better you concern yourself with what kind a woman you are—or aren't." Daniel says, setting bait he knows I will take.

"Oops!" Nicole puts in, anticipating an emotional explosion from me. I don't keep her waiting.

"Was wondering when the old Daniel would show up. Welcome home, a-hole!"

———— ∿ ————

"Are you sleeping?"

"Yep."

"Kimi."

"Daniel."

"I'm sorry."

"Tell me something I don't already know."

"Could you turn over and look me in the eye while you insult me?"

And have my eyes collide with that massive, not to mention extremely attractive, chest of yours? I don't think so. "I don't feel like doing this tonight, Daniel."

"Should I turn off the TV so you can get some sleep?" he offers, sounding innocent.

"You know better than that. In eighteen years have you ever known me to sleep in the dark?"

"No."

"Then stop playing. I've got a lot on my mind. A lot of decisions to make."

"Speaking of decisions, I quit the gallery this morning."

"What?" I ask, shocked. I turn over to face him after all. "Why didn't you say something earlier? That would have been one less worry for me to carry around."

"So you have one less worry now," he says, getting up and heading for the bathroom.

I follow, enjoying the movement of his tight butt in his fitted boxers. He is purposely missing my point. I'm sure of it.

"Thanks, Daniel," I say. "I know it couldn't have been an easy thing for you to do."

He doesn't answer right away. He continues peeing. He has washed his hands and turned out the bathroom light before he issues a bland "No problem."

"I'm so sick of this yo-yoing with us, Daniel. I'm mad, you're mad—no, I'm mad; no, you're mad. We can't go on like this."

"Well, I suggest we fix this relationship, because I've had a taste of life without you and I'll pass."

He goes back into the bedroom, but I remain at the bathroom door for another full minute, stunned by his admission.

"What did I do to deserve that?" I ask, getting under the covers. I make sure my body comes in contact with his as I settle in. He responds to my overture and pulls me into his arms.

"Shocked your behind, didn't I?" he says with a knowing grin. I'm married to the most complex man in the universe.

"No comment," I mumble.

"No need to," he teases.

"I shouldn't have gone out with him," I admit, surprising myself.

"Wish you hadn't," Daniel murmurs.

"I shouldn't have kissed him."

"I definitely wish you hadn't kissed him."

"Forgive me?"

"Kimi, we both know I'm in no position to judge you."

"You're my husband."

"I've acted like anything but for a long time. I've lied when my wants conflicted with what was best for us. I've clung to my mother's skirt when I should have turned to you. I've taken out my frustration regarding my nonexistent art career on you — secretly blaming you, I think."

"What for?" I'm surprised and immediately pissed by his last admission.

"Many artists I've met are my age, single, and very successful. I guess I've foolishly asked myself, what if we hadn't gotten pregnant and rushed to marry one too many times."

"You're not the only one who gave up a burning passion for love, Daniel." I'm really angry now. I try to pull away but he holds on tight.

"Not talking things out and my lying is what got us to this point, Kimi."

"I thought you were an artist, Daniel, but you're sounding a bit like a shrink." I'm slightly winded by my futile struggle to free myself of his hold.

"Maybe I sound like one because I've been seeing one."

I stop struggling. "You've seen a shrink in addition to a marriage counselor? When?"

"Every Tuesday for the last month."

"Are you done?" I ask.

"No, I'm not. Allow me to demonstrate. You're not planning on giving me any loving right now, but I'm positive I can change that." As he makes that claim his hand once again captures my breast. I lean into him as close as I can. "Now you might not be planning on opening your legs nice and wide for me, but I'm positive if I ask you real nice you will."

"Oh, yeah?" I foolishly say. I've already become breathless. This man still has it after all these years.

"Oh, yeah, Kimi," Daniel says, his lips inches from my own. "Open up and let me in." The hand resting on my inner thigh suddenly slides between my legs and I do as he commands as if he has used an imaginary key. "Told you so," he gently mocks as he settles himself between my legs.

"Oh, my," I sigh as he glides ever so slowly into me.

"I second that," Daniel says and lifts my buttocks to mold us completely. I bury my face in his shoulder in an attempt to muffle a cry of sheer bliss.

———&

"What you doing, baby?"

"Typing, baby," I answer proudly.

"At three in the morning?"

"What's wrong with three in the morning?"

"Nothing. I'm just curious how your brain functions at this hour."

"It was functioning just fine up until a moment ago," I hint.

"My bad," Daniel says in apology, getting my not-so-subtle hint.

"Apology accepted."

"What you writing about?"

"Us."

"You and me?"

"That's right, you and me."

"What's so interesting about us that you'd want to write a book about it?"

"You'd be surprised," I tell him, turning off the computer. "Besides, it was write or stuff my face," I confess, settling back under the covers.

"You looking good, Kimi."

"Thank you, Daniel," I tell him, duplicating his serious tone.

"Oh, you making fun of me?" he asks, his voice becoming quite amorous just before he buries his face in the hollow of my neck.

"I'm making fun of you," I confess, matching his voice perfectly.

"Please don't do that when we're getting busy, Kimi. Makes me feel like I'm in bed with another man, baby."

"Sorry," I say in an even deeper baritone, screeching with laughter when Daniel retaliates by tickling me. "Okay, okay, Daniel. I said okay!" I beg for mercy.

"Glad you see it my way," he says, pulling me close. I wake much later to the sound of the kids arguing in the hall, and I can't remember ever feeling so well rested, despite the Thomas Klein fiasco hanging over my head.

"You gonna handle this one, or should I?" Daniel asks in his Barry White morning voice.

"They're all yours," I say, perfectly happy to let him do the refereeing. He grunts and rolls out of the bed, and a few seconds later all is quiet.

"Are they still breathing?" I joke when Daniel returns.

"I showed them who is boss around here," he claims.

"You the man, Daniel," I playfully boast.

"Thanks. As much as I'd love to stick around and bask in the welcoming glow of your questionable confidence in me, I have to go."

"That's right, the kids need dropping off. I don't know how I forgot that. The weekend and the weekdays are starting to merge," I complain.

"I know what you mean, baby. I better hurry up and land another job. I hate that feeling of drifting from one day to the next without anything to break up the monotony."

"I'm sorry about Birkwirth, Daniel. I'm not blind to how much you wanted to stay there."

"It's like you said, God's not cruel. Birkwirth couldn't have been the break I was waiting for, baby." I'm almost convinced he means it.

"I could whip up something right quick for you guys to eat," I offer, watching him dress.

"No thanks," he says, explaining, "I already sent the kids down to make breakfast."

"Daniel, they'll wreck my kitchen."

In a flash, I am out of bed, ready to dash downstairs to save my kitchen, when my husband places restraining hands on my shoulders.

"I think they can handle three bowls of Fruity Pebbles," he says.

"Oh," is all I say at first, but then guilt quickly loosens my tongue. "I should've gotten up sooner and made breakfast—"

"Or I could've gotten up sooner and made breakfast," Daniel unexpectedly points out.

"Okay, that does it. Who are you? Where is the real Daniel Riley?" I ask in a completely serious voice, only to immediately ruin it by laughing. Daniel doesn't join in.

"Kimi, you remember the movie *It's A Wonderful Life* with Jimmy Stewart? I know you do. You used to insist on watching it every freakin' Christmas Eve, and you would always end up slobbering all over me at the end of it!"

"What's your point, Daniel Riley?" I ask grumpily.

"I felt sort of like him, you know, wishing my life had been different in some respects."

"In the marrying me respect," I add, feeling hurt.

"Anyway, Stewart gets his wish, only to discover what a freakin' mess his life would have been had things been different. I feel like I've glimpsed my life without you, Kimi, and some divine spirit has seen fit to give me another shot. Anyway—I'm gonna get a move on. I'll call you. You gonna be home, right?"

"Yeah, I'll be here," I manage to answer despite my euphoria-induced daze. That had to be one of the nicest things Daniel has said to me in—in a long time.

"He's a poet," Nicky quips.

"No, the second coming of Shakespeare," Yvonne cracks.

"You both are just jealous," I interject over their laughter.

I'm wishing I hadn't called either of them. But before I'd thought it through, I'd dialed Nicky and then used three-way to call Yvonne at work. I'm paying for it.

"Yeah, that's it, Kimi. We're jealous that Daniel discovered what a freaking mess his life would have been without you," Nicky jests. Yvonne cackles loudly.

"It's not how he said it, you two asses, it's what he meant by it. The man still loves me. So what if his manner of expressing it is a tad roughneck? I get his meaning, and so do you two wenches."

"Somebody's mad," Yvonne observes.

"Cause you making fun of the love of her life, Yvonne. What do you expect?" Nicky says with dubious sincerity.

"Oh, my, look at the time—gotta go," I lie with forced lightness.

"Hold up, Kimi. All joking aside, what's the word on the investigation?" Yvonne asks softly.

"Why are you whispering?" I want to know. "There is no one listening in except Nicky."

"You never know," she cautions, her voice still low.

"Anyway, Mike is supposed to make some calls and get back to me today."

"Sounds like he's going to consult with some of his colleagues regarding your circumstances. They will assist him in formulating a course of action."

"It took all that pretentious babble just to say Mike is gonna talk with his lawyer friends, run my problem by them, and call me back?"

"I pray every day that God delivers you from your acid-tongued ways, Kimi," Yvonne fires back.

I hear Nicole laughing softly.

"Well, Miss Holier Than Everybody Else, I better let you get back to your patients. Nicky, you hold on while I get rid of her."

"Forget you, bye," Yvonne says, beating me to the click.

"I think you hurt her feelings," Nicole says somberly.

"Don't you dare sit your ass up here and try and take me to task for taking Yvonne's conceited ass down a peg. I didn't hear you complaining when she was making sport of me."

"Yvonne needs your understanding. She's going through a real rough spot in her life right now," Nicole informs me.

"Nicky, if this is more of your horoscope bull, I swear—"

"Your friend is in trouble. Believe whatever you want. I've got a class."

And then Nicole is gone. But I refuse to let either of them put a damper on my good mood, just as I refuse to allow the "investigation" to dampen it. My creative juices are flowing unimpeded, so I go to my computer and attack the keyboard with a vengeance. I'm finishing up a chapter when the phone rings.

"Kimberly, it's Mike. Daniel has been arrested. Kimberly, are you there?"

A small part of my brain is urging me to answer, but I purposely don't. I'm struggling against that all-too-familiar feeling of overwhelming dread, which in the past has always driven me to that self-destructive panacea—overeating.

"Kimberly?"

"Where is he, Mike?" I finally ask.

"The police station on Gibson Street in Dorchester. Do you know where that is?"

"I'll be there as soon as I can." I hang up and race down to the refrigerator. I randomly select two armloads of food, including leftover chicken, potatoes, three biscuits, and two cupcakes. But I am quickly overcome with self-disgust. Resolving to reach out for help, I dump the food on the kitchen table.

Nicole answers her cellphone on the forth ring. "Kimi, I'm in the middle of a class," she whispers. "This had better be important."

"I need you, Nicky," I whisper brokenly.

CHAPTER 17

I see Mike as soon as Nicole and I enter the lobby police station. He's at the counter speaking with that Agent Whalen. Mike spots us and immediately comes over.

"What's happening, and why is he here?" I ask, hugging him briefly, and then gesturing to the FBI agent. Mike leads us over to a waiting area.

"Daniel slugged Klein and got himself arrested, Kimberly. There is talk of charging Daniel with assault and battery. Agent Whalen is here because it involves Klein and Big Brother is always looking after his own interest."

"What are we gonna do? What's Daniel's bail?" I ask, wringing my hands. "What's wrong?" I press for answers when Mike's expression turns pessimistic.

"They're in cahoots, Kimberly."

"Who is?"

"The DA and the Feds. They're not going to make this easy unless—"

"Unless she does what they want her to," Nicole says. "Those bitches can't do this! You're a defense attorney, right? So you need to defend her. Do your job," she demands.

"I'm doing the best I can," he says, his voice crisped. "I've called in favors that I've been saving for a rainy day to help keep this whole affair from the press. I'm fighting

SANDRA FOY

for your sister every which way I know how. God only knows what hoops I'll have to jump through when this Cauplum-Bronzen-Thature matter is settled."

"I appreciate everything you're doing, Mike. We all do," I add, nudging Nicole in the side.

She grunts and walks off.

"She's just upset, Mike."

"I understand," he says, but he doesn't make eye contact.

"What are their demands, exactly?" I ask.

"Same as before: your help nailing Klein. Only this time they're waving Daniel's freedom as incentive."

"What will happen if I still refuse?"

"I'm not sure how long they can justify keeping Daniel here, perhaps a week, if they try really hard—and they will try hard. He's in big trouble, no mistake about it. According to the arresting officer, Daniel knocked Klein on his ass in front of half a dozen witnesses—on school property, no less."

"Angela and Alex?" I ask.

"All adult witnesses. The kids were already in class. Still, this couldn't have happened at a more inopportune time. Daniel will likely be charged with assaulting Klein and be portrayed as the jealous spouse viciously attacking his wife's lover, which will call into question your credibility down the road when Klein fingers you in court as his cohort," Mike concludes, sighing wearily.

"If I agree to help them, then what?"

"Daniel walks—now."

"What about Thomas? He'll still press charges, won't he?"

261

"You help the feds bring down Klein and the rest of his band of thieves and his cries of being knocked on his ass will fall on deaf ears."

"Agent Whalen told you that?"

"That, along with reminding me I still have to work in this town when this matter is settled," he answers.

"Mike, I know you and I haven't been what you would call friends, despite the close relationship between Yvonne and me, but I want you to know I'm indebted to you for all time for this."

"You don't have to say that . . . I . . . Yvonne wouldn't have it any other way."

"I know that's right, but still, thank you."

"I'll make the deal—if you're sure, Kimberly. Make no mistake, this is serious—and very dangerous. You never know how a person is going to react to being set up," he warns.

"I have no other choice, right?" I ask.

"I'll make the deal," he says solemnly. "Daniel should be right out. I'll contact you later at home."

Mike starts toward Agent Whalen, but I grab on to his elbow.

"Not a word to Daniel or Eve or Nicky."

At first I think he is going to balk, but he exhales loudly and says, "Lawyer-client privilege."

With that assurance I let go of him and he walks away slowly. I want to scream at him to stop, that I can't go through with it, but I don't. Suddenly, he stops and looks over his shoulder, and I know without a doubt he was hoping I would stop him.

It takes over an hour before Daniel emerges from custody. I give him an earful as soon as he is in earshot.

"What the hell were you thinking, Daniel Riley?"

"Who says I was thinking?" he says. "I was reacting."

"That's good, Daniel, play word games. Make light of the whole thing. But the fact remains, if not for Mike's connections you'd still be locked up for assault!"

"And you think I don't realize that? Do you think I set out to knock Klein on his ass?" he asks, his voice now raised.

"Guys, please, can we just go?" Nicole begs, having returned shortly before Daniel emerged. Taking hold of my elbow and Daniel's, she urges us toward the door of the police station. We heed her plea and head outside.

—∾∾—

"After dropping off the kids at school, I intended to head over to Klein's house." Daniel's sudden disclosure breaks the charged silence in the car.

"I hope you kept that very incriminating tidbit to yourself when you were under arrest," Nicole says in wise-guy fashion.

I brace myself for Daniel's rebuttal. It doesn't materialize. He continues, as if he hadn't heard Nicole.

"I'm preparing to leave the school when I see Klein strutting out of the building acting as if he didn't have a damn care in the world. I approached him."

"Lucky for you he wasn't assaulted at his home. You would have been charged with trespassing, too," I point out.

"Kimi's right. Lucky you caught up with his lying ass at a public place," Nicky reflects.

"I know that's right," Daniel agrees.

I roll my eyes, and then start the car.

"Isn't Mike coming?" Nicole asks, looking back toward the police station.

"He'll be awhile. He's taking care of a few loose ends. He'll get in touch with me later." The drive home is a silent one, but once inside Daniel won't allow me to sulk. He and Nicky join me on the sofa.

"I'm sorry I worried you, Kimi."

"Let's not talk about it—ever," I stiffly suggest.

"He's a man, Kimi. You had to know he wouldn't sit idly by."

"Thank you for your unsolicited observation, Nicky. I should've dropped you at home. Your kids—"

"Are with Mildred. She loves having them. Says it makes being apart from her kids more tolerable. Her life hasn't been easy. Sort of got a bad-movie-of-the-week quality to it. Anyway, the kids like her well enough. Besides, I wanted to see you settled."

"Lucky me."

"What did Mike have to say?" Daniel asks the one question I've been dreading.

"He's positive he can work things out. You're all set," I assure him.

"I hate to run off, but I can see you two need privacy," Nicole says, rising. "But first, I'm gonna raid your refrigerator."

"I'll give you a lift. Just give me a minute to use the bathroom," Daniel offers.

"I'll take you up on that, bro-in-law. Dougie is stopping by after work tonight. If I'm lucky I can spend quality time with my kids and get 'em tucked in before he gets there; otherwise, the three of them will start horsing around and it will be at least another hour before I can have him all to myself."

Despite Nicole's supposed agitation, I can see she's thrilled that her new man and her kids have hit it off. What mother wouldn't be? What does have me baffled is the chumminess she and Daniel have been displaying since we picked him up at the police station.

"I've misjudged him." Nicole's words are muffled. Half her body is in my refrigerator as she makes her impromptu confession.

"Excuse me?" I say, hitting her lightly on her butt.

"I've misjudged Daniel," Nicole repeats, emerging with two armloads.

We're in the kitchen waiting for Daniel to reappear.

"What do you mean you've 'misjudged' him?" I ask, supplying her with empty plastic containers.

"You're gonna make me say it, aren't you?" she asks, balking.

"Say what?" I ask, genuinely confused. "I honestly don't know what you're talking about."

"Daniel's not a lowlife. He's just a man, who has made all the foolish mistakes men do while trying to love his family and make his dreams come true in the process," she observes, stuffing food into the container.

"Now who's the poet?" I ask.

"Whatever," she says, fanning away my observation.

"I can never repay you for coming to my rescue earlier, Nicky," I say, holding out a plastic bag to accommodate her bounty.

"Girl, please, you just did," she says, lovingly patting the bag containing the leftovers.

"Sillyhead. Meet me for a run tomorrow morning?"

"It will have to be early. I have an early biology test."

"Early it is."

Daniel comes into the kitchen and surprises the heck out of me by planting a deep I-want- your-sex-later kiss on my frozen lips. It embarrasses me to no end, mainly because my nosy sister not only makes no move to look away, but actually cheers him on with hoots and loud laughter. My cheeks are beet red as I happily close the door behind them.

Luck is on my side; Mike calls about ten minutes after Daniel and Nicole depart. I'm upstairs on the toilet when I hear the phone ringing, but I manage to get to it as the answering machine beeps and he's starting to leave a message.

"Mike," I say in a breathless whisper.

"Kimberly?"

I ask Mike to hold on and rush downstairs to turn off the answering machine, taking the cordless phone from the bedroom with me.

"Mike, are you there?" I ask.

"I'm here. I'm just calling to let you know everything has been arranged. They want to wire you up tomorrow."

"So soon? What could I possibly get out of Thomas this soon? Daniel just decked him. I'm probably the last person he'll expect or want to hear from."

"I agree. Unfortunately, what I think doesn't matter. The feds have a series of questions for you to ask him and don't want to wait. Hopefully, something you say will cause him to trip up."

"I doubt that. Tell me how this wiring business works."

"You will show up at his house, or it will be arranged for you to run into Klein at some public place."

"Will you go with me to be wired?"

"I'll pick you up around, say, nine in the morning?"

"No. I'll meet you at the FBI office after I come up with something to tell Daniel."

"I advise you to tell him the truth, and nothing but the truth."

"What's on your mind, Kimi? You haven't said much of anything all morning," Nicky asks.

"Trying to conserve my energy. I've still got a way to go before I can run and carry on a conversation at the same time," I huff.

Truth is, I'm distracted by the wire-tapping business, but at least the excuse I make is plausible.

"Do you want to talk about it or continue letting it eat away at you?" Nicole asks, clearly not buying my excuse.

"There's no *it* to talk about, Nicky, so drop the third degree," I say defensively.

"Fine, have it your way. I'll race you back to Stony Brook Station!"

It's no contest. Nicole's lean body and long legs easily outdistance me.

By the time Stony Brook Station comes into view, Nicole is at the door and I see her waving at me before disappearing inside. The little wench was getting even with me for staying mum. I manage to jog the last leg to my house; I'm definitely making progress.

I've showered, dressed and am ready to go down to the FBI office, and I still haven't thought of what I'm going to tell Daniel, who is downstairs looking through the want ads. If there is any way of avoiding out-and-out lying, I haven't thought of it yet.

I take one last look at my appearance in the dresser mirror and I'm somewhat pleased with the sophisticated cutie staring sadly back at me. The transformation is subtle, but it's there. I see a definite improvement in my waistline. The two-piece gray pantsuit I haven't been able to fit into since God knows how long is a definite eye-catcher. Its double portrait collar gives the illusion that my neck is longer and more slender. The elastic waist on the pants allows for comfort and easy mobility. My hair is pulled back, and I have twisted it into an attractive bun. I'm heading downstairs when I hear the phone ring once. Daniel calls up to me.

"Yeah?" I answer, my voice airy.

"Nicky is on the phone."

"I just saw her. What could she want?" I wonder aloud, going down stairs.

"One way to find out, baby," he says, passing me the phone while eyeing me appreciatively from head to toe.

"Nicky?" I ask, turning slightly away from Daniel's keen eye.

"How's my favorite sister?"

"What do you want?" I ask, bypassing her agenda-driven query.

"Now that's just nasty," she responds.

"No, that's just keepin' it real. Now, what you want, Nicky?" I repeat.

"Can you meet me with the kids this afternoon?"

"Whose kids?" I ask, just to be difficult.

"Duh," she responds.

"I know you ain't calling me for a favor and getting smart in the same breath," I say.

"Wouldn't dream of it. So you'll meet me at Victoria's Secret in Back Bay?"

"What? Girl, you crazy. I thought it was something important. You best plan on seducing Dougie on your own time."

"Please, Kimi. He's picking the kids and me up for dinner tonight at six. Girl, he's taking us to Grasshopper in Brighton. It's Asian. Have you ever been?"

"No, Nicky, never."

"I'll tell you all about it."

"No, thanks."

"Come on, Kimi. I have classes all morning. If I get the kids, I'll never make it to Victoria's Secret. Come on."

"Nicky, you have time to do that. It's what you're leaving out that you don't have enough time for," I say knowingly.

"Of course I'm getting my hair and nails done, Kimi. Dougie is taking us to a real nice restaurant," she says, all defensive now that she has been busted.

"Good for you. And I mean that, but I have a life I'm attempting to salvage here."

"Please, Kimi."

"Where's your usual backup?"

"Mrs. Leigh getting her eyes dilated and Mildred is her designated driver. No telling how long they'll be."

"Ooh, if you weren't my sister," I say weakening. You lucky both my kids have practice after school today.

"Thank you, big sis. I'll meet you guys in front of the Copley Plaza at three; no, make it three-thirty. I want to have plenty of time to pick out the perfect outfit. You know, something that makes him sit up and take notice—in more ways than one."

"Spare me. I'll be there at three-thirty sharp—unless something comes up."

"That makes two of us. Bye."

"Everything okay with your sister?" Daniel asks, reaching for my hand as soon as I hang up the phone and pulling me between his legs.

"She has a hot date with Dougie and needs my help to pull it off," I tell him, sighing long and loud.

But I'm not entirely sure I'm sighing because of Nicole's demands. Daniel's hands are now roaming over my butt cheeks.

"I was hoping we could spend some time together this morning," he says seductively.

"Daniel, you were all wrapped up in the newspaper when I got back from jogging. You didn't mention anything about us spending time together," I point out, spontaneously kissing him on top of the head to soften the sting of putting him off. But his response has me regretting my peace offering.

"You were looking like a wet mop before, not to mention you had the faintest hint of BO. Now you look like a million bucks and you smell divine. Ouch, baby," he yelps when I pinch his shoulder in response to his unflattering description of how I'd looked and smelled earlier.

"For that you have to wait until tonight," I say, pushing out of his embrace.

"That's what I get for being honest?"

"No, for being tactless," I correct him.

"Baby, I need something to help keep my spirits up. I don't see anything remotely related to my field in this paper."

"Look again. And if you still don't see anything, look again," I recommend frostily.

"That's cold, Kimi—cold!"

"See you later, Mr. Tactless," I say pointedly.

"Where are you going this early anyway?"

Damn! Damn! Damn! So close. I was so freakin' close to getting out the front door without lying.

"I have to meet Mike," I say, still managing to be truthful.

"I'm coming with you," he announces.

"No!"

"Why not?" he demands, rising, disgruntlement all over his face.

"I don't think it's a good idea, Daniel."

"On the contrary, my going is a great idea. You're my wife, and I'm going to be supportive. I'll get my shoes."

"Daniel," I call, trying to stop him from heading upstairs, but he continues going without a backward glance. I don't know what to do at this point. Panic-stricken, I impulsively rush out the front door, jump into my car and drive off.

CHAPTER 18

"Daniel is going to kill me," I say to Mike as soon as I see him at the FBI office.

"What happened?" he asks politely, though he seems distracted.

"He wanted to come along. What's wrong, Mike? You seem miles away."

"Nothing. Actually, it's Yvonne."

"Eve? What is it?"

"I'm worried about her. She's not well. She's missing church."

"Missing church? That's not like Eve. She'd rather drink poison than miss church. Did you ask her what's wrong? Has she seen a doctor?"

"Yes to the first and no to the second." His voice is strained, and he is clearly upset. "She claims she's fine and she'll see a doctor when she is good and ready."

"I'll call her as soon as I can. She'll talk, or I'll beat it out of her."

"Thanks, I think," Mike says with a tight smile.

"There's a chance that they may want to use you on the spot. Or they may schedule it for another time. It all depends on Klein's availability."

"What? I thought I'd do it this morning and get it over with. I can't go through this indefinitely. Mike, you have to do something," I plead, latching on to his arm.

"I'll see what I can do. I can't promise anything, but I'll use what little clout I have to expedite the process," he modestly assures me.

The meeting with the feds goes well, all things considered. Now that I've agreed to their demands, they seem almost friendly. After Mike has a brief and private word with Agent Whalen, I'm told they are going to try and get something on Thomas this morning.

The wire is surprisingly lightweight. Leads are attached to my waist and thigh area by a serious-faced female agent, who refrains from making eye contact. I'm instructed to drive to Thomas's house on the pretext of apologizing for Daniel's behavior. Then I'm supposed to get a confession out of him, based on gruff instructions given by Agent Sumptshon on how to steer the conversation to Thomas's accomplice and the location of the money—especially the location of the money.

I don't attend church regularly, nor do I say prayers at bedtime. I'm the last person I'd answer a prayer from if I were God, but that doesn't stop me from praying my butt off during the drive to Thomas's house in Canton. I glance in the rearview mirror for the hundredth time to reassure myself that the van discreetly tailing me is still there.

I see Thomas's car in the driveway and my heart starts pounding almost painfully. I don't think I can do this. Sweat appears on my forehead and nose. I can hear my own breathing. I'm sure he'll hear it, too, and know instantly something is amiss. I sit in the car clenching the steering wheel for several minutes before I can summon the nerve to get out.

It's a long minute before Thomas opens the door. I'm speechless. The shades he is wearing easily complement his polo shirt and khaki pants, but I don't think they are being worn for that reason. The shades are not large enough to conceal a rather ugly purple and yellowish bruising under his right eye.

"Kimberly, I wasn't expecting to see you so soon," he says.

"But you were expecting me?" I ask.

He holds his hand out and steps to the side, indicating I should come in.

"It's unfortunate that my husband took matters into his own hands, Thomas." I try to sound sincere; I'm glad Daniel punched his ass. I'm only sorry he got arrested for doing it.

"He's an extremely violent man. Has he ever beaten you?"

"What?" I'm offended now.

"His violence, has it ever taken the form of punching or slapping you around?"

"Daniel would never strike a female under any circumstances, or tell various lies about her, or ruin her good name for personal gain."

"If you say so."

"I say so."

"Was there something else you wanted?" he ask, managing to make his question sound dirty.

"I want to know why me? Why did you set me up to take the fall for you? You know I had nothing to do with your round-tripping scheme."

"I say otherwise."

"But you're lying," I say calmly. Inside I'm totally pissed by his cool exterior. He smiles that smile I used to think was genuine and engaging, but without his beautiful eyes to pull off the deception; it doesn't move me. Instead, I can finally see the cruel twist to his lips and the fact that the corners of his mouth appear to struggle to maintain the upturn sweep he's perfecting.

"Go home, Kimberly. Get a yourself a good lawyer and cut yourself a deal."

"The truth will prevail. You're going to jail, Thomas—if you continue on this course."

"It's your word against mine. I'm an affluent businessman dutifully raising my daughter alone. And you, well, you know what you are. No need for me to go into the ugly details," he says contemptuously.

"I'm going to prove you lied to the police about me, Thomas. It will go a lot easier for you if, before you take the stand and perjure yourself, you just admitted the truth and tell the feds who your real accomplice was at Thature and where you hid all that money. They really want that money, Thomas."

"Get . . . out."

———∾∾∾———

"That's a start," Agent Sumptshon says back at the FBI office. I look up from the poker-faced female agent who is removing my wire. Agent Sumptshon, along with Agent Whalen and Mike, politely avert their eyes from the thigh I'm forced to reveal.

"Didn't his calm in the face of my accusations raise questions as to his credibility?" I ask hopefully.

"Questions, yes, but we need more, much more," Agent Whalen says.

"I kept my cool." I feel the need to defend myself.

"You did well," Mike assures me. "I am sure even the most seasoned professional would have been sorely tested if confronted with Klein's calculated attack. We'll get him."

But his dejected demeanor is in sharp contrast to his words. He hangs his head and his shoulders slump and he repeatedly rakes a hand through his hair. I look around and the others seem similarly defeated. The female agent announces she is finished and all the males in the room put on optimistic faces. I look away.

"Where is your mama? I told her butt three-thirty. It's five of four," I grouse to my gloomy-faced passengers.

My niece and nephew still haven't forgiven me for attacking their mother. That much is clear to the point of embarrassment. They didn't want to come with me when I picked them up from kindergarten and pre-school. They each clung to their teachers as if the devil himself had arrived to take them away. Poor Nicolas—he had cried.

"Though I'm sure she has a good reason for being late," I say, turning to smile at them in an attempt to cover up my irritation. It doesn't work; they both look down and silently hold hands. My heart is breaking; I've made a mess of my relationship with them. I get out of the car, needing to put some distance between my victims and myself. I'm parked directly across from the Copley Plaza, so there's no chance I'll miss Nicole. I've been standing for about five minutes when she emerges through the revolving doors. She is carrying two large shopping bags and a hatbox— spending my money on more then a dress and accessories, the little wench. I wave to her, and reluctantly cross the busy street to help her with her bags.

"Don't get on to me today, Kimi, I'm too excited. I think Douglas is going to ask me to marry him over dinner."

"What? That's great. And sudden, don't you think?" I ask, taking one of the shopping bags.

"Not if you've met your soul mate," she declares, all smiles.

"Oh, God, please spare me what the stars are saying about this, please," I beg.

"Only if you save the lecture for tomorrow."

"Tomorrow," I say sternly, stopping to adjust the bag I am carrying when one side of the strap breaks.

Nicole continues walking. I can hear her call out to the kids, having spotted them in the backseat of my car. The sound of an approaching car grabs my attention. I glance in the direction of the sound. A black sports car is bearing down on Nicole. Nicole sees it, too, but she is frozen in the middle of the street.

I don't know where I got the speed or nerve to dive into the path of the car and push my sister and myself to safety, but I did it. We land hard and scream our fool heads off. Instantly, people are all around us. After what seems like forever, the police arrive, followed shortly by two ambulances. The scene is sheer bedlam. The palms of my hands ache, and my knees are throbbing. Nicole is bleeding from her nose, and she looks dazed, like she is about to faint. I remember my niece and nephew and I struggle up, despite the voices cautioning me to remain where I am.

Nicole's kids have their faces glued to the glass of the door and they are staring at me in horror, tears streaming down their faces. I can read the word 'Mama' being said over again.

After five hours in the emergency room, being examined, X-rayed, and questioned by the police, Nicole and I are released. We make our way through the parking lot, each of us leaning heavily on Daniel for support. I had reluctantly called him about half an hour after arriving, afraid that any further delayed would only make matters that much worse for myself. Despite his grim face when he arrived, he had hugged us both and told me the kids were with his mama, but other than that he hadn't said two words to me, preferring to talk to the emergency-room doctor.

I see Yvonne rushing towards us, and I attempt to smile despite my pain. She looks so worried.

"I aged ten years, Kimi," she says, holding my face gently between her hands. "Mike and I picked up Nicky's kids at the police station. A social worker there managed to calm them down a bit. Do the police have any idea who tried to run you down?"

"Nope," I say.

Mike approaches at a much slower pace. He's holding the hands of Natasha and Nicholas, who are moving as fast as their legs can carry them. Their little faces are worried. They reach Nicole and latch on to her legs and hold on for dear life.

I'm not expecting them to even acknowledge me, so I'm taken completely off guard when they turn their affections on me, racing over with joyful squeals of "Auntie Kimi". Despite the pain it causes, I bend down to accept hugs from both of them simultaneously.

"You saved Mommy!" they exclaim over and over. I grit my teeth and endure the pain shooting through my body. It seems as though I've waited a lifetime to hold these miniature people again and have my show of affection eagerly reciprocated.

"That's enough, you two. Give Auntie Kimi a breather. She's been through a lot today." Daniel's words are kind for the kids' sake, but the look he aims at me is anything but.

"Uncle Daniel's right, but may I please have one more hug and perhaps a little sugar to go with it this time?" They both converge on me all over again. This time I can't contain my cry of pain, but I focus mainly on the happy melody coming from the region of my heart. I've cheated death today and won back the love of two who are near and dear.

Not bad, Kimberly, not bad at all.

———❦———

It's close to nine when we arrive at Nicole's three-family dwelling. The porch light is on, and I can easily see the man on the porch. It's Donald Davis.

"Nicky, isn't that Dougie?" I ask.

"Oh, look at him, looking all worried," she says playfully. I can tell she's happy to see him, because she is beaming.

"Don't feel bad if he doesn't propose tonight, Nicky; you look like Geraldo's sister."

"Girl, please, after my sob story, Dougie will definitely propose to me tonight."

"Go on with your bad self," I say, laughing.

"I'll get—Dougie, is it?" Daniel says.

"Yes, it is. Go introduce yourself, Daniel; Dougie is almost family," Nicole says with pride and confidence. I cross my fingers extra hard, hoping Donald's the one.

"I'll do that. Be right back," Daniel says.

I watch my athletic husband walk up to Donald. They shake hands, exchange a few words, and then Donald is striding quickly towards us. The next several minutes are heartwarming to behold. I haven't seen my sister fussed over and cuddled so much since the day she came out of my mother's womb. Donald even lightly kisses her swollen nose. I uncross fingers, and immediately start planning what I'll be wearing to Nicole's wedding.

"I've made arrangements to have your car towed to the house," Daniel relents enough to say.

"By hook-em-up Bobby? No thanks," I bitterly retort.

"I wouldn't disrespect you like that. I'm trying to draw you back, not push you further away," he says softly, but he won't look at me.

We are driving to Daniel's mama's house. I know I need to explain my sudden departure this morning, but I'm at a loss as to where to begin. Should I plead my case and then beg for Daniel's forgiveness? Perhaps I'll go on the defensive and cop an attitude of my own.

I'm still trying to settle on a tactic when my cellphone rings. It's a welcome distraction from the awkward silence that followed Daniel's revelation. The view screen indicates it's Yvonne calling from her cellphone.

"Eve?" I say expectantly. I am surprised when a familiar male voice answers.

"Kimi, it's Eve. She fainted and hit her head . . ." he says, ending with a catch in his voice.

"Oh, my God! Where is she?"

"We're at Mass General. They're running tests."

"What happened?"

"I found her unconscious on the kitchen floor . . ." Crying in earnest now, he barely manages to get the words out.

"We're on our way. Do you hear me, Mike?"

"Okay," he says, brokenly, and then the line goes dead.

"Eve's at Mass General. It's serious. She—" I'm a basket case before I finish.

Daniel squeezes my hand and makes an illegal U-turn in the middle of the street.

"I'll drop you off, and then pick up the kids and assure them you're fine, cause I know they're worried silly," he says, maneuvering through light traffic. "Then we'll come back for you—after you've seen Eve and composed yourself."

"Don't do that. I'll have Mike drop me off. I'll call the house and let you know what's what."

"What if she has to stay, and Mike doesn't want to leave her?"

"Then I'll take his car, or I'll call a cab."

"Fine," he finally agrees.

CHAPTER 19

"Where is she?" I ask, as soon as I locate Mike in the emergency room.

"They're doing a CAT scan—that's all I know. I've been asking every couple of minutes. They can't tell me anything else."

"Where's the doctor or nurse?"

I don't wait for an answer. I spot a fellow in a white hospital coat walking purposely toward us. I take Mike's arm and we intercept him.

"Hello, I'm Dr. Palanskya. You are Mrs. Driver's family, yes?" asks the middle-aged doctor in what sounds like a Russian accent.

"Yes, I'm Kimberly Riley, and this is her husband, Mike Driver," I answer.

"Good to meet you both. Now, about Mrs. Driver, she is resting at the present time. She has suffered a minor concussion due to the impact of hitting the floor. I've been able to speak briefly with her. She recalls going into the kitchen for a drink of water. She recalls feeling light-headed. After that, she only remembers waking up here."

"Mike was told she had a CAT scan. What exactly is that, and what did it tell you?"

"A CAT scan, or CT for short, is a procedure using X-rays and computers to produce images of the brain. The scan shows no brain abnormalities. This is good, yes."

"Yes, that's very good. But why did she pass out?" I ask, relaxing a little. Yvonne's brain is okay!

"We also ran a series of blood tests, and an electrocardiogram confirms Mrs. Driver has tachycardia, a heart condition, which, in her case, I believe is temporary."

"What's that? What's wrong with her heart?" I choke out.

"Tachycardia is characterized as rapid beating of the heart. We defined that as a heart rate of greater then a hundred beats per minute in adults. We have treated your wife with oral medications and she is responding," he explains.

"So the tachycardia caused her to faint?" Mike asks.

"Depending on the cause and extent of the tachycardia, shortness of breath, dizziness as well as syncope—fainting—can result, yes."

"What caused the tachycardia?"

"After testing your wife for thyroid and numerous metabolic imbalances and after speaking with her at length, I feel reasonably sure the cause in her case is abuse of diet pills. She admits consuming the diet pill Appetite Eliminator regularly."

"What?" Mike and I ask in confused unison.

"Blood tests show she is severely dehydrated. They also show her electrolytes are abnormal. Electrolyte balance is essential for normal body function of cells and organs."

"Electrolytes are what exactly?" I ask, trying to follow his medical terminology.

"Think of it as the body's electrical system. We measure electrolytes by testing the sodium, potassium, chloride, and bicarbonate levels in the body. Too much or too little sodium can cause cell malfunction. A potassium level that is too high or too low profoundly affects the nervous system as well as the heart. Increased or decreased chloride levels can be a sign of kidney disease. Bicarbonates—"

"I can't follow all this," Mike interrupts. "Eve hasn't been sick. How could something like this happen?"

"Mr. Driver, when was the last time your wife ate or drank something?"

"Tonight, with all the craziness, we had a late dinner. I would say around nine-thirty."

"Did you see her eat?" the doctor asks.

"Of course, I saw her eat. What kind of questions are these? Look, we had dinner together. I sat directly across the table from my wife."

"And while you sat directly across from her, did you actually observe her putting food into her mouth?" the doctor presses on.

"This is crazy. I want to see my wife—now!"

Mike marches off toward the reception desk. I'm not so quick to take offense at the doctor's line of questioning. If Yvonne wasn't eating, it would explain a lot.

"Doctor Palanskya, have you asked Mrs. Driver about her eating habits?" I ask.

"I asked what she'd had to eat today; she claims not to remember."

"You said yourself, she has a concussion. Maybe that's why she can't remember," I suggest, feeling some vague need to come to Yvonne's defense.

"This is possible," he allows. "But it's just as possible that her memory loss is hunger-induced. If I were a betting man, I would wager Mrs. Driver hasn't had sufficient nourishment in well over a month."

"Sweet Jesus."

"Don't just stand there looking like you're at a funeral. Come in."

Despite Yvonne's saucy words, her voice sounds weak. I drag myself to her bedside. I offer Mike, who is on the opposite side of the bed, a quick upturn of my lips.

"I just couldn't stand all the attention you were getting earlier," Yvonne claims, with obvious effort.

"Crazy," I say tenderly, acknowledging her attempt to lighten the mood. "Did Mike tell you we spoke with the doctor, Eve?"

"Now isn't the time," Mike says, his tone hard.

"Au contraire," I disagree. "Now is the essential time." My eyes meet his; I'm ready for battle. Yvonne's health is at stake.

"I've been abusing Mike's pills I told you about," Yvonne abruptly confesses.

"The Appetite Eliminator?" I ask, remembering the conversation.

"Yes," she says, her voice cracking. "But it took away my appetite, and gave me unbelievable energy—the kind I used to have. In the beginning, anyway."

"Why, Eve? You're barely a hundred pounds, and that is with a full stomach. You're a nurse, for goodness sakes. You should have known better." I am truly baffled. She lowers her chin to her chest.

"Can you get any more sympathetic?" Mike interjects, earning another determined glare from me.

"When she deserves it, I'll give her all I've got. But when she endangers her life and my sanity foolishly—like now—she gets only my contempt!"

"Tough love," Yvonne says. "I don't care for it." She sighs deeply and adjusts her position in the bed. "Concussion or not, I recall my mother being a lot shorter, and something about your nose isn't quite right, either," she says with more than a hint of sass, finally making eye contact.

"Would you like me to call her? I'd love to let her in on how her daughter is faring in the big bad city."

"You do and I won't talk to you for a month—at least."

"Now you are just tempting me on purpose," I reply, deliberately misunderstanding her threat.

"Are you two done?" Mike butts in, clearly displeased with us both at this point.

"Hardly finished, but your wife needs her rest, so I'm reluctantly dropping the subject."

"Thank you, Jesus," Yvonne declares, with surprising vigor.

"Thank Dr. Palanskya," I correct her, just to be disagreeable. "Mrs. Driver is suffering from severe stupidity and needs to sleep it off," I say, in a dead-on imitation of the good doctor.

Mike chuckles softly, followed immediately by suspicious coughing.

"That's good," he says. "Do you do women, too?"

"Kimi's right, I've acted like a total dumb-dumb," I say, laughing when Mike's eyes bug out of upon hearing his wife's voice coming out of my mouth.

"How?" he asks, awed.

"She's weird," Yvonne suggests.

"Talent baby, pure and simple talent," I proudly profess, basking in Mike's admiration.

"That's some gift. Have you ever thought about using it professionally?" he asks.

"Nope, never wanted to go that route."

"Now who's the dummy?" Yvonne puts in.

"You still are," I answer. "Now I suggest you lie back and get some rest," I tell her. I bend and kiss her forehead.

"Did the doctor say when I could go home?"

"I'll go out and talk with him again. I suspect it'll be—tomorrow," Mike says.

"Tomorrow?" Yvonne wails.

Mike moves to comfort her, but before he gets the chance, I give him a don't-you-dare look. He reluctantly moves back and leaves.

"Count your blessings that the damage is reversible and ditch the self-pity," I order, and turn to leave.

"Do you think *he* had anything to do with what happened to you and Nicky today?"

Good old Yvonne. They don't make friends like her anymore.

"They have Thomas under constant surveillance. If he had done it, the feds would know."

"What if he didn't do it? What if someone once close to him did?" she speculates.

"Someone like—Katherine!" I say, following her drift. "He probably told her about Daniel socking his behind." "I got a bad feeling that Thomas knew my visit was a setup."

"And could have told Katherine about that, too."

"And that nutty-butty sets out to avenge her man. *Don't worry, Tommy baby. I'll get that fat bitch, honey pie.*" I channel Katherine to perfection—as usual.

"That's just not normal," Mike comments. Having returned, he's casually leaning against the doorframe. I shake my head and laugh delightedly. His expression is a mixture of disbelief and envy.

My laughter dries up when a sad thought strikes me. In all the years I've known Mike, we've never spent any significant time together, not even the minimal time it would have taken for my "gift" to come out—not until now. Desperation makes for strange allegiances—and unexpected revelations, I guess.

———⟪⟫———

"Can you do anybody you want?" Mike asks as he's driving me home.

"Excuse you?" I ask, taking convincing offense.

"The mimicking—I'm talking about the mimicking. Can you mimic anyone you want to?" Mike hastens to clarify.

"Relax, Mike, I'm just playing with you," I admit, suddenly feeling more than a little guilty for pulling his chain. He nods stiffly and concentrates on the road. "I've never tried to mimic and failed, but then I don't try and mimic everyone I meet. If I did, there's bound to be someone I just can't do." I answer his question, though it looks as if he's no longer interested. A full minute passes before he acknowledges I've said a word.

"I see. Tell me something, how do you get your voice to change to sound, say, male?"

"I just can."

He quickly looks over at me, as if he's trying to figure out whether or not I'm making sport of him again. I doubt he can make out much; the interior of the car is pretty dark—except for minimal light from the dashboard.

"I don't know any other way to explain. To be perfectly honest with you, I'm just as baffled by your inability as you are by my ability."

"Hmmm," he murmurs and then falls silent. "Do you think Yvonne's going to be okay?" he asks ten minutes later.

"The doctor says there won't be any permanent damage. So, yes, she'll be fine."

"I wish I could be as confident as you sound. How could she not eat?"

"Appetite Eliminator?" I suggest.

"And I'm the one who brought those damned pills home."

"Don't go there, Mike; Eve's a big girl—on the inside, anyway. She made the decision to abuse those pills. She knew full well she didn't need them."

"She was trying to get in the best possible shape—we both were. My mom is planning a party next month celebrating my brother passing the bar exam."

"Mike?"

"Yes."

"Eve was already in the best possible shape. Now unless you want to be planning her funeral, I suggest we help her see that."

"How?"

"Well, I've managed to get my weight down by eating better and working out."

"Now that you mention it, I have heard of that method. But in all seriousness, you're looking good. With things so crazy, I haven't gotten a chance to tell you."

"Well, now you have," I say. We have arrived at my house now. "Thanks for the lift, Mike. I'll meet you at the hospital in the morning around eight?"

"I'm thinking about heading back to the hospital now," he admits. "I don't think I can get to sleep without her. For the past ten years, hers is the last voice I've heard before falling to sleep, Kimberly." I get out and go around to the driver's side door and crouch down. With the beam from the streetlight I can see his eyes are glassy with unshed tears.

"Look, Mike, I'm not going to try and tell you what to do—you're a big boy. But I know you'll be no good to

Eve, or to my case, if you're dead on your feet tomorrow. I wish you'd go home and get some rest."

"I don't know," he hedges.

"Tell you what I'll do. If you go home, I'll call you in, say, half an hour, and I'll say good night, doing my best imitation of Eve. I could do Marilyn Monroe or Mae West, if you like," I say, with a conspiratorial wink.

He smiles politely and pats my hand to acknowledge my good intentions.

"I'll go home," he promises.

I'm unlocking my front door when a possible solution to my Thomas problem hits me. I hear the sound of screeching tires, and I'm positive the same idea has occurred to Mike.

"It's crazy," he says, rushing toward me.

"Crazy enough to work," I say, meeting him halfway up my walkway. My adrenaline is pumping; I can barely contain my excitement.

"You said yourself you can't mimic everybody," Mike cautions.

"I can do Katherine. *Would you care for a diet Pepsi, Kimberly, or perhaps a wheat thin?*" I mimic her to perfection.

Mike just stares at me.

"Trust me, that's her," I assure him.

"Are you positive?"

"Oh, yeah, I'm positive, but more important, Thomas will be positive."

"We're not even sure this Katherine person is his contact," Mike points out.

"Speak for yourself; I've been sure she is involved for some time now. Now I have a way of proving it."

"Fine, tomorrow we go to the feds."

"No, tonight I expose Thomas and Katherine."

"It would be better with the feds involved; they can tap your phone and catch the whole exchange."

"I'm not waiting."

I stand firm until Mike points out the obvious.

"I'm sure he has caller ID. If you call from your house phone or your cell, he'll know it's you."

"Damn."

"We're due back at the station tomorrow. This time we'll nail him," Mike says with confidence.

I would have said more, but suddenly my front door opens. It's Daniel, looking oh-so-yummy in a pair of fitted Calvin Klein boxers.

"How's Eve doing?" he asks.

"She is gonna be fine," Mike says. "Kimberly can fill you in. But about Klein, we were—"

"Are the kids up?" I butt in.

"At this hour, and with school tomorrow?"

"I better be getting home," Mike says. "We'll talk, after you talk with your husband."

Daniel folds his arms across his chest and stares at me. I brush past him. Once inside I intend to go straight upstairs; but seeing the missing household items back in place stops me cold. A quick check of the basement confirms the rear room door is closed again. I head upstairs without a word and throw open the closet; Daniel's missing clothes are back. He'd moved back home in the same puff of smoke in which he had departed.

"What did Mike mean by 'after you talk with your husband'?" Daniel asks, coming into the room but making no mention of moving back home.

"It has been a long day, Daniel. I'm in no mood to argue over my strategy for dealing with Thomas with you tonight."

"Fine, I'm sorry," he says, kissing me on the forehead, and heading for the bathroom.

"Hold up. Why are you conceding so easily?"

"You're right; you've had one hell of a day," he says, going into the bathroom. I follow him.

"Are you using some kind of psychological game on me, Daniel?"

"Something like that," he confesses.

"Well?" I demand.

"Well what?" he asks, stringing me along.

"What is it, Daniel?"

"Are you sure you want to know?"

"Tell me!"

"Kimi, not everyone can handle this technique," he warns, adjusting his boxers. "Should I bother washing off *King* again?" he asks seductively, eyeing me up and down.

"That depends on what you have to say," I warn.

"Fair enough. Okay, you ready?"

"Boy, will you just spit it out? Goodness."

"Fine. When I'm wrong, I plan to just admit it and apologize. That's what I did."

"That's common sense, Daniel," I point out, sure he's pulling my leg.

"Overeating leads to becoming overweight, which leads to unhealthy and unhappy. That's common sense, also. Common sense doesn't just mean knowing better, Kimi. It's means doing better, too."

I capitulate. "Get to washing. I'll be waiting," I command, laughing deeply when he hastens to comply.

"I went to the feds and got wired this morning. And then I went to Thomas's house—with the feds. I tried to entrap him. It didn't work. But I had to try. I didn't want you trying to talk me out if it—I'm so sorry, Daniel," I say, all in one breath.

Daniel says nothing for several long seconds, and then he unexpectedly pulls my naked body against his for a tight, reassuring embrace. "You realize you're not playing fair by confessing and apologizing after we've just made love," he says chidingly, lightly kissing me on the temple.

"I'm new at this apologizing thing," I explain. "Forgive me if I don't have the rules down."

"Why do I get the feeling you know exactly what you're doing, Kimi?" he asks softly.

"I haven't the faintest idea what you mean."

"Hmmm, okay, whatever you say. But I should have mentioned that the primary reason for apologizing and righting a wrong is to make amends for that wrong."

"That's elementary, Daniel."

"Example; using your feminine wiles to get over on me this morning."

"I wouldn't put it that way, but I agree with the gist of what you're saying."

"You agree, but you're doing it again to get your way. You're after forgiveness this time."

"That's not what's going on," I say, disputing his theory.

"You weaken me with wild passionate lovemaking, and then confess your misdeeds and ask for forgiveness. That's manipulation."

"That's a woman's prerogative."

"I give up," Daniel declares, not unkindly.

"That a boy," I tease.

He retaliates by going for my neck with a primitive growl. We're going for round two when the theme from the Lone Ranger stops us.

"What the hell?" I mutter.

"That's my cellphone; correction, that's the gallery's cellphone. I haven't returned it yet."

"The Lone Ranger?" I ask, snickering.

"Don't say anything; I'll make you pay for it later," he vows and shakes King at me.

"Promises, promises," I respond, watching his naked, nicely sculpted body move away. Listening to Daniel's side of the conversation, I figure someone is interested in his paintings. Who could it be at three in the morning? I'm dying to find out.

"Baby, you aren't gonna believe this!" he exclaims, turning on the ceiling light. Apparently the light from the television isn't enough.

"Who was it?" I ask.

"Blythe Richie."

"The clothes designer? He's from Los Angeles. I saw his house featured on 'Cribs' a while back. Why is he calling you at three in the morning?"

"That was his assistant. They want to talk with me about some of my artwork!" he says excitedly, diving onto the bed.

"Get out, baby, that's great! But what does painting have to do with clothes designing?" I ask. I am happy, but confused.

"He's launching a new campaign, sort of a classy urban feel, whatever that means. Anyway, last week Blythe was in Boston. He visited the gallery, saw my 'Bebop Boyz' exhibit and loved it. He may want to feature the paintings in an ad campaign for his new line. Kimi, this could be big."

"Told you fate wouldn't be cruel," I remind him, and plant a loud kiss on his smiling lips.

"We're celebrating tomorrow. You, me, and the kids are going out to dinner. I know the perfect place, Odyssey—dinner at sea."

"Odyssey! Honey, I think you should wait until you sign on the dotted line before we make reservations for Odyssey, of all places."

"Kimi, baby, they want my ideas, my paintings, I could tell. He was trying to play it cool, but I could tell. They are very interested in me. But even if this comes to nada, just having my work considered by Blythe Richie is enough to get my foot in any door."

"I'm happy for you, Daniel. I really am."

"Us—say us, Kimi. Baby, I've put you through hell at times, chasing this dream. You deserve to be just as happy as I am right now."

"From your lips to God's ears, baby," I say with feeling. "My husband is about to blow up and I'm not going to be around to appreciate any of it."

"God is not cruel," he reminds me, pulling me closer.

"I've an idea on how to get a confession out of Thomas," I say, tentatively peeking at Daniel.

"I'll punch his ass again, except this time I won't knock his ass out. I'll just stun him, then threaten to knock the fuck out of him if he doesn't confess he's a lying ass," Daniel promises, seeming quite sincere.

"That's one way to go about it," I say, pretending to consider it. "Or, I could just call him and tape the conversation and hand the tape over to the feds. What do you think, Daniel?"

"Not gonna happen. My offer to knock his bitch ass out still stands. But you aren't going near him! Got it?" he demands and abruptly leaves the bed.

"I have to help the feds get Thomas."

"No, you don't. You have a good lawyer—he'll prove you're innocent."

"Sometimes innocent people end up in jail, Daniel," I remind him.

His face crumbles at the reminder that jail time is a real possibility for me.

"They'll take you over my dead body."

"Thank you, baby," I say, unable to keep my voice from cracking or my eyes from leaking. "But I have to cooperate with the feds; your freedom depends on it, too," I belatedly confess.

"Excuse me?"

"I wanted to tell you—"

"Tell me now," Daniel cuts in, his words sharp.

"I wanted to avoid this very thing. You getting pissed, then me getting pissy right back, because I'm the one putting my ass on the line to save yours, and instead of falling at my feet to thank me, I knew you'd get indignant!"

"I liked it better when you used your feminine wiles to get your way," Daniel says.

"Does it include me using it to get you out of a jam?" I ask.

"No," he answers, too quickly for my liking.

"Daniel," I whine.

"Kimi." He tries to mock me and fails completely.

"All I'll be doing is recording a phone conversation. What's the big deal?"

"You'll be entrapping a criminal, and that's dangerous."

"The feds—"

"Are only interested in harpooning that shark Klein. If they have to sacrifice a few guppies—that would be you and me—they will do it without giving us a second thought."

"Thomas will be under arrest," I point out. "We won't need protecting after that."

"Bail. Ever heard of it, babe?"

"Funny, Daniel."

"I'm not trying to be," he claims, relenting enough to come back to bed. I'm sure my downcast expression has a lot to do with his evaporating anger. "We're just gonna have to find another way to get me out of the mess I've gotten myself into."

"No, we are not," I tell him, pushing him away and leaving the bed to prowl about the room.

"Kimi, babe."

"I said no. Look, Daniel, if there were another way to nail Thomas quickly, the feds would have done so. Mike says this whole thing could go public any day. When that happens, all deals are off. I have to get Thomas to confess before that happens or these two guppies—that's you and me—will be left to fend for ourselves."

"I'll take that chance," he says stubbornly.

"I won't," I counter just as stubbornly.

"I'm still willing to beat his ass," he again offers. "I promise he'll confess."

"I'm tempted to let you," I lie.

"Well?"

"Nonviolence, nonviolence," I answer, imitating Martin Luther King Jr.'s intonation.

"I want to be there when you call Klein," Daniel says, finally giving in. "And stop smiling."

"I wasn't smiling,"

"On the inside?" he asks. He knows me so well.

"Sorry, baby."

"Hmm."

"Tomorrow I bust Thomas."

"I'm surprised you can wait that long," Daniel observes, going to turn out the light.

"Actually, I wanted to do it tonight, but Mike pointed out that Thomas likely has caller ID and would know it was me calling."

"Not if I let you use the cellphone from the gallery—it'll just say wireless caller."

"You sure?"

"Yeah, I called Mom on it a couple of times. She says she almost didn't answer because 'wireless caller' all that was came up."

"So I could call Thomas right now if I wanted to?"

"It's four in the morning."

"Maybe Katherine calls him at all times of the night," I suggest weakly.

"Maybe they're laid up together right now. You could blow your chances of trapping Klein by being hasty."

"Shit, shit, shit. Why didn't I think of that? If they're together, my plan is as good as useless."

"Then again, he might not want to chance being seen with this Katherine person—so he's probably keeping his distance," Daniel points out, much to my eternal frustration.

"Make up your mind, Daniel. Are you gonna play devil's advocate or optimistic angel?"

"Just trying to keep you from plunging headlong into trouble. The worst thing that could happen is you call Klein posing as—"

"Katherine."

"But Katherine is lying beside him the whole time," Daniel finishes.

"Then we wait 'til morning, find out where Katherine is, and then make the call," I reluctantly offer an amended solution.

"We wait," he quickly agrees.

Daniel and I both dive for the phone when it rings about an hour later. Daniel wins only because he restrains me by placing his body across mine.

"Mike, what's going on?" he asks.

That's all it takes to get me to stop struggling. Worry over Yvonne tightens my chest.

"They were able to track down the car," Daniel says, repeating what Mike is reporting. "She's right here and listening to every word. Katherine Rings," Daniel says, letting me up. I'm off the bed like a rocket. I can't stand still. It is one thing for me to suspect Katherine, but to have it confirmed is mind-blowing.

"This can't be real. Pinch me, Daniel," I foolishly request, and then have to scurry out of his reach when he goes for my thigh. "Silly," I murmur, half smiling.

"Hold on, Mike, I'll let you tell her. This isn't the kind of news you hear secondhand."

To say I was eager to talk with Mike would be an understatement. I was fairly salivating to hear the details of Katherine's involvement.

"They have Katherine under surveillance," I say, as soon as I hang up.

"What! Why not under arrest?" Daniel asks, clearly outraged.

"It's the most logical course of action, baby," I explain, walking over and giving his stiff body a comforting embrace. I'm still trying to process everything Mike said. "If they arrest Katherine, she is entitled to make a phone call. One guess who that will be. She's also entitled to a lawyer. One guess who her lawyer will call on her behalf."

"Klein! Fuck!"

"To avoid that, Mike had to convince the feds our plan could work and won't jeopardize anything else they have in the works. They'll be here at nine to set up a trace on the phone. I'll call Thomas, he'll spill his guts, and the feds will arrest his ass."

"Not even molasses in the summertime runs that smoothly, Kimi. You foolin' yourself."

"Not true—I'm just thinking positively. You should give it a try, Mr. Negativity."

"I'd much rather deal with Klein man to man."

"Thanks, but no thank you."

"This time, I'll make sure there are no witnesses. I promise. Come back to bed, and we'll discuss it further," he says, suggestively patting the space beside him.

"I don't want to talk," I say, pretending not to know what he's really asking.

"Then don't. Just listen."

"And you'd be happy with a one-sided—conversation?" I ask, enjoying this new dimension to our relationship.

"As long as I'm *talking* to you, it would be worth it. I promise you."

CHAPTER 20

Despite her bumps and bruises, Nicky shows up bright and early the next day for a morning workout. She maintains it's for my benefit, that she doesn't want me to get lazy waiting for her to recover. I think that's only half the story. The other half is that my little sister is worried about me. I agree to go for a thirty minute walk only after bickering with her—to no avail—over the wisdom of her actions.

"You don't look good, Nicky. You should be home recuperating instead of harassing me."

"For the millionth time, Kimi, I feel better than I look."

"How did you get away from Donald, anyway?"

"I didn't tell him."

"You snuck off?"

"No, I just left him and the kids sleeping."

"I bet your ass was on tiptoes, too."

"That's gratitude for you. You think Daniel would mind giving me a ride back to my house?"

"Of course not." I assure her. When Nicky and I reach my house I can't believe what I see: Daniel and the kids are working in the front yard.

"You musta been damn good, cause aint no way a nigga gonna put forth this kinda effort just cause it's the right thang to do," Nicky whispers for my ears only.

"Forget you, Nicky." I say, leaving it at that, but I'm secretly agreeing with her as I watch my front yard being transformed.

"Hey, babe," Daniel calls out when he sees us. "We thought we'd get our own workout in before I drop the kids off, since you and Nicky were up all early showing off. What's up, Nicky?" my husband asks with a chuckle and a wink. The kids hee-haw and look at me.

Nicky hugs all three, saying, "Well, y'all go on with your bad selves," she says.

"Daniel, can you please give Nicky a ride . . ."

"Sure, Nicky, you can wait in the car. I'm gonna just wash my hands and I'll be right back. Alex, Ang, let's go get washed up. We'll pick this up after school, okay?" Daniel says, leading two smiley faces inside. I would have stayed to keep Nicky company while she waited for Daniel, but her grinning behind was getting on my nerves, so I followed my family inside.

Daniel must have pushed my sister out without slowing the car down, because he's back home before I can get breakfast on the table.

"Can Ashley sleep over Saturday?" Angela pipes up.

"We'll see," I say, stopping briefly to tweak my daughter's nose. I'm preparing a quickie breakfast. Daniel and I are in accord on one issue: The kids should know as little as possible about the Thomas Klein affair.

"Mom," Angela whines.

"Mom." My attempt to mimic falls flat. My eyes immediately shift to Daniel's. His inquiring brow only adds to the queasy sensation now filling my stomach.

"That's gotta be a first," he remarks, his voice heavy with meaning.

On the defensive, I say, "I can't do everybody, Daniel," turning away from his intense gaze.

"You've done Angela before without a problem," he insists.

"Well, I can't do everybody every time. Okay, honey?" I ground out. I do an about-face and brave the magnetic pull of his hazel eyes. I would have preferred he continued to offer some sort of objection to the Klein scheme instead of chipping away at my fragile confidence with his look of absolute panic.

Ever alert to brewing domestic discord, Alex asks, "Is everything okay?"

I make myself busy, abandoning Daniel to deal with his inquiring son.

"Everything's fine—unless you keep letting that fat-butt Michael Potts get past you during practice," Daniel informs him in a halfhearted stern tone.

"How do you know that happened, Dad? You were . . . living at grandma's at the time."

"You're still practicing at Gray Field, aren't you?"

"Yes, but—"

"No buts. Forget about how big he is. *Play the type of football you're capable of, or get ready to ride the bench.* Those are the coach's words, not mine."

"You went to see him practice?" I ask.

"Something wrong with that? A father going to watch his son play ball?"

His uncomfortable expression says my husband wants to drop the topic. I take pity on him and do so.

"You coming to watch today?" Alex asks.

"To see Potts eat your dust for a change—I wouldn't miss it," Daniel assures him, getting up from the table. "You two better get a move on," he tells the kids.

Angela is not having it. "What about me? Did you come to see me at cheerleader practice?"

"Angela, honey, I'm sure your father plans to come to watch you practice," I say, intervening to spare both my daughter's feelings and to get Daniel out of a tight spot.

"Your mom's right, Ang. I do plan to come watch you practice—again. Have you nailed the roundhouse kick yet? You were real close. Your coach, Ms. Nasser, thinks it's just a matter of follow-through. See, you have the kick down, but you need to *tighten up the loose ends*, as she puts it."

"*You* actually went to cheerleader practice?" I'm amazed.

"Something wrong with a father going to watch his daughter show 'em what she's made of?" Daniel asks with an amused wink.

"Hmm," I say, feeling warm all over. He hadn't turned his back on his kids—not completely, anyway.

"I'm gonna drop them off, then come straight back. No matter what—don't start without me," he orders sternly.

"Yes, sir, captain. Whatever you say, sir!" I bark back, mimicking a military officer.

"Are you ready, Mrs. Riley?" The lanky redhead, who looks like Alfalfa from the Little Rascals, all grown up, wants to know. He'd introduced himself as Agent Steele Waters, and I had laughed, only to belatedly realize that was actually his name. I glance at the dozen FBI agents squeezed into my cozy living room and give myself a mental shake. I feel as if I'm watching a movie playing itself out. What's taking place in my living room doesn't happen in the real world—not my world, anyway.

"Tell me again, how exactly does this wiretapping work?" Daniel asks for the fourth—maybe fifth—time. I'm beginning to suspect he's stalling.

"It's relatively easy," Agent Waters says. "Once Mrs. Riley places the call to Klein, the device we've connected to your phone allows us to hear and record their entire conversation."

"So Klein will be able to hear us?" Daniel wants clarified—again.

"Yes, he'll hear. We'll need to be extremely quiet, so as not to give Mrs. Riley away to Klein," Alfalfa patiently explains—again.

"And you're sure this Katherine can't call Klein while he's on the phone with Kimi? I'm sure the guy has call waiting."

"We're being as cautious as possible. We'll disable the phones at Thature Mathematics. At the precise moment Mrs. Riley places the call to Klein. Katherine won't be able to call Klein's home or cellphone from any phone in the place."

"And she can't use her cellphone?"

"We've arranged to have it temporarily disconnected," Agent Waters reminds him.

"Ah ha. Can you give us a minute?" Daniel asks, offering up a strained smile. As soon as we're two feet away his smile vanishes. "Say the word, and I'll throw them all out," he offers.

"Weren't you listening last night? This will work. It has to," I tell him, slightly perturbed, though I know it's his protective side working overtime. "The sooner I expose Thomas, the sooner we can get on with our lives," I explain.

"This wiretapping—posing as that punk's lover—it is not the only means to that end," Daniel insists.

"This will work. I'm doing it. I could use a bit of husbandly support. Just a tad, Daniel, a tad."

"Fine."

"Fine what?"

"Fine, Kimberly," he spits out.

"I love you," I say tenderly, switching gears.

"You should," he says, before walking stiffly away. The man is clearly in a snit.

"Daniel is not in agreement with all this," Mike says, observing the busy scene unfolding before us.

"He wants to beat a confession out of Thomas."

"Physical coercion—it'll never hold up in court."

"I believe he knows that, but his anger and frustration are causing him to conveniently overlook that fundamental fact."

"Hmmm," Mike says, and then falls silent.

"She looked good this morning. Don't you think?" I say.

"Hmmm," he says again.

"I spoke with her a little while ago. She says you're picking her up later."

"Dr. Palanskya wants to check her over once more before he releases her. And he won't be making rounds until evening," he explains politely enough, but seems subdued and miles away.

"Why didn't you stay at the hospital, Mike? This Thomas stuff will be fine. Go now, I'll call you as soon as it's over. You should be with Eve."

"To be perfectly honest—I'd love nothing better, but she wouldn't let me," he reveals, a touch of whine in his voice.

"What do you mean she wouldn't let you?"

"She insisted I be here, just in case you get into a jam," he confesses.

"A jam? For goodness sake, a dozen FBI agents are here. I'm covered."

"I couldn't agree more, but Yvonne wouldn't see reason."

"I'll call her back."

"And have her accuse me of coming crying to you? Thanks, but no thanks," he tells me firmly, and follows Daniel's example before I can insist further.

I'm heading toward the stairs, intending to call Yvonne anyway, when Agent Waters intercepts me. They are ready for me.

~∾~

Thomas answers the phone on the first ring. He sounds anxious. "It's me, Katherine," I say. In that moment of do or die, it feels as if all the air is being sucked out of the room. We all hold our collective breath, anxiously awaiting Thomas's reaction.

"Why did you hang up on me last night? Where are you? Your number is not showing up."

"I'm out. I needed to get some air." I take in a deep breath, as do all my co-conspirators.

"Where is your cellphone?" he demands.

"It fell in the toilet and I didn't feel like fishing it out. Why the third degree?" I ask, assuming a defensive attitude, and praying that it's not out of character for the Katherine he knows. God knows it's the Katherine I've come to despise.

"I was worried you'd do something crazier than trying to commit murder in broad daylight!" he yells into my ear.

"They had it coming," I say, my voice turning cold, but not for the reason he thinks.

The bastard is angry because his skank's timing was off. What about her trying to kill me in the first place? I catch Daniel's murderous expression, and motion for him to leave the room. He folds his arms across his broad chest in silent defiance.

"I can take care of myself, Katherine," Thomas retorts. "I don't need you playing vigilante!"

"You're welcome," I sneer, praying Katherine wouldn't take his verbal abuse lying down.

"I'm not going to jail because you can't keep your impulses under control!"

"Nobody is going to jail—except Kimberly Riley. You saw to that." I say, setting the bait.

"Don't get all modest on me now, Katie love—*we* saw to it. I could not have done any of this without you by my side every step of the way, my lovely co-conspirator. Don't even think of getting cold feet on me now," he warns.

"Or what? You'll frame me, as you did Kimberly Riley?" I am pushing, at which point Agent Waters passes me a slip of paper, the words "tread carefully" scribbled on it. I crumble it and toss it at him. This may be my last shot at nailing Klein, as well as getting myself off the hook. I'll jump in with both feet if I have to.

"*We*, Katie love; we set up the Riley bitch. Don't think of distancing yourself at this late date. Unless you want me spend all those millions with someone else?"

"Bastard!" I say for both Katherine's sake and my own.

"That's a girl, Katie love. I was starting to get worried you'd lost your nerve."

"Yesterday, when I ran down Kimberly and her sister, I proved I have plenty of nerve, not to mention loyalty."

"Katie love, now you're confusing nerve and loyalty with stupidity and infatuation," he says, sounding as if he were talking to a dimwit.

"You insulting asshole, I don't know how I've been screwing a dog like you for as long as I have. Just listening to your gall makes me want to vomit!" I tell him loudly, causing all the men in the room—with the exception of

Daniel, who smiles and winks at me—to throw up their hands, no doubt concluding that I've blown it with Thomas for the second time. The prolonged silence that follows my outburst has me about to believe the same.

"Somebody has a temper she has wisely kept under wraps 'til now. I think I like it," he says approvingly. "You may yet prove to be more than just another deceitful bitch hiding behind a beautiful face, Katie love."

"Does that change how much I personally stand to gain?" I ask.

"Not one nickel," he says without hesitation.

"Then can the flattery," I order dryly. He responds with a chuckle. I look reluctantly to Agent Waters for direction. He immediately passes me another slip of paper. The words 'not enough' are followed by a large exclamation mark.

"Perhaps I've been too hasty, Katie love. Why don't you bring that luscious booty on over here and we can renegotiate."

I don't answer right away; I'm busy trying to keep the bile from rising up and to choking me. Pancake-booty Katherine could spend the next hundred years on a Stairmaster and never come close to having luscious booty. I'm further distracted from answering him when an agent bumps the figurine shelf, jarring it and the figurines.

"Katherine—" Thomas reminds me he's waiting for an answer.

"That sounds—" I begin, but the agent's mishap escalates; he manages to stabilize the stand and some of the figurines. Many crash to the floor.

"What the hell was that?" Thomas demands.

"A couple of guys got into a scuffle, but everything looks under control. Law enforcement is here now; they're breaking it up," I say, truthfully. The irony was delicious; law enforcement were indeed there, but for reasons Thomas couldn't possibly know.

Grunts come from several agents standing close by—plainly said they had no trouble deciphering my words.

"A fight? Where the hell—"

"Thomas?"

"Hold on, Katherine," He says. "Someone's beeping me." He clicks off immediately.

"Oh shit," one of the agents hisses, giving voice everyone's concerns.

"Confirm where Katherine is—right now!" Agent Waters orders growls,

"What's going on? You said you had her under surveillance," Daniel asks harshly, moving toward Agent Waters. An agent blocks his path.

"We should stay calm—keep our voices down—Klein could click back over at any second," Mike reminds us, his voice so soft; I have to strain to catch his words.

Every agent except Waters hurries from the room. After several tense minutes, I hear what I think is a click, followed by Thomas indicating he is back.

"Katherine, are you still there?" he asks.

"Yeah, I'm here," I assure him.

"Katherine, there has been a change of plans. I have something I've got to take care of right away. Are we still on for dinner at Dogwoods tonight?"

"Sure," I agree, following a nodding cue from Agent Waters. My chest is nearly bursting with apprehension.

"Great, were the reservations for seven or eight?" he asks.

"Eight, I think," I say, closing my eyes tightly and holding my breath. Suddenly, I feel as if he's testing me.

"I'll pick you up at seven, Katie love."

"Seven it is," I agree immediately, and hang up.

"He's on to her," Daniel says right off.

"I'm inclined to agree," Detective Waters adds, his expression deeply troubled.

"It's fifty-fifty," I concede, refusing to admit failure.

"Kimi, that's desperation talking."

"No, Daniel, that's optimism," I insist.

—∞—

"They lost her," Mike announces when he and most of the agents return about an hour later.

"How?" Agent Waters demands.

"We had a tight tail on her," one agent explains.

"But she went into the ladies' room and never came out." Another agent further explains. "By the time we got someone less conspicuous in there to check on her, she was gone."

"The fire escape!" I loudly proclaim. I'm aghast that I had forgotten all about something so important.

"Fire escape?" Mike asks.

"There is a fire escape on that side of the building—"

"Fuck! What are the odds?" Daniel sums up our mutual thinking rather nicely. "You people should have checked the layout of the place. I'll bet a month's pay she called Klein," he adds.

"What now?" I ask the room at large.

"We locate Ms. Rings and charge her with attempted murder, for starters," Detective Waters says.

"And Klein?" Daniel asks.

"Criminal misconduct, accessory after the fact for the attempted murders of your wife and sister-and-law for starters."

"Do we have really enough evidence to convict them?" Mike asks.

"We'll throw everything we got at them and see what sticks."

CHAPTER 21

"You two should get some rest. Dougie and I will wait for Mike's call."

"Nicky, I really appreciate the offer, but—"

"But you're too stubborn to just say yes without a fight."

"No, I'm too wired to get any sleep, so I might as well wait for the call myself." I'm seriously having second thoughts about having called my overprotective kid sister. At the time I was longing for the added support to help combat all that transpired this dreadful day.

"What's taking the police and the feds so long to find them?" Daniel asks, throwing up his hands.

"Baby, it's only a matter of time before one or the other shows up."

"What about his kid? What happens to her now?" Nicole wants to know.

"She has a mother in Texas, if Thomas can be believed. I'm sure arrangements will be made to reunite them," I say, being hopeful. "Speaking of kids, I better go up and check in on my own."

"It's after ten, they're probably sleeping," Nicole says.

"Not with the long faces they were wearing. They're probably still trying to get them off the floor," Daniel says, sighing. "Alex was sulking something fierce because I didn't make it to check him out at practice today."

"Tell me about it. Angela swears that if I don't pick her up some regulation sneakers soon, they'll replace her on the squad."

"Say no more. Lay some cash on me and I'll take Ang to pick them up tomorrow," Nicole offers.

"Thanks so much, Nicky, we'd appreciate that," Daniel tells her, and then heads upstairs—surprising not only me but also my sister, if her shocked expression is any indication.

I smile proudly, but wonder, who is that considerate stranger who looks exactly like my husband?

"What about fed protection?" Nicky wants to know.

"Don't want it. Don't need it. So don't start, Nicky."

"Fine, just keep looking over your shoulder until they locate Klein and company."

I'm about to tell Nicole what I think of her smarty-pants, but Donald saves me the trouble.

"I could locate them easily," he says softly. Of course he could. It's what he does.

"Why didn't I think of that?" I say, partly relieved and partly apologetic.

"Because you're traumatized and don't know it," Nicole butts in.

"Why didn't you suggest it then, smart-ass?" I shoot back.

"Because they're dangerous criminals, and I wouldn't ask my fiancé to get involved in a dangerous situation."

"And if I volunteer for it?" Donald asks, folding his arms across his chest.

"Then I would heartily support your decision, all the while screaming my ass off—on the inside, of course."

"Fiancé?" I ask.

"Fiancé," Nicole confirms, displaying a nice diamond on her ring finger, her fleeting smile disappearing under Donald's lips.

"You know, Donald, on second thought, I'd feel better allowing the feds to deal with Katherine and Thomas."

"Was it something I said?" Nicole wonders, pulling back from her new love.

"Nope," I lie.

"Thank you, big sis," she says, seeing right through me.

"Don't mention it," I say with undisguised regret. I would have loved having Donald on the case.

"Don't I get a say in this?" Donald asks.

He gets a resounding "no" from Nicole and me in unison.

"If they still haven't located Klein by tomorrow, I'm going to take a crack at it," he says, his PI's instinct showing.

I wisely keep my mouth shut, and so does Nicole—for once.

"I've had a long day, so I'm gonna go lie down and try and get some rest." Donald takes the hint, and goes to collect their coats. Nicole isn't going out so easily.

"Who's stopping you? Go, get some rest; that's what I suggested you do in the first place, remember?"

"Nice try, Nicky. Go home and kiss the kids for me. We'll talk first thing in the morning, I promise."

"The kids are sleeping. Mildred is watching them—all night if need be."

"Well there is no 'need be,' so go home."

"Kimi."

"Don't make me regret calling you, Nicky. I don't want your life to stop because of what's going on with me. Got it?"

"Too late."

"Sillyhead." I love this stubborn woman—I swear I do.

"Your charts—"

"I don't need this right now, Nicky."

"Your charts say this is a defining time for you. This life-altering period in your life will make or break you."

"What does that mean? That could mean anything, Nicky."

"Exactly. You get to write this chapter of your life. Not everyone is so lucky. Remember that."

"O—kay—"

"I love you, nonbeliever, and I'm going, but I'll be back," she declares in Arnold Schwarzenegger fashion.

———————

The call from Mike wakes us around midnight. I wait impatiently while Daniel alternates between "I see," and "Okay," ending with, "That's a relief. I'll tell Kimi."

"Yvonne's home—in bed. They've arrested Katherine Rings, and Klein's daughter has been placed with the department of children's services."

"And Thomas?"

"Klein is still missing. He was a no-show for your dinner date—*Katherine*. Mike says the feds are gonna keep a close eye out."

"Thomas knows it was me calling and not Katherine, doesn't he?"

"Likely, but Katherine isn't talking."

"What does Mike think?"

"That it was Katherine calling to warn Klein."

"So we pray that Thomas spilled enough of his guts to earn himself a conviction, along with his lady love."

"Either way, you're cleared and I'm off the hook for punching Klein."

"Mike said that?" I ask, feeling the tension drain out of me even before Daniel confirms that we are indeed off the hook. "Well, that's somewhat anticlimactic, don't you think?" I ask, throwing off the covers and heading to the bathroom.

"Are you serious?" Daniel yells. I suspect his raised voice has nothing to do with the distance between us.

"Yes," I reply, poking my head out before soundly closing the door. I'm washing my hands when I notice the large pink diamond setting on my ring finger. My legs are suddenly mush and my naked flesh sinks to the bathroom floor. I'm bawling into my hands when I feel arms around me.

"Does this mean you like the ring, Kimi?" Daniel asks softly, his body slowly wrapping around mine.

"How?"

"Blythe Richie really really likes the Beebop Boyz, babe."

"I wasn't expecting this, Daniel Riley."

"But do you like it?" he still wants to know. All I can manage are several rapid nods. Daniel pulls me closer and kisses my wet cheeks.

"I love it," I finally assure him.

"And I love you, girl," he replies. I'm reduced to sobs all over again.

"I have something I want to share with you," Daniel says, passing me some tissues.

"Something to share? What is it?"

"Come with me," he says, helping me up from the floor and leading me back into our bedroom. "Here, put this on," he says, offering me the top to the pajama bottoms he's wearing.

"Where are we going?" I ask, putting on the top.

"I can show you better than I can tell you," he answers, leaving the room ahead of me. I follow him downstairs and down to the rear of the basement.

"Meet the Bebop Boyz," he said, pointing to a large canvas. It was a masterpiece. That is the best definition of what Daniel had created. There were four characters, all boys, who could have been anywhere from fourteen to eighteen years old. They appeared to be engaging in conversation with one another. And they were all dressed to represent various sports: one clearly played baseball, another soccer, while the last two represented football and tennis.

"I love the way you've given them each distinct characteristics. I'm loving the braids on the first fella, and the sharp sideburns on the second guy are a great touch. I like the afro on the third one; it takes me way back, Daniel. And number four's slanted eyes are sexy."

"You really like it?"

"Daniel, it's beautiful, and it's beautiful in here," I say, and really mean it. The whole room was filled with painting supplies; brushes, paint trays, paint stands, a tall wooden stool. I saw artwork at various stages of completion. Some paintings were draped with cloth and others were left undraped. There were sunsets and sunrises, snowcapped mountains and breathtaking waterfalls. It was an art studio, and it was beautiful.

"Thanks for sharing, Daniel," I tell him, too much of a coward to look directly at him.

"Come, babe, I want to share one more thing, and then we can go."

"I don't know if I can take much more."

"It has to be now, Kimi—before I lose my nerve."

That is all the warning I get. Daniel walks over and removes the cloth from a large canvas. And it's the young woman from all those years ago! It's completed now, and it's me! I burst into tears and make a run for it. "Babe," Daniel calls out, but I don't stop. I head for the front door. He catches up with me at my car. If I had to swear on my life as to my destination I wouldn't have been able to do it, I had no idea where I was running to. I only knew what I was running from.

"What's wrong?" Daniel asks, latching on to one arm.

"Nothing! Nothing is wrong! I said thanks for sharing." I'm swiping at my leaking eyes and trying to get free at the same time.

"Stop it, Kimi! Just stop! Listen! Just stop and listen! I'm sharing my soul."

"I know that!" I snap, trying to pull away again.

"Then what's wrong? Why are you angry?"

"I'm not angry, I'm upset at me. I can't believe you have a whole other side to—you. A side I don't know. You're my husband; I should know everything there is to know about you."

"Kimi, you knew I was a painter."

"I didn't know it was your gift. I didn't know you were that good. I should have; you were always so passionate about your painting."

"I'm not looking to place blame or make you feel bad. I just want to share the part of myself I had kept from you, and say I'm sorry for that."

"I should have put more energy into nurturing your dream instead of trying to get you to abandon it!"

"Well, that's true," he agrees, offering a wink and an infectious smile. I wrap my arms around his waist and hold on tight.

"Kimi?"

"Yes?"

"You cold?"

"Yes."

"Can I interest you in a warm bed?"

"Yes, yes, you can."

An hour later I had just finished showering after passionate and sweaty lovemaking with Daniel when I hear the phone ringing, then the doorbell.

"It's Yvonne," Daniel tells me, passing the phone to me. "Have a care," I say.

"Babe, I seriously doubt Klein would come boldly into the path of my fist. Bet it's the feds," he says before heading downstairs to answer the door.

"Hi, girly-girl," I say playfully, hoping to head off what I suspect will be a severe tongue-lashing. "I heard you got sprung. Which makes me extremely happy, but do you have idea how late you are ringing my phone?"

"Save that 'girly-girl' stuff for Nicky. Mike told me what you did. What were you thinking, trying to get between a thief and his ill-gotten gains, not to mention his freedom?"

"An eye for an eye?" I suggest.

"Don't play with me, Kimi," she says sternly. "I don't know what I'd do if you got yourself hurt, or worse, playing policewoman," she admits in a broken whisper.

"I'm sorry, Eve. Truly. Am I forgiven?"

"Only because God says we must forgive those who trespass against us."

"Well, hallelujah!"

"Heaven have mercy on this fool, please."

"Did Mike tell you they arrested Katherine?" I ask, switching gears.

"Surprisingly, yes, Mr. Client Privilege told me. I think it was the sight of me in a wheelchair that made him go all soft."

"Why were you in a wheelchair? Are you still weak?"

"No, mother hen, I'm fine—it's hospital policy when you're a fainter."

327

"Oh, good. You can never be too careful."

"Anyway, he told me Thomas Klein is still missing. The police and the feds are looking high and low for him—nothing. With that kind of money, they think he may be long gone."

"Maybe he's off getting laid by a new love. Maybe he's somewhere counting his millions. Maybe he's on a plane to Timbuktu. Frankly, I'm starting to not really care—as long as I'm cleared and Daniel is not gonna be charged for socking Thomas's ass, I'm all set."

"How can you say that? What if he comes seeking revenge? What then?"

"Then I let Daniel do more than sock his ass."

"Kimi."

"Hold on a sec. I think I hear Daniel talking to someone."

I put on my bathrobe and I go into the hallway, pausing briefly to look in on the kids as I make my way to the top of the stairs.

"Eve, you still there?" I ask, making my way toward the stairs.

"Who is it?" she asks. I can hear alarm in her voice now.

"The bogyman." I say, doing a spooky voice. "No, wait! It is Thomas bringing my hard-earned share of the booty."

"Don't play, Kimi."

"Fine, but it's likely the feds. Mike said they were keeping an eye out. Hmmm."

"What does 'hmmm' mean, Kimi?"

"The front door is closed. Hold on a sec, Eve. Daniel, who was that at the door?" I call down.

There is no answer, just an eerie sort of quiet.

"Daniel, honey." I call again.

"Guess again," a familiar baritone says.

I hear him approaching before he appears and orders me to join them—now. Not wanting to chance being heard talking to Yvonne, I quickly place the phone in the pocket of my robe without hanging up. Please, God, let Yvonne call the police. I doubt I have time to do it. As if to prove I am right Thomas appears at the bottom of the stairs, armed with a handgun. He's dressed from head to toe in black and wearing a hooded sweatshirt. His pants are uncharacteristically baggy. A pair of black shades tops off his outfit. I wonder crazily if they are a part of his getup, or an attempt at concealing a lingering black eye.

Thomas silently beckons me forward, using the gun as an incentive. Fear for Alex and Angela upstairs, helpless and oblivious to the danger just twenty or so feet away, gives me the strength I need not to crumble to the floor. My knees are literally knocking by the time I reach the bottom of the stairs. I give my nose a quick wipe, not because I feel it perspiring—I'm numb—but because I *know* it's perspiring. It always does when I'm under great stress.

"How are you, Kimberly?" Thomas asks, managing to sound like he gives a damn. How does he do that?

Daniel is standing in the middle of the living room in his pajama bottoms. His forehead is deeply creased and his hands are clenching and unclenching at his sides. He makes a move toward us and Thomas quickly points his gun in his direction. My heart jumps in my throat.

"Down, boy," Thomas commands before turning back to me.

"Come join the party, secret agent bitch!"

If I didn't know better, I'd swear his anger was justified. He is fairly trembling with unspent rage. I hurry past him to Daniel's side, all the while fearful he'll hit, or worse, shoot me from behind. Even with him moving toward us with the gun aimed at us, I'm relieved. My babies are safe for now.

"What do you want, Klein?" Daniel demands, maneuvering in front of me as soon as I reach him.

"I want you both dead, for starters!" he shouts, taking aim at Daniel's head.

"You won't get away with this, Thomas," I assure him, struggling against the arm Daniel is using to keep me out of harm's way. "I'm sure my nosy neighbors have your description down pat—including the black eye."

"I have a whole lot of money, a getaway car, and a chartered plane ready to take me anywhere I want to go," he gloats.

"Then just go. Why come here and risk getting caught by the feds?" I reason.

"Because this is plan B."

"Plan B?"

"Yes, plan B. I never really planned on using it. You were supposed to go to jail. I was supposed to get immunity for my help in implicating you, along with several executives from Bronzen and Cauplum."

"What can I say? Self-preservation is a bitch."

"I underestimated you—that I did. That's the root of my problem."

"Never judge a book . . . you know the rest," I taunt him, as much as I dare.

"Do Katherine for me," he orders, surprising me.

"Don't care for blondes, thanks," I shoot back, with false bravado.

"Kimi," Daniel warns, under his breath.

"So flip at the lip. I suppose once upon a time you thought that was cute?" he snipes, gesturing at Daniel.

"If you leave now, I'll give you a ten-second head start," Daniel tries bargaining with our captor.

"I've got a better one for you. If you get down on both knees and beg real hard, I'll kill you first. If not, I'll kill secret agent bitch right before your eyes."

"Thomas Klein, put that gun away! Please don't kill us!" I yell, startling both men.

"What are you up to?" Thomas yells.

At that moment, I know our time is up; we are not going to live long enough for help to arrive. I hear Alex calling my name. But instead of feeling a bullet ripping my flesh apart, that moment of distraction provides Daniel with an opening to save us. Next thing I know, they're fighting for possession of the gun.

"Get in your room, Alex!" I scream, reaching into my pocket for the phone. "Eve! Eve!" She is not there.

I toss the phone onto the chair and rush toward the two combatants. I'm betting the bank Eve has already called for help. The fight is contained within the space between the sofa and the coffee table. Thomas is on top, then Daniel, now Thomas again. The whole time, they're struggling over the gun. I grab Thomas around the neck but he head-butts me and I lose my grip. I'm struggling to my feet when the gun goes flying across the room. Both men fight their way to a standing position. Thomas makes a run for the gun, but Daniel tackles him and they both land hard on top of my antique coffee table, shattering it.

"Stop it! Leave him alone!" I scream after seeing Daniel receive several hard blows to the body. "The police are coming!"

While they struggle for the upper hand, I retrieve the gun. I have no idea how to use it. I aim it at them, but I don't try and fire it; I can't tell where Thomas begins and Daniel ends. Thomas manages to get a hand between their bodies and forces Daniel's head back so far I'm fearful his neck will snap. But he recovers quickly and goes gangbusters, delivering a barrage of body blows to Thomas.

Instead of succumbing to Daniel's assault, Thomas propels himself forward and head butts him real hard in the midsection. The impact sends them crashing into my figurine shelf. Shards of glass fly everywhere. The two struggle to their feet again—never missing a beat. Red smears appear on the floor; broken glass has injured one or both of the men.

"Stop it, damn it! Where the hell are the police?" I'm half out of my mind with fear.

Suddenly Daniel slips and goes down. Thomas doesn't waste the advantage. He goes for a broken table leg and takes a wild swing at Daniel's head. He misses, but I don't. The gun blast knocks Thomas off his feet, and he goes down screaming. Then I hear the kids screaming.

I'm frozen. Daniel is by my side and is whispering in my ear, but my mind is a jumble, and I don't understanding his words. His warm, bruised hands try to pry my cold clammy ones apart to get the gun, but they won't budge.

It seems like an eternity before I'm able to get my hands to obey my brain. A scream sneaks up on me and lodges in my throat, because I refuse to set it free. I'm suffocating. My only escape is to open my mouth and let it out. It is a long time—at least it feels like a long time—before I can relax into Daniel's embrace.

"Where is he?" I ask in a panic, breaking free of Daniel's hold. "You know what happens in the movies—as soon as we let him out of our sight, he'll attack again!" I declare with certainty.

"Okay," Daniel concurs softly. I'm sure he is only trying to pacify me. "It's over, baby," he says and points to Thomas lying motionless on the floor.

I hear sirens approaching. *Now* I believe him.

EPILOGUE

Nicole is the most beautiful bride I've ever seen, and it has nothing to do with the gorgeous gown Daniel and I sprang for, thanks to the success of his Bebop Boyz paintings. The glow of true love has transformed her. Mom and Dad come back to attend the ceremony. Watching their little girl pledge herself to Donald for life, they are overjoyed. And I secretly think they are thinking the same thing I am—Nicole is now Big D's financial responsibility. Hooray!

"I'm dying!"

"You're being overdramatic, Eve."

"I can't do this."

"You can and you will. Only six months to go."

"I've been nauseous from day one. Just the smell of food and I heave. This can't be normal."

"Everyone is different. You've had a tough first trimester. It's all downhill from now on."

"Liar!"

"I love you. Tell Mike I send my love. Bye."

"Don't even think about hanging up on me, Kimi!"

"What more do you want, Eve? My blood? I've said every comforting thing I can think of," I say, pulling on a pair of shorts and then maneuvering into a matching tank top. Me minus a grand total of *sixty pounds*—it's a pleasing sight to behold.

"Was that my phone beeping?" I ask, in all seriousness.

"Don't even try it, Kimi," Yvonne says, incorrectly assuming I'm using that old standby to get away.

"No, seriously, Daniel and I finally agreed on a new coffee table to go with the sectional. I'm expecting a confirmation call for tomorrow's delivery."

"You and Daniel agreeing on home decorating? I'm still digesting that one."

"We've agreed on the upgrades to the bathrooms and the kitchen, so digest it already. You know, that could have been my agent. I'm expecting his call. He says my first novel sold so well this one should fetch a hefty advance."

"You deserve it. Just remember, change the names to protect the innocent—namely me— this time around."

"I'll remember that. Now, can I please go? I've got a date with three of my favorite people."

"Call me later."

"Promise, promise, bye!" This time I succeed in getting off the phone, and not a second too soon. My bedroom door opens without warning.

"It's almost ten, babe. You ready?"

"Yep!" I say, smiling tenderly and walking toward the male filling the doorway.

Just as he pulls me close, the phone rings.

"Mama's persistent," I say for the both of us. Daniel beams, appreciating my congenial tone. His mama still calls every Saturday without fail, and each time Daniel informs her that *we* will all be over after *we've* spent some quality time together. I guess old habits die hard for old Dennis! Not so for Daniel. Thank you, Jesus.

The phone rings again before we can get going. I answer it; the delivery service is calling to confirm our address.

"It's the bright yellow house on the left, trimmed in gold," I say proudly. Daniel catches my eye and smiles.

——∽∽∽——

"Bring it on, both of you, blood don't mean nothing when it comes to the hoop!" Alex issues his usual challenge, and gives his father a high five.

"We've been practicing, so be prepared for a real challenge this time." I make my usual claim.

Angela and I move into position and employ our usual underhanded tricks, to no avail. Daniel and Alex tease and boast about their male superiority, but I know the sparkle in their eyes has nothing to do with their victory over us on the court. It goes much deeper.

Angela and I accept their ribbing. I bask in a similar sparkle in my daughter's eyes. It, too, has nothing to do with the thrill of competing against our male counterparts. We share a victory over the game of life, and we're celebrating on the inside. And I know it's the inextinguishable light of triumph reflecting in their sparkle that can't be contained. We are rejuvenated, prepared for whatever life tosses our way.

We settle into the car and head toward Ashmont. Daniel reaches over and squeezes my hand reassuringly. I glance into the rearview mirror. Both Alex and Angela appear to be contentedly observing the familiar view outside their window. I return Daniel's squeeze, and he smiles broadly over at me.

"God knows this life isn't perfect, but I'm living it."

The End

ABOUT THE AUTHOR

This Life Isn't Perfect Holla is Sandra Foy's first book. Originally from Tunica, Mississippi, she is now a stay-at-home mom as well as a full-time writer and resides, with her family, in Worcester, Massachusetts.

Coming in December from Genesis Press:

Chamein Canton's
The More Things Change;
the eagerly awaited sequel to
Not His Type.

CHAPTER 1

Typing at a feverish pace with the phone still attached to her ear, Catherine Chambers sat behind her new mahogany desk in her crisp blue blouse and navy skirt. Cathy was at the top of her game as an agent, and the Chambers Smith Literary Agency was doing well enough that her usually frugal partner E.D. agreed they could splurge on new office décor and new hires.

Yes, life was good, but for Cathy it would be better if Timothy Raines, the stalwart editor-in-chief for Lighthouse Publishing, would say yes to Jim Weil's latest manuscript.

"Sorry about that, Cathy. It's a nuthouse here today." He was a little out of breath.

She stopped typing. "I know how that feels." Cathy heard the sound of papers rustling. "So you're calling about Jim's *Matilda*, right?"

"Yes. I think it's some of his best work to date."

"The writing is good. But then again, he's always been a solid writer."

"I know." She paused. "I'm waiting for the other shoe, Tim." Cathy tapped her pen on the desk.

"I think the concept of *The Secret Life of Walter Mitty* meets *10* is genius," he added.

Cathy had worked with Tim long enough to know when he'd passed on a project before he said so. "Still, you're passing on it. Why?"

"Well, to be honest, I find Ray unsympathetic. Though his wife is a shrew and he's falling into financial ruin, all he wants to do is get his rocks off with hookers."

Cathy sighed. "Tim, you've been a women's fiction editor for too long. The target market is men, not women."

"I know."

"No, you don't know, Tim. Otherwise you wouldn't dismiss it so quickly."

"You never mince words, do you?"

"No. Have I not brought you four bestsellers in the last three years?"

"Yes."

"So you know I'm not one to blow smoke up your skirt."

"My skirt?"

"You know what I mean." She paused. "Listen, Tim, Lighthouse Publishing is going after the untapped men's market to prove that men aren't complete Neanderthals and will actually read something other than a how-to-build-a-deck manual."

"True."

"So men will relate to the protagonist Ray and see that he's not all bad. His wife doesn't work, so all the pressure is on him to keep the house afloat and the kids in college."

"When you say it like that, I see what you're talking about."

"Then he tops it off with a little sex."

"A little sex? Jim pulled out the stops."

"His writing style paints a picture," she agreed, "but you don't hear a bad porno guitar riff, right?"

Tim laughed. "To be honest, if a guy pays attention, he could pick up some tips."

Cathy chuckled. "Now that's a selling point. Most guys would never buy a sex how-to book, but disguise it in a novel and you might have another bestseller on your hands."

"Hmm."

Cathy could hear the wheels turning in Tim's mind.

"You know, Jim should write a sex manual or at least hold a seminar or something."

"A seminar like that would require a live demonstration, and I think that's a felony in all fifty states. Besides, how would he conduct the question and answer session?" Cathy asked.

Tim howled with laughter. "That is priceless."

"Enough so that you will take another look at it?"

"Okay, Cathy, I'll give it one more read."

"Only this time read it from a man's perspective. I know you've been in women's fiction for ten years, but I'm sure you haven't grown ovaries yet."

"Very funny, Cathy," he said dryly.

"I couldn't help myself."

"I'll give you a call about this early next week."

"Good."

"Before I go, how is Marcus? Is he getting ready for spring training?"

Of course he's getting ready for spring training. What kind of question is that? she thought, knowing she had to be ready for the polite party line answer. "Oh yes. It is that time of year."

"By the way, I heard a rumor that you're heading to sunny Florida."

"As a matter of fact, I will be in Florida for a little while."

"Aren't you lucky?"

"I know." Cathy crossed her fingers.

"Tell Marcus I wish the team good luck. Maybe this is the year we bring the championship back to New York."

"That's the plan, Tim." She looked at her clock. "Okay, I've got run. I'll talk to you next week."

"Take care, Cathy."

"You too, Tim."

"It's almost time to wrap it up," she said aloud.

"Knock, knock."

"Hey, Michelle, what's up?"

Michelle glanced around Cathy's office. "Not much at the moment. I'm taking a break from playing phone tag with your favorite client's publisher-assigned PR person."

"I'm sure Morgan is swamped. He does have other authors besides Steven."

"I know, but I didn't like tag as a kid and I really hate phone tag."

"You're preaching to the choir, Michelle." She paused. "So how is Martin?"

A warm schoolgirl smile came over Michelle's face. She'd been dating Martin Spencer for more than a year. Always one of those big girls with a pretty face, she'd met Martin, an investment banker, at a Large and In Charge party. He was six feet, one inch tall with sandy blond hair, and was an unapologetic chubby chaser who adored Michelle.

"He's good, thanks." She smiled as she walked over to a pair of strappy sandals Cathy had in a box near her desk. "Nice." She held them up. "That's some heel."

Cathy looked up. "I know."

Michelle examined the soles of the shoes. "Are these new?"

"No, I've had them for a while now."

"Really? How do you keep them from falling apart?"

"If you must know, they're my come-hither pumps."

Michelle fell out laughing. "Is that right?"

"Of course, I can't walk in them. Look at the heel."

Michelle marveled at the heel. "My God, Cathy, they must be at least three inches."

"They're three and a half inches, to be exact. I just slip them on and let nature take its course." She winked.

"Can I borrow them?"

"No."

"Thanks a lot. I thought you were my best friend." She feigned being upset.

"You'll get over it."

Michelle laughed. "Wait a second, what are your 'do me' pumps doing here in your office?"

Cathy kept working. "Don't you have to play tag or something?"

Michelle smiled impishly. "You go, girl. There's nothing like a little heels- over-head to liven up the work day . . . or night," she said as she headed for the door.

Cathy knew she was fishing. "I know, and the answer is still no."

"You're no fun." She paused. "Oh no, my bad. You are fun."

"I'll ask you again, don't you have a game of phone tag to get back to?"

"Morgan can wait."

"But you can't. Now go get Morgan."

"I get the hint. I'll report back later, fearless leader." She saluted on the way out.

"You do that." Cathy shook her head.

A few minutes later Arlene Gaines knocked on the door. Arlene was a new junior associate they had hired after Michelle was promoted to head of their small PR department. Married for over fourteen years, she was an attractive African American woman with neatly kept locks, big brown eyes and an adorable figure. She was also the mother of twin 13-year-old boys Donovan and Darren, so she'd occasionally tap Cathy for advice. For her part Cathy rather enjoyed the idea of being the senior mother in residence of twins.

"Can I come in?"

"Sure."

Arlene took the seat in front of Cathy's desk. "What's up?"

"First, I wanted to let you know that Haddon & Associates has a meeting with a D & H Productions to pitch *Swiss Journey*."

Cathy smiled. "That's good. Jim will be pleased to hear that. I'm so glad they're handling our Hollywood stuff. It makes life tons easier. "

"I know."

"Keep me posted on any developments."

"I will." Arlene looked distracted.

"So how are the kids?"

"Good." She chuckled. "Their voices are starting to change now and they're really sensitive about it."

"So you have to resist the urge to giggle."

"Let's just say I've been biting my bottom lip a lot lately."

"I did the same thing. Have they started paying more attention to girls yet?"

"It's not the girls in school. It's the women on television."

"And in your Victoria's Secret catalogs, too. "

"My catalogs still make it to my room." Arlene quickly dismissed the thought of her boys ogling the scantily clad models in her lingerie catalog.

"Of course they make it to your room, but I'll bet by the scenic route."

Arlene shuddered at the thought. "It's a little disconcerting to see your babies grow up, all the body changes and moods."

"I remember when I first realized I had to look at my sons from the waist up in the morning."

Arlene laughed. "Get out of here."

"I'm serious. Donovan and Darren are thirteen now, right? I'm sure they've joined the pack and are now unconsciously or consciously obsessed with their lower half."

Arlene seemed shocked. "Pardon me. They're still in middle school."

"You can ignore me if you like, but I promise you the sun isn't the only thing that rises in the morning."

"Oh, my God, Cathy, I don't even want to think about that." She was unnerved.

"Believe me, I know you don't. Heck, I didn't want to either."

"What did you do about it?"

"What could I do about it? It's a normal and natural part of growing up. So I dealt with it."

"They're only thirteen."

"I know. Right now Victoria's Secret is pretty tame stuff. It gets more interesting."

Arlene shook her head. "It gets more interesting? I'm not sure I could take that."

"You're a parent, Arlene, you have to take it."

"You know, they don't tell you this stuff when you leave the hospital with them." Arlene leaned back in the chair.

"That's why the maternity ward is the happiest place in the hospital. They know you don't have a clue of what lies ahead, and they get a kick out of it."

"I bet they do."

"I remember the nurses telling me that I'd be back." Cathy smirked.

"They thought you'd be back?"

"Oh, sure they did. The nurses kept saying I had to come back to get that girl. And while I loved the stylish plastic I.D. bracelet, next time anyone saw me in the maternity ward I'd be wearing a stylish visitor sticker."

Arlene fell out laughing.

"It's been twenty years and I haven't been back."

"Wait a second. What about Marcus?"

"What about him?"

"He doesn't have children. What if he wants kids?"

Cathy thought for a moment. "I think that's putting the cart before the horse. Marcus and I are in a relationship and things are good, but . . ."

"I know. I'm just saying,"

"I know what you're saying, and I'd love to have a baby with Marcus. However," Cathy flashed her naked ring finger, "see this? There's nothing on it and, until there is, I don't even think about more kids."

Arlene rubbed her forehead. "Whatever you say." She stood up.

Cathy yawned.

"Tired?" Arlene asked.

"Yes. I'm so glad I'm taking tomorrow off. I've been running at full throttle lately, and I think it's caught up with me."

"Well, in the last year you planned your sister's wedding, organized your dad's sixty-fifth birthday bash and threw a twentieth birthday party for your sons, in the Bahamas, no less. Am I missing anything?"

"Let's see. There was my Thanksgiving dinner for twenty-five, and the holiday season overall."

"God, Cathy, you've barely had time to breathe." Arlene smiled.

"That's why I'm spending a quiet day at home vegetating."

"You certainly deserve it."

"As a matter of fact, I think I'm going to skip out early," Cathy said as she shut off her computer. "I need to make a quick stop at my post office, and if I leave now I might actually make it."

"I won't tell."

"Good." Cathy got up from her desk, put her coat on and grabbed her briefcase and purse. "Help me sneak over to the elevator."

Arlene checked to see if the coast was clear, and then she and Cathy made a dash for the elevator.

Arlene pressed the call button. "I'll see you later this week."

"Definitely."

Cathy stepped in when the elevator doors opened. "A hot bath and a warm bed are calling my name." She smiled as the doors closed.

She made it to Penn Station in time for the two o'clock train to Babylon. Despite leaving before peak hour, there were a lot of commuters headed for the island. Nevertheless, she found a sparsely inhabited car. Cathy took a seat near the window and settled in for the ride.

Although she could easily take a car service from Manhattan to Amityville, Cathy preferred to take the train whenever possible. The train offered her sanctuary from ringing phones, neurotic clients and her own workaholic nature. Even though she was familiar with the stops, she always made a point to look for something new she hadn't seen before or she made up stories about the people she saw passing by on the street below. After representing writers for so many years she'd developed a sponge-like tendency to absorb sights and sounds of the suburbs that surrounded her.

Cathy arrived at the Amityville station a little less than an hour later. She hopped into her car and drove to the post office on Ireland Avenue. She'd made friends with the postal clerks there over the years as a result of the many submission packages she mailed from her home office. Often there were so many Cathy referred to it as the strength training portion of her workout.

One of the secrets to good service at the post office was to come in the afternoon as opposed to when the crowds were there in the morning. Dayla, a postal employee who often worked in the front, had let her in on that one. When Cathy walked in there was one person on line. Dayla, a lovely African American woman with short bobbed hair, finished up with the customer and smiled at Cathy. "Hey, Cathy."

"How are you, Dayla?"

"I'm good. I haven't seen you much these days. I guess you're hanging out in the city a lot with that shortstop of yours." She grinned.

"I've been in the city a lot these days. It's been so busy. Speaking of busy, how is your thesis coming along?"

"It's getting there slowly." She shook her head. "I don't know how you writers can come up with those crazy word counts."

"I'm pretty sure I don't know, either. You just sit in front of your computer and write as furiously and as quickly as it comes to you. That's my best advice."

"I'll keep that in mind." She got up. "I think we have your mail here on the side."

"I'll get it," Henry volunteered. A tall, good-looking man with brown hair, Henry was one of nicest and best looking postal clerks in the county, at least in Cathy's and Anna's estimation.

"Here you go." He placed the bin on the counter. "It's kind of light for you."

"Good. I'm too tired to do any heavy lifting today."

"Do you need anything else?"

"No, this is it," Cathy said, picking up the bin. "I'm heading home to slip into a hot bath and maybe a light coma."

"A light coma?" Dayla laughed.

"Yes. I don't want anything too heavy, just enough so I can get some rest for a change."

"I hear that. I'll see you later."

"Have a good one, Dayla. You, too, Henry."

He waved.

Cathy walked out of the post office and got into her car. Within five minutes she was home. The minute she entered she dropped the bin on the floor and made a bee-line for the upstairs.

"I'm coming, bathtub. We have a long hot date," she said as she climbed the stairs.

———✧———

I'm so tired, Cathy sighed as she lay in bed staring at the ceiling. *I'm just going to relax.* Just as she snuggled under the covers, the aroma of fresh coffee wafted through the air. *That's the end of that.*

As she made her way downstairs Cathy heard the coffee maker beep.

"Perfect timing," she said aloud.

Her coffee fixed, Cathy sat down at the kitchen table to enjoy the quiet.

"Hey."

Startled, Cathy turned around. "Good grief, Anna, you scared the daylights out of me."

"Sorry. I was on my way to Motor Vehicle to take care of some business when I realized I didn't have my title. I thought I did, but it wasn't in my papers. I came by figuring I might have left it in a drawer or something."

"Did you find it?"

"Yes, thank goodness. It was stuck in between the dresser drawers."

"Good thing you found it."

Anna looked around. "No fresh baked goodies today?"

"It's just me here now. Why make a dozen muffins for one person?"

"Maybe, but I'm sure Marcus would love it."

"I know he would, but we're getting close to spring training so carbs have become a four letter word."

"I see what you mean."

"Besides, I need a break after a month of cooking around the clock for the boys."

"Oh yes. I guess they really miss their mom's cooking now." She paused. "So you're here by yourself?"

"Yep."

"What's happening with Marcus?"

"He had an early meeting with Ben."

"So, speaking of spring training, are you ready? It's only a couple of weeks away."

Cathy thought for a moment. "I'm as ready as I'm going to be."

"Gee, Cathy, you don't have to sound so enthusiastic," Anna said sarcastically.

"Oh, don't get me wrong, I am happy to go with Marcus. I'm just not looking forward to the commute from New York to Florida and vice versa."

"Well, it's not like you have to commute, Cathy. Have laptop, will travel. You just don't like Florida all that much."

Whether Cathy wanted to admit it out loud or not, Anna had hit the nail on the head. Cathy wasn't crazy about Florida.

"Well, I'm sorry. The bugs there are the size of some small farm animals, and it doesn't matter where you live or how clean your place is, they just fly in."

Anna shuddered. "You're talking about the flying roaches."

Cathy made a face. "Oh, God, they're awful."

"Still, you have a big, wonderful guy to kill them for you."

Cathy smiled. "You're right. But there's the hair thing, too."

"The humidity shouldn't be too bad. It's still sort of wintertime."

"From your mouth to God's ears." Cathy clasped her hands together.

"You'll be okay."

"I hope so. If not, I'll have to rock a tight school teacher's bun, that's all."

Anna laughed. "Sounds like a plan." She looked at her watch. "I'd better get going."

Cathy looked at the clock. "It's kind of late for you. Aren't you off?"

Even though she looked like a model with her even brown skin and dark brown hair, Anna was a no-non-sense accountant and auditor for New York State's Comptrollers Office. At nearly six feet tall, she stood head and shoulders above most of her co-workers and supervisors.

"Normally I'm off, but I'm covering for Paula."

"That's a bummer."

"Tell me about it. My only consolation is I get another pass day." She looked at the clock. "I've got to bounce. I'll see you later."

"Okay."

Cathy shuddered at the thought of flying cock-roaches. "Yuck!" she said aloud and then glanced toward the heavens. "You know, Lord, love is the only reason I'm willing to deal with bugs, snakes, humidity and a higher than usual number of Sunday drivers. Oh well, Marcus is more than worth it. I wonder if Raid comes in three-ounce cans. This way I can start spraying the minute I get off the plane."

2008 Reprint Mass Market Titles

January

Cautious Heart
Cheris F. Hodges
ISBN-13: 978-1-58571-301-1
ISBN-10: 1-58571-301-5
$6.99

Suddenly You
Crystal Hubbard
ISBN-13: 978-1-58571-302-8
ISBN-10: 1-58571-302-3
$6.99

February

Passion
T. T. Henderson
ISBN-13: 978-1-58571-303-5
ISBN-10: 1-58571-303-1
$6.99

Whispers in the Sand
LaFlorya Gauthier
ISBN-13: 978-1-58571-304-2
ISBN-10: 1-58571-304-x
$6.99

March

Life Is Never As It Seems
J. J. Michael
ISBN-13: 978-1-58571-305-9
ISBN-10: 1-58571-305-8
$6.99

Beyond the Rapture
Beverly Clark
ISBN-13: 978-1-58571-306-6
ISBN-10: 1-58571-306-6
$6.99

April

A Heart's Awakening
Veronica Parker
ISBN-13: 978-1-58571-307-3
ISBN-10: 1-58571-307-4
$6.99

Breeze
Robin Lynette Hampton
ISBN-13: 978-1-58571-308-0
ISBN-10: 1-58571-308-2
$6.99

May

I'll Be Your Shelter
Giselle Carmichael
ISBN-13: 978-1-58571-309-7
ISBN-10: 1-58571-309-0
$6.99

Careless Whispers
Rochelle Alers
ISBN-13: 978-1-58571-310-3
ISBN-10: 1-58571-310-4
$6.99

June

Sin
Crystal Rhodes
ISBN-13: 978-1-58571-311-0
ISBN-10: 1-58571-311-2
$6.99

Dark Storm Rising
Chinelu Moore
ISBN-13: 978-1-58571-312-7
ISBN-10: 1-58571-312-0
$6.99

2008 Reprint Mass Market Titles (continued)

July

Object of His Desire
A.C. Arthur
ISBN-13: 978-1-58571-313-4
ISBN-10: 1-58571-313-9
$6.99

Angel's Paradise
Janice Angelique
ISBN-13: 978-1-58571-314-1
ISBN-10: 1-58571-314-7
$6.99

August

Unbreak My Heart
Dar Tomlinson
ISBN-13: 978-1-58571-315-8
ISBN-10: 1-58571-315-5
$6.99

All I Ask
Barbara Keaton
ISBN-13: 978-1-58571-316-5
ISBN-10: 1-58571-316-3
$6.99

September

Icie
Pamela Leigh Starr
ISBN-13: 978-1-58571-275-5
ISBN-10: 1-58571-275-2
$6.99

At Last
Lisa Riley
ISBN-13: 978-1-58571-276-2
ISBN-10: 1-58571-276-0
$6.99

October

Everlastin' Love
Gay G. Gunn
ISBN-13: 978-1-58571-277-9
ISBN-10: 1-58571-277-9
$6.99

Three Wishes
Seressia Glass
ISBN-13: 978-1-58571-278-6
ISBN-10: 1-58571-278-7
$6.99

November

Yesterday Is Gone
Beverly Clark
ISBN-13: 978-1-58571-279-3
ISBN-10: 1-58571-279-5
$6.99

Again My Love
Kayla Perrin
ISBN-13: 978-1-58571-280-9
ISBN-10: 1-58571-280-9
$6.99

December

Office Policy
A.C. Arthur
ISBN-13: 978-1-58571-281-6
ISBN-10: 1-58571-281-7
$6.99

Rendezvous With Fate
Jeanne Sumerix
ISBN-13: 978-1-58571-283-3
ISBN-10: 1-58571-283-3
$6.99

2008 New Mass Market Titles

January

Where I Want To Be
Maryam Diaab
ISBN-13: 978-1-58571-268-7
ISBN-10: 1-58571-268-X
$6.99

Never Say Never
Michele Cameron
ISBN-13: 978-1-58571-269-4
ISBN-10: 1-58571-269-8
$6.99

February

Stolen Memories
Michele Sudler
ISBN-13: 978-1-58571-270-0
ISBN-10: 1-58571-270-1
$6.99

Dawn's Harbor
Kymberly Hunt
ISBN-13: 978-1-58571-271-7
ISBN-10: 1-58571-271-X
$6.99

March

Undying Love
Renee Alexis
ISBN-13: 978-1-58571-272-4
ISBN-10: 1-58571-272-8
$6.99

Blame It On Paradise
Crystal Hubbard
ISBN-13: 978-1-58571-273-1
ISBN-10: 1-58571-273-6
$6.99

April

When A Man Loves A Woman
La Connie Taylor-Jones
ISBN-13: 978-1-58571-274-8
ISBN-10: 1-58571-274-4
$6.99

Choices
Tammy Williams
ISBN-13: 978-1-58571-300-4
ISBN-10: 1-58571-300-7
$6.99

May

Dream Runner
Gail McFarland
ISBN-13: 978-1-58571-317-2
ISBN-10: 1-58571-317-1
$6.99

Southern Fried Standards
S.R. Maddox
ISBN-13: 978-1-58571-318-9
ISBN-10: 1-58571-318-X
$6.99

June

Looking for Lily
Africa Fine
ISBN-13: 978-1-58571-319-6
ISBN-10: 1-58571-319-8
$6.99

Bliss, Inc.
Chamein Canton
ISBN-13: 978-1-58571-325-7
ISBN-10: 1-58571-325-2
$6.99

2008 New Mass Market Titles (continued)

July

Love's Secrets
Yolanda McVey
ISBN-13: 978-1-58571-321-9
ISBN-10: 1-58571-321-X
$6.99

Things Forbidden
Maryam Diaab
ISBN-13: 978-1-58571-327-1
ISBN-10: 1-58571-327-9
$6.99

August

Storm
Pamela Leigh Starr
ISBN-13: 978-1-58571-323-3
ISBN-10: 1-58571-323-6
$6.99

Passion's Furies
AlTonya Washington
ISBN-13: 978-1-58571-324-0
ISBN-10: 1-58571-324-4
$6.99

September

Three Doors Down
Michele Sudler
ISBN-13: 978-1-58571-332-5
ISBN-10: 1-58571-332-5
$6.99

Mr Fix-It
Crystal Hubbard
ISBN-13: 978-1-58571-326-4
ISBN-10: 1-58571-326-0
$6.99

October

Moments of Clarity
Michele Cameron
ISBN-13: 978-1-58571-330-1
ISBN-10: 1-58571-330-9
$6.99

Lady Preacher
K.T. Richey
ISBN-13: 978-1-58571-333-2
ISBN-10: 1-58571-333-3
$6.99

November

This Life Isn't Perfect Holla
Sandra Foy
ISBN: 978-1-58571-331-8
ISBN-10: 1-58571-331-7
$6.99

Promises Made
Bernice Layton
ISBN-13: 978-1-58571-334-9
ISBN-10: 1-58571-334-1
$6.99

December

A Voice Behind Thunder
Carrie Elizabeth Greene
ISBN-13: 978-1-58571-329-5
ISBN-10: 1-58571-329-5
$6.99

The More Things Change
Chamein Canton
ISBN-13: 978-1-58571-328-8
ISBN-10: 1-58571-328-7
$6.99

Other Genesis Press, Inc. Titles

A Dangerous Deception	J.M. Jeffries	$8.95
A Dangerous Love	J.M. Jeffries	$8.95
A Dangerous Obsession	J.M. Jeffries	$8.95
A Drummer's Beat to Mend	Kei Swanson	$9.95
A Happy Life	Charlotte Harris	$9.95
A Heart's Awakening	Veronica Parker	$9.95
A Lark on the Wing	Phyliss Hamilton	$9.95
A Love of Her Own	Cheris F. Hodges	$9.95
A Love to Cherish	Beverly Clark	$8.95
A Risk of Rain	Dar Tomlinson	$8.95
A Taste of Temptation	Reneé Alexis	$9.95
A Twist of Fate	Beverly Clark	$8.95
A Will to Love	Angie Daniels	$9.95
Acquisitions	Kimberley White	$8.95
Across	Carol Payne	$12.95
After the Vows	Leslie Esdaile	$10.95
(Summer Anthology)	T.T. Henderson	
	Jacqueline Thomas	
Again My Love	Kayla Perrin	$10.95
Against the Wind	Gwynne Forster	$8.95
All I Ask	Barbara Keaton	$8.95
Always You	Crystal Hubbard	$6.99
Ambrosia	T.T. Henderson	$8.95
An Unfinished Love Affair	Barbara Keaton	$8.95
And Then Came You	Dorothy Elizabeth Love	$8.95
Angel's Paradise	Janice Angelique	$9.95
At Last	Lisa G. Riley	$8.95
Best of Friends	Natalie Dunbar	$8.95
Beyond the Rapture	Beverly Clark	$9.95

Other Genesis Press, Inc. Titles (continued)

Blaze	Barbara Keaton	$9.95
Blood Lust	J. M. Jeffries	$9.95
Blood Seduction	J.M. Jeffries	$9.95
Bodyguard	Andrea Jackson	$9.95
Boss of Me	Diana Nyad	$8.95
Bound by Love	Beverly Clark	$8.95
Breeze	Robin Hampton Allen	$10.95
Broken	Dar Tomlinson	$24.95
By Design	Barbara Keaton	$8.95
Cajun Heat	Charlene Berry	$8.95
Careless Whispers	Rochelle Alers	$8.95
Cats & Other Tales	Marilyn Wagner	$8.95
Caught in a Trap	Andre Michelle	$8.95
Caught Up In the Rapture	Lisa G. Riley	$9.95
Cautious Heart	Cheris F Hodges	$8.95
Chances	Pamela Leigh Starr	$8.95
Cherish the Flame	Beverly Clark	$8.95
Class Reunion	Irma Jenkins/ John Brown	$12.95
Code Name: Diva	J.M. Jeffries	$9.95
Conquering Dr. Wexler's Heart	Kimberley White	$9.95
Corporate Seduction	A.C. Arthur	$9.95
Crossing Paths, Tempting Memories	Dorothy Elizabeth Love	$9.95
Crush	Crystal Hubbard	$9.95
Cypress Whisperings	Phyllis Hamilton	$8.95
Dark Embrace	Crystal Wilson Harris	$8.95
Dark Storm Rising	Chinelu Moore	$10.95

Other Genesis Press, Inc. Titles (continued)

Other Genesis Press, Inc. Titles (continued)

Hard to Love	Kimberley White	$9.95
Hart & Soul	Angie Daniels	$8.95
Heart of the Phoenix	A.C. Arthur	$9.95
Heartbeat	Stephanie Bedwell-Grime	$8.95
Hearts Remember	M. Loui Quezada	$8.95
Hidden Memories	Robin Allen	$10.95
Higher Ground	Leah Latimer	$19.95
Hitler, the War, and the Pope	Ronald Rychiak	$26.95
How to Write a Romance	Kathryn Falk	$18.95
I Married a Reclining Chair	Lisa M. Fuhs	$8.95
I'll Be Your Shelter	Giselle Carmichael	$8.95
I'll Paint a Sun	A.J. Garrotto	$9.95
Icie	Pamela Leigh Starr	$8.95
Illusions	Pamela Leigh Starr	$8.95
Indigo After Dark Vol. I	Nia Dixon/Angelique	$10.95
Indigo After Dark Vol. II	Dolores Bundy/ Cole Riley	$10.95
Indigo After Dark Vol. III	Montana Blue/ Coco Morena	$10.95
Indigo After Dark Vol. IV	Cassandra Colt/	$14.95
Indigo After Dark Vol. V	Delilah Dawson	$14.95
Indiscretions	Donna Hill	$8.95
Intentional Mistakes	Michele Sudler	$9.95
Interlude	Donna Hill	$8.95
Intimate Intentions	Angie Daniels	$8.95
It's Not Over Yet	J.J. Michael	$9.95
Jolie's Surrender	Edwina Martin-Arnold	$8.95
Kiss or Keep	Debra Phillips	$8.95
Lace	Giselle Carmichael	$9.95

Other Genesis Press, Inc. Titles (continued)

Last Train to Memphis	Elsa Cook	$12.95
Lasting Valor	Ken Olsen	$24.95
Let Us Prey	Hunter Lundy	$25.95
Lies Too Long	Pamela Ridley	$13.95
Life Is Never As It Seems	J.J. Michael	$12.95
Lighter Shade of Brown	Vicki Andrews	$8.95
Love Always	Mildred E. Riley	$10.95
Love Doesn't Come Easy	Charlyne Dickerson	$8.95
Love Unveiled	Gloria Greene	$10.95
Love's Deception	Charlene Berry	$10.95
Love's Destiny	M. Loui Quezada	$8.95
Mae's Promise	Melody Walcott	$8.95
Magnolia Sunset	Giselle Carmichael	$8.95
Many Shades of Gray	Dyanne Davis	$6.99
Matters of Life and Death	Lesego Malepe, Ph.D.	$15.95
Meant to Be	Jeanne Sumerix	$8.95
Midnight Clear	Leslie Esdaile	$10.95
(Anthology)	Gwynne Forster	
	Carmen Green	
	Monica Jackson	
Midnight Magic	Gwynne Forster	$8.95
Midnight Peril	Vicki Andrews	$10.95
Misconceptions	Pamela Leigh Starr	$9.95
Montgomery's Children	Richard Perry	$14.95
My Buffalo Soldier	Barbara B. K. Reeves	$8.95
Naked Soul	Gwynne Forster	$8.95
Next to Last Chance	Louisa Dixon	$24.95
No Apologies	Seressia Glass	$8.95
No Commitment Required	Seressia Glass	$8.95

Other Genesis Press, Inc. Titles (continued)

No Regrets	Mildred E. Riley	$8.95
Not His Type	Chamein Canton	$6.99
Nowhere to Run	Gay G. Gunn	$10.95
O Bed! O Breakfast!	Rob Kuehnle	$14.95
Object of His Desire	A. C. Arthur	$8.95
Office Policy	A. C. Arthur	$9.95
Once in a Blue Moon	Dorianne Cole	$9.95
One Day at a Time	Bella McFarland	$8.95
One in A Million	Barbara Keaton	$6.99
One of These Days	Michele Sudler	$9.95
Outside Chance	Louisa Dixon	$24.95
Passion	T.T. Henderson	$10.95
Passion's Blood	Cherif Fortin	$22.95
Passion's Journey	Wanda Y. Thomas	$8.95
Past Promises	Jahmel West	$8.95
Path of Fire	T.T. Henderson	$8.95
Path of Thorns	Annetta P. Lee	$9.95
Peace Be Still	Colette Haywood	$12.95
Picture Perfect	Reon Carter	$8.95
Playing for Keeps	Stephanie Salinas	$8.95
Pride & Joi	Gay G. Gunn	$15.95
Pride & Joi	Gay G. Gunn	$8.95
Promises to Keep	Alicia Wiggins	$8.95
Quiet Storm	Donna Hill	$10.95
Reckless Surrender	Rochelle Alers	$6.95
Red Polka Dot in a World of Plaid	Varian Johnson	$12.95
Reluctant Captive	Joyce Jackson	$8.95
Rendezvous with Fate	Jeanne Sumerix	$8.95

Other Genesis Press, Inc. Titles (continued)

Revelations	Cheris F. Hodges	$8.95
Rivers of the Soul	Leslie Esdaile	$8.95
Rocky Mountain Romance	Kathleen Suzanne	$8.95
Rooms of the Heart	Donna Hill	$8.95
Rough on Rats and Tough on Cats	Chris Parker	$12.95
Secret Library Vol. 1	Nina Sheridan	$18.95
Secret Library Vol. 2	Cassandra Colt	$8.95
Secret Thunder	Annetta P. Lee	$9.95
Shades of Brown	Denise Becker	$8.95
Shades of Desire	Monica White	$8.95
Shadows in the Moonlight	Jeanne Sumerix	$8.95
Sin	Crystal Rhodes	$8.95
Small Whispers	Annetta P. Lee	$6.99
So Amazing	Sinclair LeBeau	$8.95
Somebody's Someone	Sinclair LeBeau	$8.95
Someone to Love	Alicia Wiggins	$8.95
Song in the Park	Martin Brant	$15.95
Soul Eyes	Wayne L. Wilson	$12.95
Soul to Soul	Donna Hill	$8.95
Southern Comfort	J.M. Jeffries	$8.95
Still the Storm	Sharon Robinson	$8.95
Still Waters Run Deep	Leslie Esdaile	$8.95
Stolen Kisses	Dominiqua Douglas	$9.95
Stories to Excite You	Anna Forrest/Divine	$14.95
Subtle Secrets	Wanda Y. Thomas	$8.95
Suddenly You	Crystal Hubbard	$9.95
Sweet Repercussions	Kimberley White	$9.95
Sweet Sensations	Gwendolyn Bolton	$9.95

Other Genesis Press, Inc. Titles (continued)

Sweet Tomorrows	Kimberly White	$8.95
Taken by You	Dorothy Elizabeth Love	$9.95
Tattooed Tears	T. T. Henderson	$8.95
The Color Line	Lizzette Grayson Carter	$9.95
The Color of Trouble	Dyanne Davis	$8.95
The Disappearance of Allison Jones	Kayla Perrin	$5.95
The Fires Within	Beverly Clark	$9.95
The Foursome	Celya Bowers	$6.99
The Honey Dipper's Legacy	Pannell-Allen	$14.95
The Joker's Love Tune	Sidney Rickman	$15.95
The Little Pretender	Barbara Cartland	$10.95
The Love We Had	Natalie Dunbar	$8.95
The Man Who Could Fly	Bob & Milana Beamon	$18.95
The Missing Link	Charlyne Dickerson	$8.95
The Mission	Pamela Leigh Starr	$6.99
The Perfect Frame	Beverly Clark	$9.95
The Price of Love	Sinclair LeBeau	$8.95
The Smoking Life	Ilene Barth	$29.95
The Words of the Pitcher	Kei Swanson	$8.95
Three Wishes	Seressia Glass	$8.95
Ties That Bind	Kathleen Suzanne	$8.95
Tiger Woods	Libby Hughes	$5.95
Time is of the Essence	Angie Daniels	$9.95
Timeless Devotion	Bella McFarland	$9.95
Tomorrow's Promise	Leslie Esdaile	$8.95
Truly Inseparable	Wanda Y. Thomas	$8.95
Two Sides to Every Story	Dyanne Davis	$9.95
Unbreak My Heart	Dar Tomlinson	$8.95

Other Genesis Press, Inc. Titles (continued)

Uncommon Prayer	Kenneth Swanson	$9.95
Unconditional Love	Alicia Wiggins	$8.95
Unconditional	A.C. Arthur	$9.95
Until Death Do Us Part	Susan Paul	$8.95
Vows of Passion	Bella McFarland	$9.95
Wedding Gown	Dyanne Davis	$8.95
What's Under Benjamin's Bed	Sandra Schaffer	$8.95
When Dreams Float	Dorothy Elizabeth Love	$8.95
When I'm With You	LaConnie Taylor-Jones	$6.99
Whispers in the Night	Dorothy Elizabeth Love	$8.95
Whispers in the Sand	LaFlorya Gauthier	$10.95
Who's That Lady?	Andrea Jackson	$9.95
Wild Ravens	Altonya Washington	$9.95
Yesterday Is Gone	Beverly Clark	$10.95
Yesterday's Dreams, Tomorrow's Promises	Reon Laudat	$8.95
Your Precious Love	Sinclair LeBeau	$8.95

ESCAPE WITH INDIGO !!!!

Join Indigo Book Club©
It's simple, easy and secure.

Sign up and receive the new
releases
every month + Free shipping
and
20% off the cover price.

Go online to www.genesis-
press.com and click on Bookclub
or
call 1-888-INDIGO-1

Dull, Drab, Love Life?

Passion Going Nowhere?

Tired Of Being Alone?

Does Every Direction You Look For Love

Lead You Astray?

Genesis Press presents
The launching of our new website!

RecaptureTheRomance.Com

Ignite
The Flame!